TEARDROP

SUE AMOS

First published in Great Britain in 2024
by Indie Novella Ltd.

INDIE NOVELLA www.indienovella.co.uk
Hackney, London

Editor: Damien Mosley
Cover Design: Luke Bird

Editorial Support from Kate Pasola,
Sam Burt, Hannah Walker, Shreyas M

A CIP catalogue record for this title is available from the
British Library
Paperback ISBN 978 1 738 44210 2

Printed and bound by TJ Books in the United Kingdom.
Indie Novella is committed to a sustainable future for our readers and the world in which we live. All paper used are natural, renewable and sustainable products.

Indie Novella is grateful that our work is supported using public funding by
Arts Council England.

Supported using public funding by
ARTS COUNCIL
ENGLAND

LOTTERY FUNDED

For Dad, and One Big Family

PART I

THE FALL OF THE GECKO

PROLOGUE

In the cool and cloudy hills of Badulla, the Gal Oya begins its journey east towards the Indian Ocean. For thousands of years its waters have flowed beside the stone remains of lost dynasties and ancient cave temples, murmuring beneath the branches of kumbuk trees and groves of coconut palms as it winds through forests and plantations, carrying silt and seeds and pollen until it reaches the rocky whirlpool known as Makara Kata, where it roars and readies itself for the big drop.

On one particularly wet day during the height of the monsoon season, at the last moment before the fall through the Mouth of the Dragon, something else joined the river, jolting its way across the boulders and rocks before tumbling with the current, the water roaring as it descended into the basin of water below.

Hours later, when night had fallen, in the silvered moonlight something white gleamed, a hint of bone; a bound mass drifting to the shallows before coming to rest, trapped against a formation of sharp stones.

It rocked back and forth gently, waiting to be found.

From the notebook of Jazz Barthelot

1

JANUARY 1953

The first hint of saffron on the horizon brings an explosion of birdsong to the city; mynahs, sparrows, and parrots suddenly awake and trading gossip from the overhanging trees. Below, the daily procession of overloaded buses belching diesel, motor cars, bicycles and rickshaws are filling up the streets of Pettah and Fort. Although Colombo is a modern metropolis, the remnants of its garden glory fringe the urban sprawl like ripples of fraying silk: emerald doves in the yellow cotton trees, purple-faced langurs scavenging for guavas, and further beyond, marsh crocodiles paddling in the wetlands.

A swarm of fruit bats swoops low across the roofline towards the banyan tree, ready for sleep. She glances at her watch. Six am. She had risen earlier to watch the sunrise from the seating area at the top of the garden, enjoying the brief stillness of the world before the uncertainty of the day.

'Jacintha? Jacintha! Oya koheda?' The maid, Bimali, is calling, the sounds drifting from the open shutters of the house.

Easing the tension from her neck and shoulders, she readies herself to face the day.

~

'Please let me out here, Uncle. I would like to walk into office on my own.'

Angelo Crozier, already heavily perspiring as the car comes to a pause in the clogged-up streets close to the clock tower, ignores the request. 'Jacintha, I'm looking for a parking space, please use your eyes, also!'

'Uncle...'

He curses at a bullock cart driver with a cargo of plantains who has careered straight into his path causing him to swerve. Not for the first time on this short but frustrating drive, she wonders why, when he employs a full-time chauffeur, he has insisted on driving himself to work on such an important day.

A police officer on traffic duty is frantically waving his gloved hands giving the order for the car to stop. She grabs her handbag, pulling open the door, narrowly avoiding a collision with a rickshaw.

'Jacintha!'

'I will see you later!' She slams the door and steps onto the pavement, matching her rhythm to the flurry of movement alongside. An office worker, briefcase tucked under one arm, has the morning edition of the *Colombo Courier* spread wide as he waits at a tram stop. Prime Minister Dudley Senanayake stares out at her from the front page, with apparently 'Not Much to Smile About.' A graph underneath illustrates his declining popularity, the article documenting how he has failed to keep his election promises from the previous year.

Halfway down Chatham Street she arrives at the three-storey building which houses the *Colombo Courier*, entering its dark hallway. There are no signs to indicate where she should go. She concludes that she should after all have waited for her uncle, but the door opens once more and an older woman in a lemon-and-lime sari sweeps in, tapping the dust of the street from her shoes.

'Excuse me…'

'Yes?'

'I'm looking for Walter Jayatilake. The Editor?'

'I'm Mr Jayatilake's secretary. Do you have an appointment? There's nothing in his diary.'

'He's expecting me. My name is Jacintha Barthelot.'

The woman gives a long, suspicious stare. Jacintha straightens the collar on her blouse and smooths down her skirt. Eventually the woman says without smiling, 'Follow me. Up the stairs.'

She hadn't even noticed the staircase. The building is run down, smelling of something sour. Her uncle has plans for refurbishment, amongst other goals. His appointment had come about suddenly due to the previous chairman having to retire on the grounds of ill-health, and over the past weeks, in a flurry of half heard telephone calls and hastily convened late night meetings in her uncle's study, she had gleaned that his ultimate plan is to expand the *Courier's* output across the island.

At the top of the stairs, she follows the patterned sari down a corridor, typewriters clattering, raised voices coming from various rooms, finally entering the main reporters' room where a cluster of tired-looking men barely glance at her. The woman ushers her into a glass-walled room where a well-built, middle-aged man has his feet up on his desk, smoking a cigarette. 'What is it, Pearl?'

'This is Miss Barthelot to see you. You are expecting her?'

'Board meeting starts in twenty minutes, I don't have time to deal with anything until after that.' Shaking his head, he scrabbles around on his desk, retrieving a scrap of paper underlined in red. He meets Jacintha's eyes with a cool gaze. 'You're the new girl?' A tinge of judgement in his tone.

'Yes.' Beside her, an exhalation of surprised displeasure.

'New girl? Walter, we don't need...'

'Pearl, check the conference room and make sure refreshments are ready. First meeting of the new Board; everything must be set up correctly.'

'Of course, but Walter I was not aware of any job advertisement—'

'Hurry up please! Take Miss Barthelot to Sonny, he can settle her in.'

'Sonny? But—'

He motions them away with his hand. With a curl of her full lips the woman, Pearl, closes the door, motioning to an empty chair at the back of the office.

'Sonny hasn't arrived yet. Wait here for him.'

'Okay. Could I just ask—'

'I can't stand here chatting, you heard Mr Jayatilake.' Pearl disappears in an acid swirl of colour.

She sits on the edge of the chair, discreetly observing the rhythms of the office. Apart from the occasional interplay of voices, mostly people seem to be working with a quiet intensity, a brief look upwards from the desk with an absent smile, the collective groan as the office boy arrives with a stack of letters, a grumbled enquiry as to when the tea might arrive. As the minutes tick by, she takes from her handbag a short letter and re-reads it, drawing comfort from the familiar teasing tone behind the words of a friend from England, who has written to wish her luck in her new job.

At ten, a tall man who looks to be in his mid-twenties, rumpled with tired eyes, makes an entrance and the quiet room comes to life. The reporters look up with broad grins, whistling across the room.

'Late again, Sonny!'

'Too much arrack again, isn't it?'

'How much did you lose last night?'

The newcomer takes it all in good humour as he slumps into his chair. 'Where is Pearl? I need tea.' He looks around and catches Jacintha's eye. 'I'm Sonny de Roye, the crime reporter. Waiting for me, is it?'

'Yes. My name is Jacintha Barthelot, I'm the new girl.'

'Ah.'

'Mr Jayatilake is in a meeting with Pearl. He asked you to settle me in.'

Sonny looks surprised, then gives a shout of laughter. 'Walter's way of telling me he knows I'm not busy. Okay, well, allow me to officially welcome you aboard. Have you met everyone?'

'Not yet.'

'Come, come.' He jumps up and she follows, trying to keep up with his wide stride.

'Everyone, say hello to the new girl.'

Now they look at her; a brief smile from Suresh Kandasamy, the Politics and Economics Editor, a wink from one of the sports reporters, Shyam on his way out to the cricket, and from the Cultural Editor, Ganesh, a well-bred eyebrow raised in her direction as he sips his tea. They pass another office which she is told houses the International News Editor and his team, the persistent hum of the teleprinter connected to the Reuters newswire service follows them down the hallway.

Another corridor, more doors and desks. 'Copy editors in there. Next door are our photographers.'

'And the room at the end of the hall?'

'That's Pearl's office. Watch your step because she knows everything.'

'Well, I don't think she knew I was coming. She seemed annoyed.'

'Pearl is always annoyed about something; you'll get used to her. Now, next door are the typists but last night was a late rush, so Latha and Ranji will come in mid-morning. They like to think they know everything, but don't stand any of their nonsense. Downstairs is the office boy, Douglas. He generally claims to know nothing but trust me, he's the best of them.'

Jacintha gives a smile.

They have arrived back at his desk. Sonny gestures around the untidy office. 'As you can see there are always files and papers piled around that the typists are supposed to deal with, but never find the time. Maybe you should start on the filing until Pearl returns.'

She hesitates, sits down again. He looks at her, a slight frown falling over his handsome face.

'Mr de Roye...'

'Please call me Sonny.'

'Sonny, I believe there's been a misunderstanding. I am not a typist; I'm the new junior reporter.'

He is unable to hide his surprise.

She gives a warning snarl. 'What's the matter? Women can't be reporters? You think we should all be at home, going marketing and doing the cooking?'

'I'm not judging. It's just unusual. You have tiger eyes. Anybody told you that before?'

'I...what do you mean?'

'Tiny flecks of amber dotted across your irises. They match those claws of yours.' He smiles across at her and she can't help but respond. He gives a sudden exclamation of pain, rubbing his shoulder gingerly.

'What is wrong?'

'You won't believe what happened this morning. Crazy thing, a gecko fell from the ceiling while I was sleeping and landed on my shoulder. Woke me up with a hell of a shock.'

'Maybe put some balm on it, if it's painful.'

He looks at her intently. 'Do you know the meaning of a gecko falling on your right side?'

'Well, one could say it was bad luck. Also, not so great for the gecko...'

'You know what the aunties would say: a falling gecko to the right signifies a terrible death.'

The overhead fan blows, sending a shiver to the back of her neck. 'Well,' she says eventually, 'as you work in crime that must be auspicious.'

He gives a snort of laughter. 'Enough talk about lizards! Let's get you settled in.'

'Okay.'

'I'll sort out a desk for you.'

'Righto.'

She stands, feeling awkward while he drags an unoccupied desk opposite his own. She picks up a chair and sets it in place. Sonny drops back into his seat and begins to shuffle papers around his desk.

'What should I do? Is there something I can help with?'

She sees a fleeting look of worry cross his face. 'I have to be honest, I'm not that occupied at the moment. But don't worry, I can find you something to do.' Eventually he passes her a dishevelled collection of notes and cuttings and tells her to find any mention about rice sanctions. Satisfied, he puts his feet up on the desk and tilts back in the chair.

'Rice sanctions? I thought this was the crime desk.'

'Of course, but Suresh has too much to deal with. Walter wants to run this story tomorrow so I'm lending a hand.'

'Not many criminals in the city at the moment?' There is a long pause. She assumes he hasn't heard her but then she hears the faintest of sighs.

'There are criminals everywhere, they're just not getting caught at the moment.'

2

'I found that damned gecko still lurking in my room when I got home yesterday evening.' She has been in the office for half an hour before Sonny appears, rubbing sleep from his eyes.

'What did you do with it?'

'I grabbed my torch, got hold of the beast and took it downstairs to let it outside. I thought it would scamper away, but it just sat there blinking in the darkness, staring at me. It gave me the creeps.'

'I don't like them either.' She pauses. 'Do we have anything new today?'

Walter had called her into his office the previous afternoon and officially welcomed her to the team. Apparently, she was to remain in Sonny's charge for the next six weeks, gradually rotating around the different desks. As she had left his office, Walter had given her a small grin which she hoped was a symbol of acceptance.

Something had nagged at her on the way home, silent in her uncle's car, as to why the name Sonny de Roye had seemed familiar, until Angelo Crozier had begun to talk about him, and she had remembered. Four years ago, Ceylon had been enthralled with a shocking case; what became known as the Ratnayake Killing, the school-boy killer who had been convicted of murdering his twin brother. Sonny had been first on the scene to report the murder and then subsequently the trial, and afterwards had been the only journalist granted an interview with the sister of the twins, resulting in yet more sensational headlines.

'Come on,' Sonny says briskly. Although the Colombo court rooms are still remarkably quiet, he has decided to take her to a hearing. They sit in the courthouse, half asleep, lulled by the large fans lifting the heat around the rooms, listening to the case of a maid who had slashed her married lover across the face as they had argued in the shaded grounds of Wolvendaal Church.

Sonny leans across as she takes notes.

'Your shorthand is very good. Mine is mostly cobbled together. And you are much speedier than I am.'

'I did a Pitman training course while I was in England.'

'Write it up,' says Sonny on their way back to the offices of the *Courier*, 'and I'll take a look.'

Later that day she asks him what it had been like to work on the Ratnayake case.

'Well, you know, of course it was horrifying but at the same time exciting. It was a great opportunity for me. But there was a lot in that story to keep me awake at night. I used to wonder if the twin that died had a sense of what was coming.'

'Horrific. You may never get another story that big.'

'Maybe not.'

'That must be a dull prospect for you, no?'

He waggles his head. 'It's good to know that the streets of Colombo are not full of people like Ratnayake.' The slack day concludes in silence.

~

They are browsing for rice-related material in the library housed on the top floor of the building, shelves of books and clippings, cabinets of dossiers and a huge archive of photographs at the disposal of the journalists. Jacintha would have been content to continue the search, but before noon Sonny looks up from a pile of photographs and proposes they take a walk along Galle Face Green.

'Now?'

Glancing across at his pale face, she sees he had drunk too much the previous evening and needs fresh air. 'Where did you go last night?' she asks, aware that the city's journalists tend to congregate after work in certain favoured hotels and bars in the Fort area, sharing stories and information.

'Hotel Ratnagiri to meet a couple of the boys from *The Times*. Turned into quite a night.'

'Did they have anything useful to tell?'

'Not this time. They were asking me for leads and, of course, I had gone to meet them with the same hope.'

He purchases two portions of murukku from one of the street vendors, and they eat as they walk along the promenade. A boy stands with his feet in the waves, flying a dragon kite, its scarlet and orange trails weaving across the sky.

'Look at him.'

'Lucky bugger. Having fun.'

'So carefree. His whole future lies ahead, not yet dreamed of.'

Sonny is looking out across the ocean, his eyes dark with melancholy.

After a while she asks, 'Tell me about you.'

He turns to her with a grin. 'I like your style, straight in with the open-ended question.'

'Of course.'

'Okay, okay. I'm twenty-four. I come from Badulla, been in

Colombo for five years now, more or less. I came looking for work and a bit of life. I found both.'

'Tell me something about you that not many people know.'

He gives a burst of laughter. 'Okay...when I left school, I wanted to be a poet.'

'Well, if that's your darkest secret, that's probably the end of my career as an award-winning reporter.' She pauses waiting for him to laugh. There is an awkward silence. She picks it up quickly. 'So...do you have a poetry collection you're working on?'

'No. I used to write poems but now I rarely do.'

She looks across at him and, seeing something in his face, changes the subject. 'So, next question. How does living in Colombo compare with home?'

'I don't miss home.' A decisive tone. 'I love the pace of the city with the never-ending buzz running through my brain even while I sleep, the people, the bars, the distractions. I enjoy living in a place that is constantly changing.'

He gestures to Galle Face Green, the promenade surrounded by the din and clamour of construction, new buildings climbing into the sky. 'Here we are, wandering and chatting freely but did you know that a hundred years ago in the same space, the British Army paraded their troops and sentenced them to hang if they disobeyed orders. On a scaffold placed over there, in fact.'

She stares, picturing the recalcitrant soldiers far away from home, heads in the nooses under the unfamiliar sun. Sonny possesses a quicksilver way of darkening or lightening the mood. She wonders if it is something he has cultivated as a reporter.

They cross the road and stroll by the seafront. Sonny lights a cigarette, taking a deep satisfying draw as his eyes follow the rise and fall of the waves. 'What about you, what made you choose journalism?'

'I was always good at English at school. I loved writing stories.

I still do, I suppose.' She aims for a careless laugh, but Sonny is razor sharp.

'Let me guess – you're working on a novel?'

'Not exactly. Not yet.'

'Waiting for that lightning strike of inspiration?'

'Something like that. I'm in the habit of making notes about anything that interests me or little things that happen in the day.'

'And tell me, where did you go to school? In Colombo?'

'Actually, I went to boarding school in Batticaloa.'

'Ah. My sister now lives in Batti.'

'After I finished school, I went over to England. My aunty, Ada, has an old school friend living in a place called Caversham, and I went to stay with her family while I studied English at Reading University.'

'How lucky for you.' He lifts his eyebrows.

'Tell me something, Sonny. I've been meaning to ask how you normally find your stories? Do they begin in the court rooms?'

'It depends. Sometimes I'm lucky to get wind of something very early on in the investigation stages. Let's hope for my sake something happens very soon.'

She catches his tone. 'Why?'

He snorts. 'Day before you arrived, Walter had me in his office and spent twenty minutes shouting that I needed to do better. Be more productive. He likes me, he was giving me a warning. There's been a reshuffle on the Board at the *Courier*, you see.' He gives her a sly look. 'But you already know that, right? You're related to Angelo Crozier? You are staying in his house, no?'

Word has gone around quickly. She guesses it has come from Pearl, obviously less than impressed at Jacintha's newly created position. Jacintha returns his look, determined not to be apologetic. 'That's right. Uncle Angelo is my father's younger brother.'

'I see. But wait, your surname isn't Crozier?'

They stop by a bench and sit to catch their breath in the searing heat. 'Smart boy,' she says.

'What's the story?'

She sighs. 'I saw your face when I said I'd been to university in England. And, of course, you know I've walked straight into a reporter's job. You think I've had an easy life and that can't be denied.

'But before you judge me, I should tell you that all the inherited wealth that went to Uncle Angelo should have been shared with my father, the eldest brother.'

'So then, what happened?'

'My father met and fell in love with my mother, a Tamil ayah. My grandfather removed him from the family business, threw him out of the house and cut all ties with my father, when he refused to give her up. Daddy retaliated by marrying my mother, changing his name, and moving far away from the Croziers, to where my mother's family lived.

'I was born in a tiny house in Kalmunai. I remember my early days as being a much-loved child. Then Mummy got sick and died when I was four. My father had trained as a forester and his work took him all across the country, so he was unable to take care of me. By this time my grandfather had died, and Uncle Angelo wanted to try and repair some of the mischief that had been done to Daddy. He and Aunty Ada were living in Galle at the time, and they took me to live with them for three years. I had been used to the simple life, so this was quite a shock at first. When I was older they paid for me to go to boarding school. They have always done their best for me.'

Sonny has been listening to her, his eyes unreadable. 'You're from Kalmunai?'

'Yes. Why?'

He doesn't elaborate, instead turning his gaze to a lone ship far out on the horizon.

'I'm sorry,' he says finally, turning to face her.

'What are you sorry for? That I had a Tamil mother? Or that I had a lowly start in life?'

'I'm sorry she passed away,' he says gently.

Shaking her head, she gets up and strides away from him along the shoreline. She feels raw, exposed. She can feel Sonny watching, wondering whether to follow.

After a while she turns around. The bench is empty.

Not yet ready to return to the office she continues her walk, drawn to the fracas surrounding the port where a huge development scheme is underway, with a new quay due to open next year. She remembers her uncle's scathing response towards the improvement plans for the city's warehousing and ship repairing facilities, his opinion being that in the not-too-distant future, air cargo routes will play an equally important role. She has heard him on more than one occasion, pontificating about his role on an advisory board lobbying for equal amounts of money to be made available for aviation improvements.

She can see the building work is going at quite a pace, the area much more built up now than when she was last there the previous summer, when she had sailed from London back to Colombo after finishing university and, to her surprise, had been greeted by a new lighthouse at Galbokka Point.

When she returns to her desk there is no sign of Sonny. She puts her head down and continues to work on the piece about the rice sanctions. Late in the afternoon she looks up to find him standing by her desk with tea in a fine china cup and saucer from the good set that Pearl keeps for guests. He gives a quick smile and places it on her desk.

'Sorry about earlier, Jacintha, I meant no offence.'

She nods and takes a sip of tea.

'The piece you wrote about the maid was good. I barely had to use my pencil,' Sonny says. 'I think you show a lot of potential.'

She finishes her cup and looks up at him. 'Call me Jazz, okay?'

He assures her that he will.

3

She has completed a second week at the *Courier* and is heading back to the Crozier household for a quiet weekend; some letters to write and maybe a telephone call from her father in Kalmunai. Sonny comes up alongside her as she leaves the building. 'Jazz! Coming to the party at the DBU tomorrow night?'

'Party?' She's not really paying attention, worrying that her uncle will come out at that exact moment. She knows by now that everyone is aware she is the chairman's niece, but she wants to keep it as low key as possible.

'Cecil's tenth wedding anniversary celebration.'

'Sorry, Cecil? Who is he?' The name sounds familiar, but she still can't be sure who half the people in the building are. Some of the reporters are scarcely in the same place two days running.

'Cecil Stork. He works alongside Ganesh.'

'I haven't had an invitation.'

'You'll be coming with your uncle, no? Everyone from the *Courier* is going.'

'Well, in that case I will see you there.'

A well-heeled crowd is thronging on Reid Avenue outside the Dutch Burgher Union Hall, taxis pulling up sharply, temporarily blocking the intersection between Havelock Road and Bullers Road. The creamy white building rises from a deep lawn, its porch crowned with an upper storey arched window, flanked on each side by two gabled wings: the fabled meeting place, and depository for wills, photographs, certificates, and letters relating to the intertwining family histories of the small, unique group on the island, known as the Burghers.

Created to preserve the legacy of the Burghers on the island and to promote their social standing, the receptions and celebrations held within the walls of the DBU are legendary in Burgher society.

Jazz steps from the car directly outside the old colonial building, taking her uncle's arm to walk through the vestibule into the large hall, crowds of people drinking and laughing beneath the dazzle of the overhead lights. At one end of the room, the sprung teak dance floor waits in silent splendour, at the other a buffet table looms long and low, waiters coming and going, setting down platters of hoppers, dhal, rice and curries.

Ada Crozier had gone ahead earlier to help set up; they find her standing in the midst of the stalwarts of Burgher society, the van Driesens, the Ferdinands and the Hingerts. She nods as they approach. 'Ah, here you both are at last! Everyone, I'm sure you all remember our niece, Jacintha?'

'Lovely to see you again, darling.'

'Jacintha, how well you are looking! You must come to our place for lunch next weekend. Our son, Frederick, is home at the moment and I'm sure you would get on well.'

'I have a nephew, Anthony, who would also love to meet you,

he has a prominent position now in an insurance company you know...'

She smiles at each one politely, explaining that she is busy at work and has not much time for outings, making sure to avoid her aunt's disappointed eyes. After a while her uncle looks across and nods his permission for her to go and find her colleagues. She climbs the carved wooden staircase to the bar where she comes across the *Courier* crowd being guarded by Pearl's unwelcoming glare. Jazz slips in beside young Douglas, the office boy, who is gulping a glass of beer, his unruly mop of hair combed unnaturally flat. He looks at her, blushing when she greets him. Shyam and his pretty wife give her a wave, but her attention is arrested by the sight of Sonny. He is standing away from their group at the far side of the bar looking handsome in a navy suit, white shirt, and polished shoes, and has evidently just finished relating a highly amusing story to a crowd who roar appreciatively.

She suddenly understands Pearl's rumoured devotion.

Sonny's gaze falls on her, and he shouts across. 'Join us, Jazz! What are you drinking? Lemonade?'

'Don't forget the port,' she fires back smartly, moving over to join him.

Clutching her drink, enjoying its coolness in her warm hands, she turns slightly to find that Pearl has followed her. 'Good evening, Pearl.' The woman nods at her stiffly, running her eyes over Jazz's pale satin cocktail dress.

Jazz persists. 'I love the colour of your sari,' she lies. The green tint makes Pearl's neck look sallow, but the older woman's demeanour softens. Jazz is on the brink of drawing her into conversation, but the opportunity dies as soon as Pearl notices Jazz exchange a smile across the crowd with Sonny. She immediately moves away, nostrils flaring.

Suresh Kandasamy comes up alongside. 'Make sure Pearl

doesn't catch you flirting with him when the lights go down on the dance floor. She'll poison your tea.'

'Silly nonsense.' She rolls her eyes, and he fetches her another drink as penance. The rest of their colleagues have now joined them, and Jazz stands listening to stray fragments of conversation rising into the hot smoky air: Shyam and Douglas reciting a litany of cricket stats, Pearl, now ensconced next to Shyam's wife, discussing the forthcoming coronation of Queen Elizabeth and the State Visit she will be paying to the island the following year. Sonny and Suresh are having one of their habitual disagreements, this time about how best to boost the country's economy.

'Look man,' Suresh is saying, 'the Colombo Plan is simply a ploy to stop the country toying with communism. Nothing more, nothing less.'

'Suresh, you're wrong, it's a good, solid initiative. Why shouldn't we accept help from the West?'

'Because there's the suspicion that by giving us money, they will demand certain allegiances.'

'But surely if they're willing to share business connections and teach us new skills that's all that matters, no?'

'Well, it all depends on what strings are attached, and how long they stretch.'

Before Jazz can put forward her own opinion, from downstairs the Master of Ceremonies is calling, declaring the buffet open and there's a wave of movement towards the stairs.

After the dinner, hot and uncomfortable in her tight dress, Jazz steps outside into the empty garden away from the din.

'All alone?' Sonny has materialised beside her. From behind she hears the drawl of a saxophone. They turn to watch through the window as the six-piece band, already hot in their suits and bow ties, begin their first set, the dance floor filling quickly with rotating couples.

Sonny lights a cigarette.

'May I have one, please?'

'Of course. I didn't realise you smoked.'

'Only now and again. When Aunty and Uncle aren't looking.'

'Well, I won't tell them. Are you enjoying yourself?'

'Yes. It's been a good night.'

'It will go on until the small hours.'

'I imagine so.'

'We have to enjoy this while it lasts. These days are coming to an end for us Burghers.'

'We can't know that for sure.'

'Ah, Jazz. You know it's true.'

She knows, of course. The Burghers, who had been quick to swear allegiance to the new British conquerors when they sailed in to replace the Dutch in 1796, are slowly fading to a shadow of their former selves, isolated and undervalued now that the British are no longer in control.

'We are loud tonight, but we have to remember what a tiny minority we are in this country,' he says.

'We're part of this nation's history.'

'And yet, we have also remained distant, slightly apart.'

'You are saying we have no role in its future?'

'We have to face facts. There's change coming. Say, for example, they go ahead with these rumoured plans to eventually replace the English language with Sinhala. All lessons taught only in Sinhalese, government matters no longer conducted in English, creating a rising nation of those who will not be able to communicate and keep up with the rest of the world. Politicians rushing to put distance between our new independent nation and its colonial past, with no thought that this may perhaps be backward looking instead of forward focused. It's great to be our own nation, but why erase the positives from the map? It's…unimaginative.'

'Uncle says this is what happens when a country gains its freedom. Nationalism can be brutal.'

'There will be no place for us. Or our newspapers. Are you sure your uncle is doing the right thing, investing in the *Courier*?'

'He is of the opinion that English language newspapers will continue to remain prestigious.'

'A lifeline for the minority who will still be able to read them, perhaps.'

They look at each other. Sonny lets out a theatrical groan. 'I'm sorry. I've ruined the mood.' He takes a hip flask from his jacket pocket and unscrews the top, offering it to her.

She shakes her head. 'I've had enough.' She thinks perhaps he has also had more than his fair share of alcohol.

'Oops.' He stumbles as he tries to stub out his cigarette on the ground. 'Look at me, I'm making up my own dance moves. Good to see Cecil and his wife enjoying themselves. He's a lovely chap.' The celebrating couple are still moving energetically to the beat of a jive.

'Would you like to dance?' She smiles at his request and moves towards him, but he staggers forward and his arm shoots out to save himself. Jazz catches him by the sleeve.

'Ow! Ouch!' She draws her hand back sharply.

'What is it?'

'Something jabbed me.'

'Oh. I...you're bleeding. Here, let me.' He fumbles in his pocket for a handkerchief and offers it to her. She dabs at the blood spatter.

'What was that?'

'I am so sorry Jazz. I lost my cufflinks. I had to pin my sleeves in a rush to contain them in my jacket. So sorry,' he says again.

In the distance, Jazz can see her uncle striding towards them. As he approaches his eyes narrow at the sight of the blood.

'Good evening, Mr de Roye,' he says stiffly, 'is everything okay here?'

'Good evening, Mr Crozier, just a little accident...'

'Everything is fine, Uncle,' interjects Jazz.

'Very well, Jacintha. Aunty has a headache; I've ordered the car to take her back. Will you go with her?'

'Yes, Uncle, I will go. Well, goodnight, Sonny. See you on Monday.'

'Fellow is drunk,' mutters Angelo Crozier as they make their way to the front of the building, 'and not just tonight but on many nights, so I am hearing. It's a shame that he has fallen so low after such a promising start. I can't understand it. I need to have a word with Walter Jayatilake to ascertain whether Mr de Roye is still capable of doing the job.'

4

At the start of the new week, she is uneasy. The conversation about the bleak future of the Burgher community has set her wondering if she should have been braver after finishing university, perhaps tried to find an opening on one of the English newspapers. Her friend Vera, who occasionally finds time to send a scrawled letter, is progressing well on the *Manchester Guardian*.

She wonders if it is the general Burgher unease that gives Sonny his devil-may-care attitude. She knows the rumours about him: the late-night gambling, the bars and toddy shacks, the loss of ambition. She watches him spend his time smoking and lobbing paper aeroplanes around the office, alternatively disappearing for hours on end before coming back reeking of alcohol. Alarmed, she wants to warn him of her uncle's displeasure, but he is never around long enough to be able to broach the subject.

Late on Wednesday afternoon, almost time to go home, the telephone on Sonny's desk jangles. Sonny, rooting through his drawers for his spare pack of Peacocks, steadfastly ignores the sound.

'Shall I answer for you?'

He draws a cigarette from the pack and lights it with a sigh. 'Sure, Jazz. Thank you.'

'Hello, who is calling please? Yes, he is here.'

'Who is it?'

She offers him the receiver. 'It's a police officer. Superintendent Ludowyk.'

'Give it to me. Hello? Yes, Uncle. That's right we have a new...' Jazz widens her eyes. He gives her a grin. 'No, not a typist. Junior reporter. Yes, a girl. What's that, the line is not good?'

She begins to gather her things together, ready to leave. Sonny seems relaxed, feet up on the desk, head back, ready for a long conversation. She is about to signal her departure when Sonny's demeanour freezes. His legs come down onto the floor abruptly as he listens to what she can make out as rapid-fire sentences at the other end of the phone.

'Right,' Sonny says with a snap in his voice, 'I will let Walter know. Thank you for the call, Uncle. Goodbye for now.'

She watches him replace the receiver in its cradle, playing with the tangled telephone cord, winding its coils around his fingers, his eyes darting backwards and forwards in the silence following the call, face pale, eyes wide.

'Sonny? Is everything alright? Who is this superintendent fellow?'

He looks across at her, for a brief second having no idea who she is. Finally, he finds his focus. 'Superintendent Charles Ludowyk from the Colombo police force. He's my father's closest friend. He's also my godfather.'

He catches her questioning look. 'When I first joined the newspaper, he promised that he would tip me the wink about interesting cases, whenever he could. It was his influence that gained me such close access during the Ratnayake case. As he was fond of saying at the time, he led me to the water, and I drank the well dry. We do try to keep our relationship low profile but every now and again, he gives me a ring or brings me back to his place for a meal.'

She's impatient to learn what has just been relayed to him. 'Okay. But Sonny this telephone call…what did he say?'

'This call was not a social one.'

Jazz looks at him.

'What is it, Sonny?'

'I need to talk to Walter.'

'Okay.'

'Why don't you go home, and I'll see you tomorrow.'

She follows him to Walter's door. He gives a shrug and holds it open for her.

Walter, heaving his jacket on, looks up in annoyance. 'What is it? I'm meeting a crowd at the Nippon Hotel in five minutes.' He looks at Jazz curiously before moving his gaze to Sonny.

'I think I might have a story.'

There is a pause. Jazz can hear the clock ticking loudly in the large office beyond. 'Yesterday morning a body was discovered in the waters of the Lanka Samudraya,' Sonny says finally.

Jazz stares. She thinks fleetingly of the gecko landing on his right shoulder.

Walter bangs the top of his desk. 'My God! Imagine it! A body in the swanky new reservoir!' He gives a roar. Jazz can almost see the increased copies rolling off the presses, reflected in his eyes.

'Is this an exclusive?'

'Yes.'

'Then don't hang around. I want you on the train tomorrow.'

'Of course.'

'And I will go also?'

They turn to her in surprise.

'Just one person out in the field, Jazz,' says Sonny gently.

Walter regards her silently. 'Jacintha will also go,' he says after a long pause.

'Jazz – but why?'

'She will go with you because...' Walter is rummaging on his desk for a map, 'she will know the region well and she can speak Tamil better than you can.'

'Superintendent Ludowyk didn't specifically say it was murder...we don't need two of us running up there for something that might turn out to be nothing.'

'Whatever it is, it's a good story, enough to keep you both busy.' Walter gives another thump on the desk. He turns impatiently, bellowing down the hall. 'Pearl, I need you to reserve two train tickets to Batti.' He looks at them. 'Why are you still here? Go home and pack. I want you on that early morning train - don't be late.'

5

Due to worker shortages and repairs to the trains, they are unable to leave the next day. At one point, it also seems as if Jazz will not, after all, be making the trip; her aunt raising an objection to her travelling with Sonny, her uncle concerned that Jazz is being placed in danger. In the end, Angelo Crozier bows to Walter's judgement in the face of Jazz's adamant stance and a telephone conversation with Jazz's father.

They leave on Friday, the first train out to Batticaloa, the 6.05. Her uncle's driver, Ajit, drives to the Fort Railway station, taking charge of her bags, ascertaining which platform the train will depart from. Having finally persuaded him that she is capable of getting on the train without further assistance, she stands in the midst of a huddle of porters in sweat-stained lungis and vests, wrinkling her nose against the stale aromas, waiting for Sonny.

As the activity around her on the platform increases, finally she sees him, his face radiating exhaustion, crossing the forecourt, picking his way through boxes and barrels, the hordes of flies massing over food remnants, and the huddles of beggars, hawkers, and travellers. By the time he has arrived at her side, the train doors are being flung open, the carriages filling up quickly, mostly men in short sleeved shirts and longs.

Douglas appears, panting, bleary eyed, clutching an envelope, some files, and their train tickets.

'You're an early bird today, Dougie,' says Sonny. 'You will catch not one but two worms.'

'Will I receive something good?'

'We'll ask Jazz to give you a kiss on the cheek, no?'

'I say.' Douglas, who is barely out of school, waggles his head and mutters something.

'Don't be such a tease, Sonny,' she says looking at Douglas kindly.

'Mr Jayatilake says be sure to get receipts for everything.'

Sonny dismisses the half-asleep boy with a gentle tap to the head and a handful of rupees, and they climb aboard in search of their reserved seats. She follows Sonny up the aisle of the train, cautious as to what his mood might be, aware that he had not wanted her on the assignment, perhaps annoyed that she would get in the way of his drinking time. She will have to tread carefully and make the most of this chance to work on a potentially big case. Lucky for her it has come along at the start of her career, and so close to her home turf.

Home. Much as she is enjoying the progressive freedoms of the city, there have been occasions when she has yearned for the landscape of her youth: the dry lowlands of the Eastern Province, wooden houses nestled above coastal lagoons, the camaraderie of the women in the paddy fields, elephants roaming through the dense forestation. A place where a girl growing up with a fertile imagination could conjure all sorts of stories to pass the long nights.

'My aunty always used to say the East Coast was cursed. A

place of devils.' It comes out louder than she intended. He whirls around.

'Devils? What the hell are you talking about?'

'Sorry, I was just being silly.' She winces at the acid in his tone, forcing a smile, which he returns with a blank stare.

Tersely he offers her the window seat, hefting her baggage in the hold above, silently taking his seat beside her. She notices he keeps hold of his portable typewriter in its case, placing it with delicacy by his feet.

A few fellows moving back and forth along the aisle look slyly in Jazz's direction, whistling and winking. She keeps her face towards the window, watching the clouds of steam drifting over the platform as the train edges out of the station, a hesitant rattle before picking up speed as they slip through the awakening city and out into open country. Glimpses of shanty huts perilously close to the tracks, washing hanging on a line slung low between palm trees, a small temple. The sun rises over a creek where a single stork wades in the shallows and finally Sonny speaks.

'So, a place of devils, you say?' He's back to his normal self, bantering and soft eyed.

'It was nothing, I was just remembering a few tales from the past.'

'Tell me. I'm listening.'

'Sometimes I would spend holidays with my Aunty Chitty, my mother's sister. She would sit for hours with her winnowing basket, telling her tales as she flung the rice husks high into the air. The legend of Prince Vijaya, the conqueror from India, and the demoness Kuveni who fell in love with the Prince and vanquished his enemies with her wicked sorcery. Do you know that one? My gosh, it was so terrifying. I was just a tiny girl who had to sleep on her own and I would spend hours trying to keep awake, scared that I had invoked the fury of the demoness who would cast a spell upon me and send me to sleep forever. That's when I first started to write my own stories, to stop me falling asleep.'

'You'll have to show me one of your pieces.'

'Maybe some day.'

Sonny stands. 'Now the train is going at a good pace, let's get breakfast. On expenses, of course.'

Jazz follows Sonny along the corridor in a gyrating dance to the buffet car where they are the first to be seated and served. A plain omelette for Jazz, three eggs, three rashers of bacon, and a side order of string hoppers and pol sambol for Sonny.

'Business breakfast, travelling to the scene of a crime, I'm really starting to feel like a reporter.'

'Hush,' Sonny says warningly, as a couple take the table next to theirs.

She lowers her voice. 'And of course, I'm looking forward to seeing my father again this evening.'

They are due to arrive in Batticaloa in the late afternoon. The nearest town to the Lanka Samudraya, Kumburapola, is two hours further, so they will be breaking their journey with an overnight stay. Jazz will be going home with her father to Kalmunai; she assumes Sonny has made his own arrangements.

She eats slowly. Sonny clears his plate quickly, sitting back once he's finished to scrutinise the other passengers.

'Looking for somebody?'

'Checking to see whether there are any reporters on board from rival newspapers. There shouldn't be but you can't be too sure.'

As the buffet car begins to fill with hungry passengers they leave. Their carriage is quiet, practically empty.

'Okay,' says Sonny, 'let's get started. I want you to pull together everything we know about the development of the region.' He passes her the files that Walter has supplied.

'How does this connect to us reporting on the murder?'

'Nobody has mentioned murder, Jazz.'

'No, but I thought…'

'It's bound to be some poor fellow accidentally drowned while out fishing or swimming. But the timing of this tragedy, just weeks after the reservoir was officially opened, will make good copy. Imagine the headline! Just write up a couple of paragraphs. I didn't get much sleep last night so I'm going to have a doze.'

'Yes, okay. But Sonny…'

He has already tipped his head back and closed his eyes, surrendering to the rhythm of the train against the track.

Deepa, the archivist, must have been working night and day. There are copious press cuttings going back to the start of the Lanka Reservoir Project in the late nineteen forties, when the government decided to set the newly independent country on an ambitious modernisation path. The first stage had been to initiate a modern irrigation system, a step up from the ancient water tanks currently in places such as those at Anuradhapura and Polonnaruwa.

By 1951, Jazz's second year in England, the construction had hit its peak. A vast reservoir was in the process of being built alongside vast land clearances ready for future cultivation.

The lake was named the Sea of Lanka or the Lanka Samudraya, the largest reservoir the country has ever seen — Jazz writes — *with its tributaries and streams quenching the thirsty soil of over 7,000 formerly dry hectares.*

'Quenching the thirsty soil.' Sonny is awake and reading over her shoulder in a dramatic tone. 'Sounds like something to include in your novel, perhaps?'

She feels her cheeks redden. 'I'm just trying out words on the page.'

'Relax, I'm teasing you.'

'Well, anyway, the town of Kumburapola is growing quickly,'

says Jazz, leafing through articles. 'New shops, houses, and a hotel. There are even plans to turn the surrounding land into a National Park. It's anticipated that the completed project will set Ceylon on the world stage.'

'Hmm. Could be more to this story then. Something underhand, a deliberate act to darken the triumph of the government. If it does turn out to be murder.'

'That's a bit extreme, isn't it? Murdering somebody to sabotage a celebration?'

'Politics is a dirty business, Jazz. Best we don't waste time speculating. We might as well wait until we meet with Uncle Ludo, that is, Superintendent Ludowyk, and get an update.'

It is Jazz's turn to nod off and she doesn't stir until the customary commotion, hours later when they have reached Gal Oya Junction. As the train comes to a standstill, those with window seats draw up the glass anticipating the pedlars appearing alongside, holding aloft trays of snacks, incessant calls of 'Ah, vadai, vadai! Ah vadai, vadai!' echoing through the station as they walk the length of the train.

Waking abruptly, she sees Sonny stand and stretch at the window, pity spreading across his face as he throws a coin to a limbless beggar sprawled in the dust.

'Ah, you're awake. I got refreshments.' He hands her a dusty bottle containing an orange liquid which she drinks thirstily, watching as the travellers disperse like a shuffle of playing cards across the platform, some heading for the exit, some running across to the Trinco train, while others join their own train to Batticaloa. Newcomers totter up and down the aisle in their carriage and a plump man in his early thirties takes a vacant seat opposite.

She and Sonny exchange a brief look of annoyance. Jazz tucks the files and her notebook away.

'Just got on?' enquires Sonny of their new companion.

'No. I boarded at Colombo. I've been in the buffet car. Good arrack. I managed to persuade the fellow behind the bar to fill up my flask. When I came back to my carriage, some bugger had fallen asleep in my seat. I tried to wake him, but it was no good... ah, what the hell. Have a shot, man.'

He is the type to ignore women. She turns away towards the window and lets the conversation rumble on. Sonny takes a deep draught before handing back the flask.

'Travelling on business, is it?'

'Yes. I've been transferred to the new branch of the Island Bank in Kumburapola, but I have to travel back to Colombo quite a bit. Also, I have a little side-line going. It's turned out to be rather lucrative. But on second thoughts, forget I said that.'

'Of course,' says Sonny.

'Remember, I haven't told you anything.' Jazz watches his reflection in the glass as the stranger places an unsteady finger against his wet lips.

'We're also going to Kumburapola. Our boss wants to see whether we could open a new sector out there.'

'What kind of business are you in?'

'Insurance,' Sonny says smoothly.

'Well, if you need any assistance while you're there, give me a call.' A printed card is handed over from a small leather case. 'R. S. Chandimal,' Sonny reads. 'Good to meet you.'

Chandimal's voice is sleepy. 'My name is Ray,' he says and seconds later his swine-like emissions are filling the carriage.

'He's probably drunk enough to bring an elephant to its knees.' Jazz is out of sorts from the long hours of travel. Her hair, normally silky smooth against her shoulders, is full of knots from having slept in her seat. Muttering, she tries to untangle it with her fingers. She looks up and catches Sonny gazing at her.

He coughs and looks away. 'Don't worry Jazz, not long to go, we're almost there.'

'No doubt my father will already be pacing the platform.'

'When was the last time you saw him?'

'Not that long ago. We were together for Christmas at Uncle's place. But I've not been home for some time.'

Sonny grunts, something shifting in his eyes. Christmas was the biggest event in the Burgher calendar.

She looks across at him. 'Sonny, you didn't go home? Your family must have missed you, no?'

'Well…'

'Let me guess, too many parties and celebrations in Colombo.'

He gives a wan smile. 'My mother was so angry when she found out I wasn't coming home.' He pauses. 'She's just about speaking to me now, but only after I sent a grovelling telegram.'

'Which part of Colombo do you live? Lodging with friends or family, is it?'

'No, not nowadays. When I first arrived, I stayed with Uncle Ludo and his wife for a couple of months until I got taken on at the *Courier*. Then I found myself a room just off Darley Road.'

'I see,' says Jazz. She is familiar enough now with the city to realise that he must be referring to the sprawling two-storey warehouses in that area, roughly developed to provide single living rooms and shared outdoor cooking facilities for as many as fifty people in each building. Her uncle had pointed them out to her once, on a drive through the city. Built in colonial times by rich merchants to store their wares nearer to their shops, these days they display patched roofs and long rows of mean windows, many with broken panes covered with cardboard, others adorned with makeshift shutters to guard occupants from the searing heat.

He avoids her eye. 'After my success on the Ratnayake case, I meant to move to a better place, somewhere bigger, but I've never got round to it. Farnsworth Place is just somewhere to lay my head at night.'

'I understand,' says Jazz. She hopes she doesn't sound patronising. Sonny doesn't appear to be offended, his attention turning to the landscape as the train slows pulling into Batticaloa. 'We've arrived.'

'Ah, yes indeed.' It is monsoon season on the East Coast. The sun is setting and through the window the air blows a refreshingly cool breeze. She gives an expectant sigh.

Ray Chandimal gives a final snort and resurfaces, jumping up and muttering under his breath.

'Is everything okay, man?' Sonny asks. Ray looks at him as if he's never seen him before.

'Yes, very good,' he replies shortly and says nothing further, picking up his briefcase and holdall and departing without a goodbye.

'Odd fellow,' says Jazz. The guard is rattling the windows imploring passengers to leave quickly. They alight, stretching their cramped limbs, blinking in the open air.

'Jacintha!' Guy Barthelot, tall and well-built with grey hair, face lit up at the sight of his only daughter.

'Daddy, this is Mr de Roye, my colleague from the newspaper. Sonny this is my father.'

'A pleasure to meet you, Mr Barthelot,' says Sonny shaking his hand.

'Can we offer you a place to stay?'

'Thank you but my brother-in-law is coming to collect me.'

Jazz raises her eyebrows. 'You didn't say.'

'My sister, Gail, and her family live in Batticaloa. My brother-in-law is Assistant Government Agent for the district.'

Her father says, 'Bernard Alvis? I know of him. A good chap.'

'Yes, he's a nice fellow. I'm fond of him.'

'Well, my dear, we had better get going. There's quite a bit of traffic around.' Her father puts an arm around her.

'Righto. Sonny, see you tomorrow.'

He gives a wave of his hand. Stupidly she feels a pang at leaving him. He turns back as if he has read her mind.

'Have a good evening, Jazz. I'll see you at the bus station tomorrow at nine.'

6

'So, Jazz, come on, what is this Sonny de Roye like? Handsome bugger, no?'

After a quiet dinner with her father catching up with the news, she had been heading for bed when Marlee, her old school-friend, had appeared on the veranda with a half-opened bottle of arrack and a dozen questions.

Although given the opportunity, Marlee chose not to go to university with Jazz. She spends her time helping her older sister with her young children or cooking alongside her mother in the house, with one eye always on the horizon in search of a husband. Jazz knows there is a growing distance between them, but still when they meet, they are able to enjoy shared memories and long discussions about what the future may hold.

Seated around the teak table, the bottle now almost empty, Jazz opts for silence, feeling her cheeks grow warm. She is glad her father has gone to his bed. Marlee persists. 'Yes, yes, I remember his picture from the paper.'

'I mean, he is a good-looking boy, but a very complicated sort of fellow. Not somebody to get entangled with.'

'What do you mean?'

'He drinks more than he should. Keeps very late hours with all the journalists in Colombo. He's a closed kind of fellow.' Her deliberately terse description omits Sonny's easy charm, his kindness, and the fun-loving side of him.

'Show me a Burgher who doesn't drink too much. Still if you think he's not suitable…'

'He would not be suitable.'

'Or have you marked him for yourself?'

'No, of course I haven't.'

'Ah yes, you are the career woman now.'

Quick to divert from the subject of Sonny de Roye, Jazz launches into tales from the *Courier*, office politics, the Colombo courts, all of which hold Marlee's attention until Jazz mentions Pearl, which leads them inevitably back to Sonny.

'Pearl sees you as a rival, no? You are much younger, have the great career, and naturally you stand to get the man she wants.'

'Oh my gosh, Marlee, stop your nonsense. Firstly, Sonny is not interested in me. Secondly, I'm on the newspaper because I want to become a successful journalist. And as for Pearl, she is an older lady, like an aunty.'

'But don't you want a boyfriend to take you to the pictures at the Savoy in the evenings, and buy you ice cream from Alerics at the weekend?'

Jazz shrugs.

'You don't know how lucky you are to be in Colombo with all the restaurants, cinemas, and dances at the hotels. And yet you seem to be excited to be back here.'

'It's my first story.'

'In Kumburapola of all places. Not some juicy Colombo crime.'

'It's just the way it is.'

'I see. This big story that you won't tell me anything about.'

'Sorry. I can't.'

Marlee snorts. 'Did you know that Daddy worked for a while as a Colonisation Officer in Kumburapola recently?'

Jazz's ears sharpen. 'Can you remember anything about it?'

'I do remember him describing the noise and the chaos. Remember Jazz, when we were children, it was just a few roads, a couple of huts and dirt tracks and now it's all modern buildings and lots of people, mostly colonists. Also, others who come to the region trying their luck for work, usually on the building sites.'

'Tell me about the colonisation. It's still going on, isn't it?'

'My gosh, yes, there seems to be no end.'

'How easy is it to apply?'

'Lots of rules and regulations, Jazz! The eldest child of the colonist family must be a son, and the family must not currently own any land, not even an inch. Daddy says the new villages in the valley are being filled with so many more Sinhalese families than Tamils.'

'Really?'

'There has been a bit of unrest. Friends of Mummy and Daddy recently hosted some of the new Sinhalese families overnight on their way to the settlements and had to have a guard standing outside the house the entire night.'

'There's been trouble?'

'Some of the Tamils in the area are annoyed because they didn't meet the strict criteria. They feel land-owning opportunities are being taken away from them for no good reason.'

'I see.'

'Since this new settlement, everything feels different in the area, it doesn't feel as friendly, you know? There's a strained atmosphere.' She pauses. 'Are you going to be scribbling away all night?'

'I might. Don't look at me like that, it's my job.'

Marlee pouts. 'Well, then it's time for my bed.'

Jazz hugs her tightly. 'Come and stay with me when I get back to Uncle's place. We'll go to the cinema and have ice cream together. We don't need boys for that. Okay?'

'Okay. And don't work too hard, it makes you scowl, your face will grow old and wrinkled.'

After settling down under the covers she jumps up again, finds a packet of sandalwood soap that promises radiant skin in the morning, and gives her face a thorough scrub before returning to bed.

7

Jazz and Sonny catch the morning bus, delayed for two hours seemingly without reason, from Karaitivu, an old coastal village just outside Kalmunai. Three women travelling with sacks of flour have taken up seats at the back of the bus and their raucous chatter fills the air. The bus is filled to capacity before it has started along the route heading inland to Kumburapola.

Sonny has barely said a word since boarding. 'Sorry, Jazz,' he says, leaning his head against the window, hot from the sun's rays. 'I'm going to snatch forty winks.'

Clearly, he had drunk too much arrack with his brother-in-law the previous night. She wonders how he can sleep with the chatter and laughter from the women going marketing, a baby howling at the front and a lively conversation in the seats behind. Two engineers are discussing extensive tree felling, on their way to inspect the site of a proposed air strip. She wonders why they are roughing it on the local bus rather than being chauffeured. The bus rumbles on. There is no sign of impending rain, so there won't be delays from flash flooding or mudslides as sometimes happens. The scenery flashes past, forest and shrubland interspersed with paddy fields, lakes, and coconut groves, now and again a minaret, a Hindu temple, hints of stone emerging from the greenery.

Sonny opens his eyes and smiles at her. 'Your father seems a pleasant chap. Did you enjoy your evening at home?'

'Yes, thank you, we had a nice meal, and then one of my class-mates came over. Did you have a nice time with your sister?'

He frowns. 'She wasn't feeling well. I mainly chatted with my brother-in-law. Played with the children a while before bed.'

'Ah, how many do they have?'

'A boy, Joe, almost five and twin three-year old girls, Marjorie and Millie. Scamps, the pair of them.'

'Twins? That sounds like hard work, no?'

Sonny gives a brief nod. By the time they arrive at their desti-nation it is late afternoon. They are bathed in sweat and have to peel themselves away from their seats. Standing, bags at their feet, they face a mix of the usual kades overflowing with wares. In one, a fierce looking man is weighing Maldive fish for a customer, open sacks of rice and lentils spilling out across the floor, while in the cramped space next door, a young man fights to extract a single candle from a complicated arrangement dangling at the front of his booth. Sonny buys them lunch from the hopper stall by the roadside and they eat quickly before walk-ing on.

The new modern shops are practically empty, the locals still perhaps intimidated by the carefully arranged displays of pottery and household goods behind glass windows, the sanitised version of mercantile trading which Jazz considers soulless and which she is surprised to find outside Colombo. Clearly the region is modernising at a fast rate.

A few cars and motor bikes are parked on the fresh new road that shimmers in the heat. Spilling out across the newly paved street is a market, bright with the rainbow colours of the fruit and vegetables, the cries from the stall holders filling the sky like the calling of hungry birds. A man hawking thambilis moves hopefully towards them.

Jazz and Sonny turn a corner where a small area of huts and outhouses stand, housing rows of damp washing reeking of woodsmoke. 'According to the notes, last century, the British built these to use as a resting place during their hunting trips,' Jazz says.

From out of nowhere come violent raindrops, the last ballad of the fading monsoon. Women halfway through their marketing wind up their saris, running in sandaled feet for the nearest place to shelter, the men on the streets covering their heads with their newspapers.

'Well, we're the hunters now.' Sonny has started to run, shaking raindrops from his fringe. 'Let's go and find the story.'

~

They find Superintendent Ludowyk under the canopy of the police station, where he is giving orders to a handful of officers dampened in the rainstorm.

'Sonnah boy! How are you? I was expecting you sooner.'

'Yes, Uncle, the usual train delays in Colombo and then also the bus this morning.'

The Superintendent waves his arms at the surrounding crowd. 'This is Sonny de Roye, from the *Colombo Courier*.' Sonny raises a hand in greeting.

'Please give any help you can to Mr de Roye, you have my permission to answer all reasonable questions. Sonny, do you hear what I'm saying? Reasonable questions. I can't say fairer than that. And who is this delightful young lady?'

'Jacintha Barthelot. Junior reporter.' She holds out her hand firmly. Superintendent Ludowyk takes her small hand in his large one and pats it briefly.

'Very pleased to meet you.' He turns to Sonny. 'Inquest was yesterday afternoon, such a shame you were delayed. Come, come, the rain has stopped. Let's find somewhere to talk.'

Further down the road is an older style tea boutique. Superintendent Ludowyk waves them towards a table in the window and goes to order. Sonny closes his eyes while Jazz watches a street barber at his work, customers squatting or standing in the road, the barber lathering foam in a brass bowl, a brown dog asleep by his feet.

The tea arrives accompanied by thin slices of butter cake. She opens her notebook and turns to the superintendent. He meets her gaze, wiping his mouth.

'The girl is keen, Sonnah boy, no?' He gives a shout of laughter. 'Okay, let me update you. On Wednesday morning Superintendent Madugalle from Batticaloa district was asked to visit the scene of the Lanka Samudraya where a body had been discovered. He was accompanied by a Crown Counsellor from the Attorney General's Department. They carried out a survey of the scene and then arranged for the Judicial Medical Officer in Batticaloa to conduct a postmortem examination.'

'Why is it you were called over from Colombo?' Jazz asks.

'The LRP were panicking. They didn't want a lot of hulla-balloo around the new reservoir. I've got friends on the Board, so they called on me as a favour to get things processed with discretion.'

'LRP?'

'The Lanka Reservoir Project.'

'Ah right.'

'The inquest was held on Friday before the District Magistrate in Batticaloa. Magistrate gave a ruling of death of an unidentified person caused by gunshot wounds to the chest and heart. One bullet has been found, trapped within the rib cage.'

'So, it was murder. Not a drowning accident.' She is quietly jubilant. She turns to Sonny who is staring impassively at the superintendent.

'So, we are now starting to gather evidence to take to the magistrate. The first thing of course, being to establish the identity of the body. I am going to be running the case from Colombo in order to keep it a respectable distance from the reservoir project.'

Superintendent Ludowyk swallows the remains of his tea. 'If you are both refreshed, shall we go?'

'Go? We've only just come.' Jazz is beginning to realise the unrelenting pace of being out in the field.

'We'll go and see the place where the body was found.'

'Of course.' She glances across at Sonny who gives a small shrug. As they make their way outside, she nudges him. 'Are you okay? I thought you would be delighted it's going to be such a big story.' He raises his eyebrows. She reminds herself that Sonny has reported on countless crimes, but she is surprised that he has so little enthusiasm for the task.

An officer in a khaki uniform is waiting in an open-top jeep with police insignia painted on its doors. He jumps down and stows their bags in the boot. Superintendent Ludowyk is already settling himself in the front. 'Let's go.'

They drive through the town, frenzied building work everywhere, office buildings, factories and warehouses rising up through rivers of concrete. Their driver, a softly spoken Tamil, points out places of interest.

'That site over there will be District Central Dispensary, opening next year. Also, a maternity hospital, much needed here. At the moment only small clinics serve the district.

'This building on the left will be a school. Lots of Sinhalese children coming to the area, from settler families.'

Remembering her conversation with Marlee the previous evening, Jazz glances at him but the constable is expressionless.

'How do you feel about all these new developments?' she asks.

The constable waggles his head. 'I live here my whole life. Lots of changes happening all the time, engineers from Britain, the United States and Canada, and foreign builders coming from all over.'

She notes he has not expressed an opinion either way.

The road leading away from the town begins to disappear. The sturdy vehicle comes into its own once the road has disappeared into deep rutted tracks. There are signs of land clearances as they drive further. Jazz nudges Sonny. 'This must be part of the development of the new National Park.'

'You will see elephants,' says their driver without turning his head. 'Also leopards and red deer. Many birds coming across the water, storks, eagles, and herons. And crocodiles, also.'

'Ah,' says the Superintendent looking uncomfortable in the rural surroundings. Jazz thinks he is probably wishing himself back in the police station in Colombo behind his desk, the roar of the city streets much more to his liking.

They travel around a bend along a stony road shaded by trees and suddenly, before them, are the sparkling waters stretching as far as the eye could see. In the distance the mountain peaks of the majestic Inginiyagala rise, topped by low rain clouds. Superintendent Ludowyk directs the constable to drive about half a mile round before stopping.

'Stay with the car, Constable. Keep a look out for elephants, jackals and whatnot. You two come with me.'

'How big is this reservoir?' asks Sonny glancing across at Jazz. They have read the reports, but even so they are unprepared for the forbiddingly huge expanse of water.

'Nine miles long and four and a half miles across at its widest point.'

There are fishing boats out towards the centre, tattered sheet sails billowing in the strengthening winds. A flock of cormorants fly up from one of the islets scattered around the waters. It is eerily quiet. Jazz turns to Sonny who is tracking something in the far distance with his eyes. 'Baby elephant,' he murmurs. 'Look, there in that bit of scrubland. Poor fellow looks a bit lost.'

'Come, come.' Superintendent Ludowyk is striding towards the edge of the lake and a waiting boatman, Jazz is keeping pace ahead with Sonny silent alongside. She clambers into the boat, followed by Sonny who sportingly takes the dampest spot with a wry grin.

The boatman pushes away from the shore, and they head across at a fair pace. The Superintendent's voice booms across the vast expanse of water. 'We're heading for the spot where a couple of young chaps out fishing found the body.'

They fall into silent contemplation, Jazz's eyes combing the rocky outcrops filled with birds in the bright daylight, wondering if the crime had been committed on one of them during a night full of shadows.

'When I say body, I actually mean a partial skeleton, in fact.' The superintendent's voice makes her jump.

Jazz thinks for a moment she has misheard. 'A skeleton? But how long was the body in the water?'

'The body is still undergoing tests so we cannot say.' Superintendent Ludowyk becomes stern. 'Please do not put that in print until we have more facts.'

They have almost reached the far side of the lake. Sonny sits unblinking, his face an unreadable mask.

'Sonny,' she says, 'are you okay?'

He answers in a flat tone. 'Of course.'

They have come to a stop at the other side of the lake. Superintendent Ludowyk clambers out first, holding out his hand to Jazz and then Sonny. He leads them to where a couple of small buoys mark the spot where the body had been retrieved at the shore. Further out two more are lying where the body had first been spotted.

Jazz shades her eyes and stares across. 'Superintendent, would it be possible to have the fishermen's details, we would like to hear their story?'

'Yes, I'm happy to share that information with you.'

'So, Ludo, do we have any idea who the victim is?' Sonny is suddenly alert.

'Not a single clue. As I mentioned before, the body has been taken back to the hospital morgue for further investigation.'

'I wonder what on earth happened to our mystery man? Shot, then ending up in the reservoir,' says Jazz.

'Who says the body was a man?' Sonny says. 'You didn't actually say, Uncle?'

'That's one thing the Chief Medical Officer would say with any certainty.' The superintendent walks to the far edge of the section marked by the buoys and gazes across the glistening waters to one of the islands. 'It was a man.'

8

At the front of the vehicle, Superintendent Ludowyk and the constable converse in low murmurs, Jazz and Sonny silent in the back seats, looking out of their respective windows. The rain has arrived and a mist is forming around the perimeters of the lake as they drive away. She gives a shiver, wondering about the dead man. Surely somebody must be missing him, wondering where on earth he could be.

She feels a sudden need to make small talk, share a laugh with Sonny, at the constable's huge billowing khaki shorts, clearly made for someone of a much bigger build, or Superintendent Ludowyk's flyaway hair escaping in the breeze of the open-top jeep, giving him the look of a wild forest goddess, the *Kukulapo Kiri Amma* maybe, another of Aunty's tales. She almost risks a joke but looking across at Sonny's set jaw, she thinks better of it, joining him in contemplative silence.

Driving back through the town they finally stop in a small lane off the main street of Kumburapola outside an unusual two-storey house. Superintendent Ludowyk turns around.

'This is the place, organised for you by your boss, no? You will be well looked after here. I'm told the lady is a Burgher widow who will make you feel very welcome.' The constable nods approvingly from the driver's seat.

'Well, Sonnah boy, why don't you both settle in and take it easy. I'll see you both tomorrow; we have a reservation for lunch at 1pm at Still Waters, a place I think you might find interesting. I will come at half past twelve.' The superintendent gives a brief wave as the vehicle drives sharply away.

They pick up their bags without speaking, Jazz following Sonny across a trimmed lawn surrounded by pink and green zinnias in a neat border. The house has a veranda at the front and the sides and a sign: 'The Lanka Welcome Guest House.'

'Place looks far too nice for our pockets. Still, if Walter has booked it, it must be okay. Strange though.' Sonny hovers at the door.

Jazz realises her presence on the trip has prompted Walter to book somewhere far superior to the places Sonny would normally stay. No doubt at her uncle's insistence. 'Let's go in.'

Jazz pushes gently past him through the open front door and they pass into the cool interior of a large hallway. Fragrant spices waft through the air. A fan overhead is creating a pleasant breeze, underneath which a Persian cat is lying half asleep, whiskers lifting in the cool air. To one side is a wooden desk with a bell, to the other a dark wooden staircase. Sonny jangles the bell, its tinny clamour bringing a woman clattering down the stairway.

'Good evening! Welcome, my name is Mrs Andrado. I was told to expect a Sonny de Roye from a newspaper in Colombo, and a colleague.' She looks with surprise at Jazz. 'I'm very happy you have chosen my place. What exactly are you reporting on, may I ask?'

'The Lanka Samudraya,' says Sonny.

'Ah. I see. Well, of course the opening of the reservoir has been in the news for many months now. Come, come, let me show you your rooms.'

They follow behind.

'House was built in the 1830s by a wealthy British trader for his 'native' wife and family, a safe distance from his English wife and children, who came to join him a few years after his arrival on the island. Such a complicated way of living!

'I've lived in the house all my life. Parents both sadly have passed, followed by my husband two years ago. We weren't blessed with children, but I had my brothers and their families, my nieces and nephews while they lived close by. Then both families moved to Canada last year. So now, it's just me.' She pauses. 'Was that the police constable dropping you off just now?'

Sonny and Jazz, wishing to keep the murder story quiet, exchange a look.

'Well, I'm sure I was mistaken; my eyes are not as they used to be. Now, we are quiet at the moment, it's the rainy season, you will have the place to yourselves. Towels are included and also breakfast. Come, come.'

She leads them to a front-facing room, neat and clean, dark wood furniture, light coloured walls and a bed made up with floral linen. 'I'm sure this will be comfortable for you,' says Mrs Andrado looking at Jazz, 'Miss…?'

'Jacintha Barthelot.'

'Barthelot?' Mrs Andrado wrinkles her eyes. 'You have a look of a man with that name, a forester working around this region, many years ago.'

'That's right. My father, Guy. Retired now.'

'I always used to say to my husband that the world is such a small place.'

'Yes, I suppose it is. The room is very nice, thank you.'

'Bathroom is at the end of the corridor. I will leave you to settle in. When you are ready come downstairs and I will make you some tea. And now, I'll show you to your room, Mr de Roye, the best room which has had some modifications to it, its own shower, constructed a few years ago by one of my long-term guests, a reservoir engineer from abroad. He did not wish to share a bathroom.' She calls over her shoulder for Sonny to follow.

'Sonny, why don't you take a nap?' Jazz suggests. 'You're still looking tired.' Although she thinks it may be something more than tiredness, his verve and bounce gone, his eyes deep pools overflowing with worry.

'Yes, okay,' he says slowly. 'See you later.'

She watches as he follows Mrs Andrado to the end of the corridor where a small staircase concealed behind a door leads to the top of the house. As they tread the stairs, she can hear the landlady announce that she has made mutton curry for the evening meal. Gently, Jazz closes her door.

Half an hour later, she makes her way downstairs. Cups of tea and a plate of Maliban biscuits await her on the veranda. Before sitting down, she takes one of the cups upstairs and knocks gently on Sonny's door, creeping into the unlocked room when there is no answer. The shutters have been closed but she can distinguish Sonny's sleeping form, almost as if he has passed out, still in his clothes on top of the bed.

She checks his breathing which is soft and even on her cheek when she bends down. Leaving the cup on the table she creeps away.

Heavy rain drumming on the windowpane wakes her just after dawn. She raises herself feeling stiff after two days of travel. The room is momentarily cool without the heat of the sun. She stretches and eases herself out of bed, walking towards the windows to open the shutters onto the misty garden. The lawn is beaded in silver and at the end of a pathway, teardrops fall from the branches of a papaya tree.

In the big kitchen Mrs Andrado is frying eggs on an open fire in the corner. Jazz is pleased to see Sonny seated on a stool. He looks up as she enters and gives her a small grin. 'Mrs Andrado is making breakfast.'

'How are you this morning?'

'Right as rain. Slept all afternoon and through the night.' He pats his flat stomach. 'I have an empty bundy that needs filling.'

'It won't be long, Sonny.' Mrs Andrado gives a delighted laugh. 'So nice to have people to cook for again. Guest house has been empty, these last few months.'

Mrs Andrado dips her head. 'I will serve out on the veranda. Sonny, did you want to tell Jacintha about your visitor from the police? Your godfather?'

Jazz looks across enquiringly.

'He called around briefly. Our lunch has been cancelled.'

'Oh.'

'And apparently, Walter has asked him to pass on a message for us to get in touch. We'll go to the post office after our visit.'

'Okay.'

While they eat, Mrs Andrado switches the radio on and begins her housework at the back of the house, warbling along to a popular tune playing on the Radio Service, a vaguely unpleasant sound. They meet each other's eyes and laugh.

'Sorry about yesterday, Jazz, I'm feeling okay today.'

'You're looking better, I must say.'

He lowers his voice. 'I'm fine. It was a surprise to see the superintendent first thing, lucky I was up early. I don't think Mrs A yet realises we are following a police enquiry, so let's keep it that way for now. We will go and speak to the fishermen who found the body. I got the address from Uncle. Have you finished? Shall we get going?'

'I'm ready.'

Mrs Andrado appears beside them, carrying rags and cleaning equipment. 'Rain is stopping,' she says cheerily. 'Are you going out now?'

'Yes. We're going to look up a couple of acquaintances living at this address. Is it far?'

She glances at the address. 'Turn right out of the house, left onto the main road and keep walking. It's a little place about a mile away.'

9

It was two boys who had found the body, the Wijesinghe brothers. 'Sinhalese fellows,' says Jazz. 'I suppose they are part of the recent influx, looking for work.'

It takes a while to find their place, a small shack in a row of similar dwellings, recently sprung up in a hamlet a mile outside the town. Rapping on the partially open door, they enquire for the two sons. A middle-aged woman, the mother, directs them to a small brick-making factory half a mile down the track.

They enter a yard filled with noise, three wooden structures housing mountains of bricks along one side, the kilns housed in a structure in the centre giving off heat and odours. Men in sarongs and vests, heavily sweating, are coming in and out of the kiln house, others are preparing the mix of clay, sand and water while several are methodically pressing the wet mixture into brick-shaped moulds. Nobody looks up at their arrival.

'We're looking for the Wijesinghe brothers. It's okay, they're not in any trouble,' calls Sonny in the general direction of the labourers. One of them raises his head and shakes the remnants of clay mixture from his hands. He comes over, glancing at Jazz curiously, releasing a spiral of Sinhalese. He's young, probably no older than seventeen. Sonny pulls out his reporter's card and shows it to the young fellow who glances at it and waggles his head.

'Ayubowan, my name is Sonny, and this is my colleague Jacintha. What shall we call you?'

'Nihal.'

'Nihal, we want to ask some questions about the body you found with your brother at the Lanka Samudraya. Would that be okay?'

The young man turns pale. 'Already go to inquest, sir. Amme made us wash and tidy first. Felt very scared to stand and speak to everybody but I told magistrate everything, sir. Boss man not happy because we miss two hours work here. Don't want trouble, sir.'

From his pocket Sonny draws a handful of rupees and a packet of Peacocks. 'No trouble, Nihal. You tell us also, what happened?'

Nihal brightens. 'Right, sir.'

Sonny takes a cigarette from his own pack, lights up and hands it to Nihal, then lights his own.

Ready with her notebook, Jazz says, 'What day did this happen, Nihal?'

'Early hours of Wednesday morning, Miss. We work here in the day, go home, and have some sleep then wake up sometimes to go night fishing.'

'Did you catch a lot of fish that night?'

'Catch lot of carp, Miss. New reservoir mean nice, clean water, so fish very fresh. We spend a few hours catching fish for Thatha to sell in market. Five o'clock start to go back. No good to be late for work here. We always busy with all new buildings in town.'

'When did you first see the body in the water?'

'My brother, Ranil, see something floating towards us. Tied up. He stand up and there is danger, boat rock like cradle. He use oar to pull the thing close. He think it might be big fish caught in net. When we see what it is, we vomit.'

'Can you say what it looked like, Nihal?'

'Covered in a net. Very thick rope. Ranil shout at me and say not to look, but I want to see, so I open my eyes.'

'I'm sorry about this, it's not nice to have to speak about it all over again. Where is your brother now?'

'Brother has left area after inquest. Too upset to stay.'

'Okay.' Sonny finds some more coins in his pocket and presses them into Nihal's hand. 'Thank you, you've been very helpful.'

They watch him return to his piles of mud and buckets.

'Horrible thing to have happened. He seems very shaken by the experience.'

'Yes, and who can blame him, poor fellow.'

They make their way back through the streets of Kumburapola. 'Jazz, I'll go and queue for the telephone in the post office, no need for both of us to hang around. I'll see you back at the guest house.'

'Are you sure?'

'I'm sure. You will be sick to death of this post office before too long; every day a visit to pick up messages from Walter, send him our copy or queue to use the telephone.'

'Righto, Sonny.'

It is one o'clock as she slows her steps at the gate of the guest house where pleasant cooking aromas are scenting the air. 'Jacintha, there you are!' The landlady appears on the veranda. 'I have cooked lunch if you are hungry?'

She suddenly realises she is.

'Sonny is not with you?'

'No.'

'Well, I am sure he knows his own business. Come, come, we can eat and save him a plate.'

After lunch Jazz seats herself in the parlour while Mrs Andrado supervises the servant girl to clean and tidy the kitchen. Jazz feels her eyelids closing. She wakes in a darkened room. She cannot believe she has slept right through to nightfall. She rises in alarm. The landlady coughs gently in the darkness.

'Jacintha? Come and sit with me.'

'What's the time? Did I really sleep all afternoon?' She looks around for Sonny.

'You have just taken forty winks.'

'Oh, but it's so dark.'

'I have closed the shutters. Sit, sit.'

Obediently she rises to join her landlady at the large table which fills one half of the room. 'Opposite me,' instructs Mrs Andrado switching on a table lamp. 'Now give me your hand.'

Relaxed from her nap, Jazz obliges.

'You have a good long lifeline.' Mrs Andrado has taken her hand across the table and turned her palm upwards, looking approvingly across the criss-crossing lines. 'Shall I read for you?'

'If you want.' She does her best to hide her amusement. She remembers a time in England with her friend Vera when, in Brighton for the day, they had visited a clairvoyant, somewhere on the seafront. Her friend had just lost an aunt who had always promised that after she died, she would do her best to send a message from beyond the grave. Nobody had come through for Vera or Jazz, but the old woman had wrinkled her nose at them and told them they still needed to pay.

Mrs Andrado is continuing to peer into her hand.

'Where did you learn to read palms?'

'My granny taught me, and also how to cast horoscopes. I'm gifted that way. You are not supposed to hide your light under a bushel, isn't it? Would you like me to cast your horoscope?'

'That's okay, Mrs Andrado, please don't trouble yourself.'

'Let me see now.' The landlady is concentrating, eyes squinting. 'I am looking Jacintha, and I am seeing something unusual here.'

'Ah, here you both are.'

Neither of the women has heard Sonny's approach.

'What's going on here? Having a bit of a manicure, is it?'

Jazz looks at him sharply. He's kidding with them, but his heart isn't in it.

'Sit, sit, Sonny. Your turn. Give me your hand.'

'Red is not my colour, Mrs A, I probably need a lighter shade, just to warn you.'

'Oh, stop your nonsense now, let me concentrate.' Mrs Andrado gazes long and hard before releasing his palm abruptly. 'I can't stand around all afternoon chatting. I will fetch your food,' she says, hurrying from the table.

'Women's talk and whatnot, is it?'

'Something like that,' says Jazz rising. 'I'll see if she needs a hand.'

Mrs Andrado is taking food from a covered pan ready to turn it onto a plate.

'Do you need help?'

'I have everything ready.'

'Is something wrong?'

'Ai, nothing.'

'You seem a little upset.'

'I thought I saw something horrible for both of you. Anger. Darkness. And...'

'Yes,' Jazz coaxes her gently.

'A body. Lifeless.'

'I see.' At first Jazz thinks the canny landlady is fishing for information but observing her closely she can see the woman is genuinely distressed. 'Mrs Andrado, please be calm. Look, I'll let you into a secret. We are not here to do a piece on the Lanka Samudraya, at least not in the way you believe. We are reporting on a murder.'

'A murder?'

'Hush,' says Jazz looking over her shoulder to see if Sonny has followed them into the kitchen.

'Oh my. But...well okay. That would explain what I saw.' Mrs Andrado looks across at her. 'Thank you for telling me. I will not tell a soul.'

Jazz hears Sonny scrape back his chair. 'Let's not mention this to Sonny. Shall we just forget about it?'

'Yes, yes, I will be happy to do that. And I will not say anything about your case.'

10

'What did Walter say? You seem a little annoyed.'

Sonny is bolting his food. He looks at her without speaking, empties his plate, then addresses her shortly. 'I'm going to get my stuff and I'll meet you outside.'

'Righto.' She can't imagine what has happened.

They leave, Sonny setting a pace, Jazz struggling to keep up. 'Slow down,' Jazz says, 'just tell me what is going on.'

'Apparently, arrangements have been made to rent office space for us.'

'Is that usual when we are reporting in another district?'

'No.'

'But why, then?'

Sonny's voice is cool. 'I thought you might know something about it.'

'Me? Of course not.'

'This is my idea of hell. I hope you realise that.'

'Come on Sonny, what exactly did Walter say?'

He doesn't answer her. They have come to a halt in the middle of a row of newly built shops, one filled with woven mats and rugs, another smaller one, half empty, closed, full of shelves waiting to be put up. Alongside is another, newly painted. Sonny produces a key and steps inside. She follows.

'Apparently there's a filing cabinet coming tomorrow; for now, we just have desks and chairs. Welcome to the East Coast branch of the *Courier*. You and I are now its official correspondents.' He gives a mirthless smile and places his typewriter on one of the desks.

'Seriously?'

'I think I see what the deal is here. Your uncle thinks if we are working in an office environment, this will put minds at rest regarding your safety.'

'Sonny, you have to believe that I had nothing to do with this. I just want to be treated like everybody else. How do you imagine I feel?' She pauses, her eyes flashing. 'Uncle is wildly ambitious you know. He must view this as the first step towards expansion. I have heard him say he wants the *Courier* to eventually be a national newspaper.'

He grunts. 'Well, whatever the reason, the Board have decided that our presence here heralds a new phase for the *Courier*. I spoke to Suresh briefly and he couldn't believe it. And as for Walter, well he thinks it's a crazy idea, but he says for the moment, his hands are tied.'

'I wonder how long we will have to be here?'

'In my case, until I learn to behave better, I am guessing. I get the feeling your uncle is not keen on me.'

Jazz is impressed at how perceptive he is. Her uncle has found a way of keeping Sonny away from whatever causes him such trouble in Colombo. She senses her aunt's hand in this also, probably happy for her unconventional niece to be out of sight, hidden in the back of beyond away from their influential friends.

As if reading her mind Sonny says, 'I do think this is unfair on you, Jazz. To have the bright lights of the city dangled before you and then snatched away.'

'Well, treat it as my card being marked.'

He looks at her and nods. 'We'll have to make the best of it. Although how, I don't know. I've got a feeling this murder is going to dwindle away into nothing. No leads to go on. Unknown identity of the victim. Once we break the story that's it.'

'We'll just have to find other stories then.' Her tiger eyes are still glinting.

'Exactly.'

'Our landlady will be pleased, anyhow.'

'Oh yes. She will now have plenty of opportunities to cast your horoscope. She's probably got lots of Burgher acquaintances with sons needing wives, who would swoon at the sight of you with your hair running down your back like a waterfall, and those eyes of yours.'

She is not sure what kind of reply she should give.

He gives an awkward laugh. 'I'm going to have to keep an eye on you.'

'Really? I thought it was more likely to be the other way round.'

He grunts good naturedly. 'Let's get this report typed up. Prop the door open a little, it's so stuffy.'

He sits down at the desk, fixes a sheet of paper into his Remington, and begins to tap away at the keys. Every now and again Jazz prompts him from her notes, strengthening the narrative with descriptions of the hauntingly beautiful reservoir, the stillness of the waters, the young fishermen in their boats and the shocking discovery. They keep their word to Superintendent Ludowyk, making no mention of the skeletal aspect of the body.

When Sonny is satisfied, he places the typewritten sheets on the desk. 'We need envelopes, paper and pens.'

'I will go and get them.'

'You go to the post office and dispatch this to Walter. I'll get some supplies. Meet back here in half an hour.'

Sonny's supplies include a bottle of arrack and some mugs. He pours them both a measure when she arrives back, hot and thirsty.

'Might as well have a drink to christen the new place. Cheers.'

She glances around the office, files, reams of paper and envelopes now stacked beside his Remington. Curious she asks, 'Does the typewriter belong to the *Courier*?'

'No. It's mine. Given as a gift when I left home for Colombo.'

She takes another slug of arrack when it is offered. 'A gift from whom?'

'Well, that's a bit of a story. I worked hard at school, got top grades in Senior School Certificate, and was all set to do my High School Certificate when my father got sick and was no longer able to stay in his job. I had to leave school to find work to support the family.'

'That's rough luck.'

'I took the first job I was offered, a position on one of the tea estates as a junior office clerk which I hated; long hours in a boring office where nothing ever happened. A few months later I saw an advertisement for the post of junior reporter at *The Badulla Times* and was lucky to get taken on. I realised quite quickly that I loved the job but after a while I grew restless reporting about lost cats and random pilfering from market stalls.

'When I turned nineteen, I decided to leave for Colombo to try and get onto one of the big newspapers. My school friend, Victor, came with me. He had been working in one of the hotels owned by his father and he fancied spreading his wings and trying his luck in one of the Colombo hotels. The night before we left, Victor's father gave me this.' He pats the Remington. 'It had been used by one of his staff who used to travel with it between offices. It's my pride and joy.'

She grows quiet. He probably considers her a spoilt princess with her stories about life at Reading University.

'Jazz? You're a million miles away.'

She shakes herself. 'Sorry. What did you say?'

'I said that I think we should make our own way to Still Waters tomorrow and find out what we can about the people who've been designing and building the reservoir. Maybe one of them will have had a reason to put a body in that lake of theirs.'

11

'During this current Maha crop-growing season, all the signs are pointing towards a great harvest.' Listening to Mr Karunaratne's prepared speeches is like dealing with a radio presenter unable to deviate from a script. Jazz does her best to maintain a semblance of enthusiasm, but Sonny she can see, is lost in faraway thoughts behind the plumes of his habitual cigarette smoke. She makes notes diligently, although Ashoke Karunaratne, who is there to promote the merits of the newly formed reservoir region, is ignoring her presence, choosing to direct his speech to Sonny.

'I assume you are familiar with paddy cultivation, Mr de Roye?'

Arriving with an air of innocence at Still Waters, they had asked to speak to somebody about rice cultivation. Impressed with their Colombo credentials, Mr Karunaratne had readily agreed but it is proving impossible to shift him even a fraction of an inch away from the agreed topic.

Jazz catches Sonny's eye and he gives a wry shrug. She glances over Mr Karunaratne's shoulder into the plush interior lounge of the clubhouse known as Still Waters. An attractive woman, probably the wife of one of the engineers, is sitting down to lunch. Unexpectedly the woman smiles at her, a vaguely sympathetic look. Jazz hopes she will still be there after they have finished with Mr Karunaratne.

Sonny is valiantly trying to divert Mr Karunaratne towards a more pertinent topic. 'I understand the settlers are given several acres of paddy land, plus the necessary farm implements. Can you expand a little on that theme?'

'Well, yes, if you like. In the beginning all the land, of course, had to be prepared,' said Mr Karunaratne. 'We were lucky that the company brought in bulldozers to complete the task quickly. Traditionally wild buffaloes would have been used to level the ground, but the Lanka Reservoir Project spared neither expense nor manpower to clear the ground. Then they had to ensure that only the finest quality rice seeds were planted. There are, of course, many different types of rice but at the moment the settlers are mainly growing the keeri samba variety.'

'These settlers,' interjects Jazz, 'were they farmers previously? Were they all happy to have been moved here just to grow rice?'

Mr Karunaratne blinks. 'Certainly, many of them have agricultural experience, but in their former homes they lacked their own land. They are all grateful to have been given a plot of their own.'

'And are the settlers equally split into two groups - Tamil and Sinhalese?'

'Roughly speaking it is so.'

'And will it continue in the same way?'

'I don't actually have the answer to that just now. But if we return to the question of the paddy fields you will see that—'

'I've heard,' says Jazz, 'that not all the land is being handed out in a fair manner. For example, the Sinhalese settlers have been given the land on the upper parts of the area, very close to the dam, while the Tamils and Muslims have been placed lower down where presumably the water reach is not as good.'

'Well...it was felt it would be best to keep the communities separate.'

'I wonder how it was decided that the Sinhalese would receive the better plots?'

Ashoke Karunaratne rises from his seat swiftly. 'I am sorry, I'm going to have to leave you now, I have some people to meet. I think I have given you all the information about rice production that you have asked me for. I hope you will enjoy your visit to our clubhouse and please sample some of our delicious food as my guests, before you leave. Ayubowan.'

He scuttles away, casting dark glances in their direction. Jazz closes her notebook. 'I'm sorry I frightened him away. Maybe I went too far.'

Sonny stares at her thoughtfully. She's convinced he is annoyed but then he says mildly, 'Not at all, you got him to reveal his discomfort around the bias towards the Sinhalese. Where did you pick up that line of questioning?'

'I had a tip-off from a friend while I was in Kalmunai. Do you think it could be connected to the case?'

Sonny shrugs. 'It's certainly a lead to follow up.'

'Don't look around but there's a woman over there who seems friendly and willing to talk.'

Instantly he turns. 'Shall we?' As they approach her table the woman looks up with a smile, holding out her hand.

'Well, hello, I was hoping you would come over. I've been dying of curiosity. Please join me. It is lunch time after all.' She has an American drawl. She claps her hands with the air of one used to being waited on and instantly a uniformed young boy arrives to receive the order of further lunch dishes and two extra glasses of wine.

'I bet you're in need of refreshment. I'm afraid poor Ash can be a little dry.' She nods in the direction of the disappearing Karunaratne.

'And rather dull,' murmurs Sonny, smoothing back his fringe and giving her a wide smile. Jazz frowns.

'My name's Peyton Emery. Please excuse my appearance, I've come straight from the tennis court.' Jazz knows the woman is completely aware that she has drawn Sonny's attention to the white tennis skirt barely covering her shapely knees.

'Sonny de Roye. And my colleague, Jacintha Barthelot. We are here to do a piece about the Lanka Reservoir for the *Colombo Courier.*'

'How interesting. Good to meet you.'

'So, tell us about yourself and this place, Mrs Emery.'

'Peyton, please.'

Sonny drinks half his wine straight off. Jazz takes some gentle sips so she can keep her mind clear.

'We came out in '49. My husband, Bob, was one of the original engineers brought in on the project in its very early days. He and Dick Fry were the first two out. Poor Dick …who knows where he is now…perhaps I shouldn't have mentioned him.'

Jazz's heart leaps. Sonny warns her with his eyes, biding his time with the American woman who cannot help gushing information like a waterfall.

'Darnit, you're reporters and here I go opening my big mouth. Look, we don't talk about Dick so could we pretend I haven't said anything? I'm sure he'll turn up sooner or later. Although…' She lowers her voice. 'There's a rumour doing the rounds that they found somebody dead in the reservoir. Imagine if that's true! Some of us are now of course wondering whether it might be poor Dick.' She looks at them sharply. 'Maybe that's why you are both really here.'

Jazz's mouth opens in surprise. Sonny raises an eyebrow.

'Mr de Roye…or may I call you Sonny? We've all been told in

no uncertain terms to stay quiet about this matter. Sometimes in this place it's hard to tell who among us are friends and who would stick a knife in your back. I'm just kidding, of course, but there's a certain amount of professional rivalry, not really among us foreign workers, more the natives, if you understand me. I don't mean natives in a derogatory way of course…'

Jazz suspects that is precisely what she means but her face doesn't slip.

'I understand. You can't say anything more in our present surroundings.' Sonny breaks off as the waiter brings fresh curries and bowls of rice. Reacting to his look, Jazz swiftly changes direction.

'So, where was it you met your husband? Bob, I think you said.'

'He was out in California at the start of a new contract. I was working as a secretary and one day I went on an earlier lunch break than usual to my favourite diner, and he was in a booth opposite me. He's British, he'd just flown in from London and was baffled by the menu. I can still see him now, puzzling over what devilled chicken and golden nugget cake could possibly be! I sat myself down opposite and helped him make his choices. That was seven years ago, and we've been practically inseparable ever since.'

'And do you have children?'

'A daughter, Janine. We moved to England after we were married; Bob's contract had finished, and he had to return home. Janine has been staying with Bob's parents while we've been out here. Our time here is drawing to a close and I really can't wait to get back to England. I've missed my baby girl so much.'

'I'm sure you have.'

Peyton lifts a delicately plucked eyebrow. 'So, what's your story, Sonny? Have you left a wife behind in the city?'

'No time for a wife. Work keeps me busy.'

'Well, you mustn't keep too busy. Everybody has to have some fun sometimes.'

The head waiter strides into the centre of the dining room. 'Is there a Mr de Roye here?'

Sonny looks up in surprise. 'Yes, that's me.'

'Telephone call for you, sir. Come this way.'

After a short while, Sonny reappears looking irritable. 'Time to go.'

Jazz springs to her feet. 'It's been lovely to meet you, Peyton.'

'You too, dear. Let's set up a lunch date so we can chat some more. How about tomorrow? Do you know the Ocean View Guest House, on the edge of town? It's a good place to meet if you want a bit of privacy away from here.' She glances around as if to indicate the prying eyes of the other wives. 'Would one o'clock suit you?'

'We'll look forward to it.'

They make their way back through the lush gardens, along the colonnaded veranda overlooking the tennis courts and the swimming pool, until they reach the fountain that stands at the entrance, flanked by a pride of stone peacocks. Sonny stops and lights a cigarette with a grimace.

'Who was on the telephone?'

'The superintendent. He was extremely annoyed to discover that we made our own way to Still Waters. He may be my godfather but when he's cross, boy, do you know about it.'

'How did he know we were here?'

'Somebody brought it to the attention of his pals on the LRP board.'

Jazz notices the tips of his ears are red. 'Did you mention anything about Dick Fry?'

'He gave me no time to speak, he mainly shouted, making it very clear that we are to leave the LRP people alone. If he had been the one to have taken us to Still Waters, that would have been acceptable, but because we came on our own, he now feels a little compromised.'

'Oh dear.'

'I will wait to hear what Peyton has to say first before mentioning anything to Uncle Ludo about Dick Fry. As it happens, he is shortly returning to Colombo. He wants to meet with us tomorrow morning before he goes.' He sighs. Jazz looks across at him, seeing how desperate he is to be back in the city that he loves.

'You can't wait to leave either, can you?'

'That's not true at all,' he says shortly. 'I am here to do a job. Tell me, what do you make of Peyton?'

'Well...she's very...' Jazz is not sure how she feels, remembering the American woman's flawless skin, largely on show, and mascaraed eyes. 'She's a little inappropriate, perhaps.'

'She's harmless, she just likes to flirt. She's probably just bored and would run a mile if anyone took her seriously.'

'Okay,' says Jazz unconvinced, 'if you say so. Maybe you want to watch yourself with her, though.'

'Sweet of you to worry about me,' says Sonny laughing.

'I'm not worried. Why would I care?' she says in a higher voice than expected.

12

Superintendent Ludowyk pulls up outside their office driving the jeep himself. He comes in and leans his frame against the wall.

'Good morning to you both. So, this is new office? Not sure what there is for you to do here, now all the witness statements have been taken.'

'We are here to look at other stories, also.'

The superintendent raises an eyebrow. 'I'm leaving for Colombo, but Sergeant Rutnam will be in charge and will be reporting back to me with any developments. As you will be hanging around, I will tell him to answer any questions you might have.'

'Okay, thank you,' says Sonny breezily.

Superintendent Ludowyk looks askance at Sonny. 'Please remember, no more harassment of the officials and members of the LRP.'

'You have my word.'

'Is there anything new to tell us, Superintendent?'

'Body is still undergoing tests, but what we do know now, is that he had been dead and probably buried somewhere for at least a year, maybe more, before entering the water.'

Jazz looks across at Sonny expecting him to burst forth with questions, but there's a hush in the wake of the Superintendent's news.

'That is surprising,' she says breaking the silence. 'Do you have any theories about that, Superintendent Ludowyk?'

'Nothing to go on at the moment.' The superintendent pauses. 'By the way, Sonnah boy, I know you will be busy here for a while but maybe you could find time to pay a visit home? Your father is constantly mentioning to me that you haven't been back in a long time.'

'I will arrange it,' says Sonny without expression.

'Well, I must be on my way.' They stand as he clambers back into the jeep. As he ducks to get into the driver's seat, he makes a little bow to Jazz and winks at Sonny. 'I'll be seeing you. We'll have a few drinks next time we meet.'

He reverses the car back onto the main road, honks his horn twice and is gone.

Jazz turns to Sonny. 'That's an interesting turn, no?'

He nods.

She persists. 'Can you believe it, though? The body may have been buried in some kind of shallow grave and then somehow found its way into the reservoir. I have heard that the rains have been very hard this season, maybe the grave got washed away.'

He holds his hand up in a plea for silence. 'I have a really terrible headache.'

She goes to fetch him some Aspro before they leave for their lunch time appointment. Sonny is becoming more and more of a puzzle since they have left Colombo. All his jauntiness has disappeared since arriving on the East Coast, save for sporadic patches that disappear as quickly as they arrive.

'I'm fine,' he assures her when she returns, 'just…you know… taking my time adjusting to being away from the city.'

She looks at the dark purple patches beneath his worried eyes. 'I thought you liked working out in the field. Especially on a big new case. I hope it's not my presence that's causing you to feel this way.'

Immediately he is protesting. 'Not at all. I like having you around, Jazz, you should know that by now.'

She can only hope this is true.

Mrs Andrado has told them the Ocean View Guest House is situated beside a creek on the outskirts of the town, about five miles away. They manage to find a dilapidated old Ford in the centre of Kumburapola whose driver assures Jazz, in his sing-song Tamil, that he is for hire.

'Sonny, are you sure you are okay to continue? Head better now?'

'Yes, yes, I am fine.' A slow crawl through the busy roads ensues, weaving in and out between bullock carts and rickshaws before a bumpy drive along the main road heading out of town. As they round a bend a mechanical crane looms high over a half-built construction, intriguingly deserted despite the hour.

'I wonder why that's all closed down?' murmurs Jazz.

'We've got a few minutes to spare, let's have a look.'

They ask the driver to stop. He puts his feet up on the steering wheel and instantly he is asleep. They walk along the outer shell of the building, a huddle of grey cement blocks and steel girders, cables snaking along the floor, stacks of empty pallets away to one side, tools and machinery standing like quiet ghosts. A sign, still half-covered in wrappers, leans on its side: 'H O T.'

'Nothing much to see,' she says. 'A regular building site. Although I can't believe they're building another hotel.'

'But where is everybody? Everything looks haphazard, like everyone left in a hurry.' Sonny spots a shred of paper attached to one of the pallets and ducks down to pick it up, shoving it into his pocket. Jazz gives an exclamation as she spies movement.

'Somebody's coming. We shouldn't be here.'

'We're not doing any harm,' Sonny reassures the burly young man who has arrived at their side looking cross. He says something in Tamil. Sonny looks at Jazz.

'He wants to know if we are from the Government office.'

'Tell him, yes.'

She hesitates for a brief moment and then nods the lie. The man utters a stream of sentences, evidently very angry. Sonny makes calming gestures with outstretched arms and palms facing the floor. The man puffs out his cheeks and finally falls silent.

'What's the story, Jazz?'

'This is Mr Chettiar, the site foreman. Today he was fired because during his shift this morning, part of a wall collapsed and two of the workers got hurt.' She asks Mr Chettiar another question and he points to a heap of rubble in one corner.

'What actually happened? And what's he doing back here? Causing mischief?'

'He's collecting his equipment. The site manager flew into such a rage this morning he didn't give him a chance. Apparently, this is the second time they have started to build, and the same thing happened before. The site manager is blaming him for shoddy workmanship. The manager told him he would have to report it to the big boss, and he was also forced to call in the Area Building Department to do a site check. He heard from the site manager that the big boss was no longer around, he thinks he probably also got fired.'

She and Sonny exchange a glance. 'The big boss?'

She turns back to Mr Chettiar and says something sharply. Even Sonny can understand the words that come back instantly: 'Dick Fry.'

~

There is no time to speculate, with Peyton Emery awaiting their arrival. The driver, who clearly thinks their behaviour odd, drops them outside the guest house, takes their money and drives off before they can ask him to return later to take them back.

They find Peyton Emery seated at a table in the otherwise empty restaurant, sipping something long and cool. She springs up to shake hands vigorously, slightly unsteady on her feet. Sonny orders vodka for himself and Jazz to catch up with Peyton's gin and tonic high spirits.

'I started without you,' she drawls unnecessarily.

'Let's order food,' says Jazz. 'These things can take a while.'

At a sign from Sonny a grey-haired man arrives, carrying a pen and pad, whose eyes turn reluctantly to Jazz when she asks him a few short questions about the menu. She turns to the others. 'How does crab curry sound?'

They nod approval and she gives the order, the man still not meeting her direct gaze.

'You are Tamil?' Peyton asks her. Sonny leans back in his chair. Jazz wishes he had offered her a cigarette as he sometimes does, but she doesn't like to ask. 'My mother was Tamil. But as my father is a Burgher, I'm considered to be a Burgher.'

'I see. Tell me what Burgher actually means, I've never quite understood it.'

Sonny leans in. 'Burgher is a term that gradually evolved to describe the descendants on the island of first the Portuguese, and then the Dutch invaders. My ancestor in the middle of the sixteenth century was a sergeant named Jan de Rooye who sailed to Ceylon on the Amber Cornelia with the Dutch East Indies Company, or, if you prefer, Vereenigde Oost-Indische Compagnie. VOC for short. One of his descendants dropped the second 'O' to anglicise the surname, during the British era.' He looks up, expecting her eyes to be darting around in their usual, restless manner, but she meets his with interest.

'Sonny that is fascinating. How would you have found this out?'

Peyton nods every now and again, registering Sonny's explanation about the meticulous record-keeping of the VOC employees and their families, now housed in the Dutch Burgher Union. She makes a discreet signal, and more drinks are delivered to their table.

'I suppose,' she says, surprising Jazz and Sonny, 'the dry facts in an archive can never fully tell the story of our ancestors. Their hopes and dreams, their fears for the future. In your ancestor's case, what could have prompted him to sail so far from home and never return.'

A gecko runs up the wall directly behind Peyton. Jazz tracks its progress anxiously, not wanting any dramatics that would impede their fact-finding.

'I found a few articles on this subject in our archive at work,' says Sonny, 'I got the impression that signing up to the VOC as a soldier was usually an act of desperation. Conditions on board were tough and when they landed at the garrison in Batavia they were expected to engage in combat with very little training.'

'Your ancestor must have thought it was worth taking the risk for an opportunity to rewrite his life,' Jazz says thoughtfully.

'Well, let's drink to his courage.' Peyton clinks glasses with them both.

'When he left Batavia and sailed on to Ceylon he would have discovered a burgeoning community that must have felt like a clean slate for him.'

'And I suppose this new community just kept growing.'

'Oh yes. Over the generations, the VOC employees intermarried with descendants of the Portuguese who had conquered the island before the British, and also of course, with the locals. You may have noticed a lot of Burghers are paler than the Tamils or Sinhalese and sometimes have blue or grey eyes.'

'I'm guessing you're Christian?'

'That's right. And as you can see, we wear European style clothing.' Sonny gestures to his short-sleeved shirt and trousers, and Jazz's skirt and blouse.

'Really, we view ourselves as being European. When the Dutch left, a lot of Burghers also left. Those that remained adopted the English language and continued to favour European rather than Asian culture. In turn, the Burghers were gifted solid administrative positions by the British. Of course, we need a smattering of Tamil and Sinhalese to get by, but the English language remains our native tongue to this day.'

Jazz wonders why Sonny is being so expansive. She assumes he is warming Peyton up to be equally forthcoming.

'And that's why you all did so well under British rule.'

'Exactly.'

'Fascinating history. I've always thought of this as an interesting island, nice place to live, wonderful food and friendly people but somehow, I was not aware of all the layers.'

Jazz looks hard at Peyton, imagining her thinking all the people looked the same with their brown faces.

Peyton tosses her hair back. 'Bob says the hope is the Eastern Province will become a new paradise for the modern tourist. Kumburapola may be starting life as a new town inland, but there are plans to edge out the borders towards the golden sands and the warm ocean. Tourism is going to take off in the region, in a big way.'

'Really?'

The food arrives and they help themselves from the heaped platters. Jazz is amused to note that this time it is Sonny who has ordered more drinks.

'Tell us about the Lanka Reservoir project,' suggests Sonny once they have begun their meal.

Snatching at her glass as the waiter places it in front of her, Peyton gives a little screech. 'Oh my, well at the start of it all, you should have seen this place when we first got here! It was a real shock, nothing more than a collection of shacks for the workers. Those of us wives who had come over to be with our husbands, had to be boarded out to families in the town while they built new homes for us'. Peyton tosses back her hair in an offended manner.

'That can't have been easy for you.'

'Well, the people were friendly to us, but our husbands didn't waste any time getting to work, some building houses for us and others beginning on the reservoir. Now, here's an interesting fact for you: when construction began, the engineers found the remains of the ruins of an ancient irrigation system on the exact same spot! Extraordinary, don't you think?'

'That is interesting. There must be some photographs of that somewhere, I'd love to take a look.' Jazz wonders if anybody has written a story about this.

'Oh, I'll ask Bob, he'll have some.'

'I suppose Bob's work is almost at an end. What lies ahead for you now?'

'Oh well, we'll be going within the next month or so. What an exciting thought! Several of the engineers who worked on the reservoir are staying on to do consultancy work on other projects; for every new building springing up, there are half a dozen new ones in the pipeline. Bob has been asked to stay on of course, but we just want to return to Janine, and anyway, he has a new contract starting in June that will take him back to England for the next couple of years so...'

Jazz is amazed at how Peyton barely pauses for breath. She finds herself only half listening until Peyton gives a loud exclamation.

'I suppose you want me to tell you about our mystery man, Dick Fry.'

At last, thinks Jazz with a sense of relief.

'Well, Dick was a larger-than-life character, everyone knew him.'

Jazz notes the past tense and sees Sonny half raising an eyelid.

'Dick did the one thing that the other engineers and builders and foreign nationals out here didn't really do; he got friendly with the natives. He was always being invited to visit strangers, sharing their ferocious curries with them at home or visiting those awful toddy shacks at ungodly hours.'

They remain silent, not wanting to interrupt her flow. Jazz notices Sonny catching sight of the gecko, now halfway across the ceiling.

'Dick was really anxious to fit in, he even used to ditch his suits and wear a sarong at weekends.' Peyton sounds affronted. 'And rumour has it, although I never saw it, he would even eat with his fingers.'

Jazz and Sonny give each other an awkward grin. Peyton flushes, eyeing them as they handle their knives and forks. 'That was rude of me. I know that it's the custom here to eat with your fingers.'

'We don't do it when we're out in public. And never if we are in the company of foreigners.'

'Quite.' They chew in silence for a moment. Having eaten her fill, Peyton continues. 'Sometime last year, Dick's behaviour became erratic. According to my husband his work got sloppy, he started drinking during office hours and he became surly and withdrawn. He wouldn't turn up for meetings and then when he did, he was shambolic and rambling. Finally, in early November, he left a note at his guest house saying he had some business to attend to back in Colombo. Nobody's seen or heard of him since. You don't think...the body...I mean could it be...?'

Jazz and Sonny look at each other. They know of course that the body can't be that of Dick Fry who has been missing for a mere matter of weeks. Sonny gives Jazz a look and she nods her understanding.

'Why has nobody contacted the police? Reported him as a missing person? Surely his bosses would have done that?' Jazz attempts to get Peyton to focus.

'I think, given Dick's eccentricity they assumed he would just turn up sooner or later. Oh dear...' Jazz thinks she does look genuinely dismayed.

'Do you know the name of the place where he lodged?' Jazz has an inkling, a heartbeat of excitement, but still she waits for Peyton to throw back her final glass and wipe her perfectly formed lips.

'Why yes, I believe I do know. Bob and I picked him up several times in the early days for evenings out. It was The Lanka Welcome Guest House.'

It was Dick Fry who had rigged up the shower in Sonny's room. Back in the guest house Sonny paces up and down on the veranda, allowing his tea to go cold.

'Is Dick Fry now officially one of our stories?'

'Yes, I think so.'

'But the murder, Sonny?'

'That story is currently going nowhere.'

'Okay. So do we need to talk to the police about Dick Fry?'

'We do. But let's see if we can give them some hard facts first.'

He goes out into the hallway and calls for Mrs Andrado. Never far away, she appears almost instantly.

'Mrs A, what can you tell us about Dick Fry?'

She looks slyly at them. 'Ah, so you have heard about him. Well, he said he was going away to visit a friend. I didn't question it; he was often gone for a day or so before coming back a little bit worse for wear. He was here for a long time and so I got used to him. He paid his rent and was no trouble to me, although I think he was probably in trouble in other ways.'

'Such as?'

'I couldn't say anything for sure. Just an impression I had. Anyway, when he hadn't returned after a week, I contacted somebody at Still Waters, and they advised me to empty his room but to keep his possessions somewhere safe for the time being. They were very good about it and agreed to pay me a small storage rate.'

'You still have his things?'

'Yes.'

'As you know us now, Mrs A, would it be possible if we could just have a little look?'

She turns on him a shocked look. 'No, that's not possible. It wouldn't be right.'

'Sorry, we didn't mean to cause any offence,' Jazz says soothingly. Mrs Andrado gives her shoulders a shake and starts to move towards the kitchen.

'Sorry, Mrs A, we're just curious; some friends of his who know we are staying in the same guest house, asked us if we had heard anything. If we could just ask in a general way, what he left behind?'

'Well, there is nothing at all of interest. A couple of novels, a few shirts and his work clothes and shoes. A bar of soap and some toothpaste.'

'No money or passport? Letters?'

'Nothing like that at all. Not that I would have looked at them, but there is nothing at all that is personal.'

Jazz and Sonny make their way upstairs to Sonny's room, in what had been Dick Fry's abode, at the top of the house.

'To be honest I've not even looked properly around the room,' Sonny says over his shoulder as he stands in the middle surveying slowly with his eyes. 'I mean, the bed is comfortable and I'm grateful for the private shower but that's as far as any room goes. I haven't even unpacked yet.' He opens and closes each empty drawer of the ebony tallboy in the corner.

Having ascertained that all drawers and cupboards are devoid of belongings, Sonny stands in the middle of the room running his eyes around the space before turning to the window overlooking the gardens. He opens it wide, and a wave of afternoon heat drifts in. He gazes up at the section of the overhanging roof.

'What are you thinking, Sonny?'

Putting his head out, he feels around the overhang and gives an exclamation.

'There's a section that has been cut away.'

'Really?'

Digging deeper with his hands he pulls out a bundle bound in oil skin which he brings into the safety of the room and carefully unwraps. Assorted letterheads for various building and supply companies, flutter onto the floor.

'What is all this?' Jazz says, taking the sheets of paper from him.

'I'm not sure. Dick made a hiding place for these so something is definitely up, wouldn't you agree?'

'It's certainly strange.'

'I can't think of a single good reason why somebody would need to hide company letterheads. Unless...'

He breaks off, staring into the distance.

'Sonny? Enlighten me, please.'

'I'm not sure. Just a hunch. We'll figure this out in the morning at the office. Let's keep this to ourselves for now.'

13

The kade that sells cigarettes and newspapers in the centre of the town has copies of the morning's edition of the *Colombo Courier*. THE BODY IN THE LAKE is announced from every shelf.

'It seems your uncle has already arranged for the *Courier* to be distributed in the Eastern Province,' says Sonny 'he doesn't waste much time, does he?'

'Perhaps Uncle thinks there will be increased demand with more tourists expected in the region.'

Sonny and Jazz buy a copy each and then Sonny goes back and buys a few more. 'My mother will be wanting to show her friends,' he mutters, 'I'll send these to her.' On the road to the police station, Jazz stops at a roadside boutique, attracted by the display of ointments and creams. A young woman is filling small sachets with a blend of herbs and roots. She looks up and smiles at Jazz, and they have a brief chat before the woman directs her to a glass bottle of lotion.

'Lovely smell,' she says to her in Tamil, 'good for your hair in this damp weather.'

'She read you well', says Sonny grinning as they walk away, the bottle clinking in Jazz's handbag.

'I like her. She grows plants and herbs and makes her own ointments, guided by spirit healers.'

'Magical potions.' Sonny clicks his tongue irritably. 'If she has something good for my eternal headache, then I will believe in her.'

'I don't think Tamil is her first language. There's something different about her, that I can't quite place.'

'I think by the look of her she might be a Vedda.'

'Ah, really? Why would a Vedda woman be here in town?'

'Mrs A was telling me that some Veddas are leaving their tribal communities and marrying local Tamils and Sinhalese.'

'I didn't know that.'

There are several bicycles leaning against the wall of the police station, the usual mode of transport for the town's police force, who up until now have mainly had to deal with the odd bit of thievery or a dispute leading to a fight between neighbours. Jazz wonders where Superintendent Ludowyk had managed to find a jeep.

She supposes it is inevitable that as the town enlarges, its character will change. Certainly, the advent of hotels will lend an entirely different air. She feels a sudden nostalgia, hoping that maybe, given the problems with construction, progress and the path of tourism might slow down. She is not sure if the East Coast is ready for such a sudden shift in values.

The police station consists of a workspace for several constables and the front desk between themselves and visitors. Behind is a door to the Sergeant's Office that the superintendent has recently vacated, and another door leading to the cells. The place is deserted when they enter but after a minute the sergeant's door opens and an officer comes out.

Sonny tries to catch his eye. 'Hello, my name is...'

'Constable Nadaraja will be with you in a moment.' The sergeant's eyes flicker to Jazz.

'Jacintha Barthelot from the *Colombo Courier*' she says seizing the advantage, holding out her hand, 'and this is my colleague, Sonny de Roye. Are you Sergeant Rutnam?'

'I am. Yes, I remember you now, friends of the superintendent.'

A constable appears, sweating and muttering, his hands covered in grease.

'Repairing bicycle chain,' he explains.

'Wash your hands and bring tea,' says Sergeant Rutnam sharply, 'these are people from Colombo. Ai,' he murmurs ushering them into his office.

They follow him into his windowless room. A small overhead fan is blowing a pile of papers from side to side. Behind the desk a wooden board displays photographs of the Lanka Samudraya and a map, an arrow pinpointing where the body had first been sighted by the fishermen, and question marks in several places accompanied by the words: MURDERED HERE?

'You have questions for me? Superintendent Ludowyk mentioned you would be stopping by every now and again.'

The constable comes in carrying a tray with cups of tea. He places them unceremoniously on the sergeant's desk and stares across at Jazz.

'Stop that staring, Constable Nadaraja. Have you been to the hospital to see how the Fernandez girl is doing?'

'Bike still not working, sir.'

'Well then, take mine. Lazy bugger,' he says as the door shuts. He takes a sip of tea which seems to put him in a calmer mood. He looks across at them and answers their mute enquiry.

'A few nights ago, a young woman was almost killed at one of the new factories. She was cleaning after all the workers had gone home and apparently one of the interior walls collapsed on top of her.'

'Interesting,' says Sonny quietly, looking at Jazz.

'Anyway, you will want to know how we are getting on with the murder enquiry.'

Sonny swallows his tea back in one mouthful. 'It will be difficult for you, of course, to pinpoint possible leads until there are more details about the body. A dead male body could be anyone.'

Sergeant Rutnam puts down his cup. 'Well, we've had some further communication from the Medical Examiner which came in this morning.' He pauses as if he is about to be indiscreet. 'The male was aged between approximately fifty-five and seventy. Possibly more likely to be towards the upper age range. We are following up leads of all men who have gone missing in the last couple of years and there are a number on file, but we have no reports about missing males of that age. All are younger men.'

'Ah, right.' Jazz makes a note. 'Well, there could still be lots of possibilities. A lone tourist perhaps, or maybe one of the naturalists that come to these parts with notebooks and drawing equipment to capture our flora and fauna. Although even a missing tourist would eventually be missed back in their homeland.'

'Every lead will be followed up. We are not the rural idiots that Colombo assume we are. Superintendent Ludowyk was quite comfortable leaving us here to run things, overseeing it from Colombo.'

'Of course, we know the police force is very capable,' Jazz says looking to Sonny who is staring into space. 'There is one thing we wanted to bring to your attention. Sonny?' He surfaces from some deep thought, looking ill at ease.

'What was that?'

'The other matter to bring to discuss with the sergeant?'

'Ah, yes indeed. We do have a lead on another story, possibly related, possibly not.' He mentions the missing engineer, Dick

Fry, leaving out the extra details of what had been discovered in the bedroom at the guest house. The sergeant looks unimpressed but makes a note and says he will make the relevant enquiries.

They rise. 'We'll get out of your way. Thank you for the tea.'

'Do not mention it, Mr de Roye. It was good to meet with you and you also, Miss Barthelot.'

Jazz feels his eyes lingering a fraction too long on her, as he says goodbye. She is about to make a comment to Sonny but outside in the street he seems eager to be alone.

'Got some errands to do, Jazz.'

'At office? I'll come with you.'

'No, not in office. I'll see you back at the guest house for lunch.'

Piqued, she watches him stride away purposefully. There is not much to do in the office, and she doesn't feel like going back to the guest house, spending an afternoon with the landlady and her threatened horoscope. She can't fathom where Sonny would be going. After a few moments of hesitation, keeping a careful distance, she decides to follow him.

She does her best to keep out of sight, but Sonny is a fast walker, and she is panting heavily as she endeavours to keep up with him. She walks a parallel path through the market, almost coming face to face with him at the spice stall where he has stopped to linger. She falls back and lets him go ahead, watching as he halts again, this time to light a cigarette. He is smoking far too much, at least a couple of packets a day, she thinks, having grown accustomed to hearing him coughing in the early hours. No wonder he is looking drawn.

She steadies herself to his pace as he strides seemingly without purpose, peering in through doorways, stopping to pet a stray cat that briefly winds its skinny body between Sonny's legs before realising there is no hope of scraps, watches his face crack into a brief smile as he calls out to a couple of street kids, tossing them some coins.

Without warning he ducks down a turning into a tiny street. Too late she realises it is a dead end and draws back sharply. Looking around, Sonny has disappeared. A row of simple dwellings stand along each side of the road with a Roman Catholic church of white stone at the end. She has never had the impression that Sonny is religious. She approaches the half open door to peer inside.

A row of votive flames flickers to the left, keeping the light alive for departed souls. She catches a vague shape in the darkness of the far pews, straining her ears as she hears Sonny talking in an urgent tone as if trying to persuade somebody to respond. She tiptoes along the side aisle, craning her head to catch sight of his companion.

The church is the perfect place to steal some privacy, away from the townspeople. Sonny has obviously arranged to meet a source, perhaps concerning Dick Fry. Or the murdered man? She wonders why he hadn't included her. She forces herself not to rush up and join the conversation, even though she is wild with curiosity.

Finally, the conversation peters out and then a long silence before Sonny gets up and makes his way down the centre aisle. Jazz shrinks into the walls thankful for the dimming light as he passes her without detection.

After he has left, she feels the enveloping silence, heavy as a priest's vestments. Whoever Sonny has been interviewing will probably wait for a suitable pause before also leaving. She walks along the side aisle, softly so as not to cause alarm. Just a discreet glance so that when Sonny surprises her with his story, she will be able to turn the tables on him, show him that she too, can deliver the unexpected. She peers through the gloom and then impatiently turns towards the pew Sonny had recently vacated.

There is no-one there.

14

Early morning rain has drenched the veranda leaving dirty puddles of water and trails of mud. Jazz watches a speckled frog assessing the depth of a wet patch at the foot of the veranda steps before making a leap, while Sonny paces, smoking, his eyes as moody as the sky. She is startled when he jumps up unexpectedly. 'Soon, soon, come. Let's go to office. Could you make a detour on the way, and check for any letters?'

They part company at the corner. After standing in the habitual post office queue, she is given a handwritten letter addressed to Sonny. Walter's writing. She wonders what their new instructions will be. Something to do with what had happened in the church, perhaps?

The previous day, she had left the church, annoyed at herself for having forgotten the side door, through which Sonny's informant had obviously managed to slip away.

Making her way back to the guest house, she had arrived at Mrs Andrado's place to discover Sonny calmly reading a newspaper, feet up on the edge of a coffee table in the small parlour set aside for the residents. He had looked up at her, totally without guile, in one of his better moods. She had waited for him to reveal where he had been, but he had produced a pack of cards and dealt her a hand, and the afternoon had passed without further mention of the investigation.

'Ah, something for me? Let's see.'

Sonny takes the envelope from her. She slumps into one of the two chairs, feeling hot and irritable in her surroundings. The place still only vaguely resembles an office, although she has tried her best to create a working environment, sticking maps and notes onto the wall, and stocking the little cabinet with pens and pencils.

'Something to do with the murdered man? Or Dick Fry?' She watches his face reading without expression.

He lets out a sigh at the end, punching the air in jubilation.

'Walter has given us a few days off. He's very pleased with us.'

'Trying to soften the blow of being stuck out here.'

'When did you get so cynical?'

They look at each other and grin.

'So, visits home then? I will go and telephone my father and tell him to expect me tomorrow. What will you do, Sonny? Back to Colombo?'

'Please don't tempt me. Jazz, I'm going to do the right thing.'

She smiles approvingly, which fades when she notes his expression.

'What? You are up to something?'

'No. Nothing. Only…I wondered if you might invite me home with you?'

'I…well of course, you would be very welcome. But…why exactly?'

'I thought it would be good if I got to know your father. It would calm your aunt and uncle down from whatever nonsense they are worrying about.'

'That is a good plan. But shouldn't you use the opportunity to go home?'

'Yes, we will do that. We can spend a night with your father and then head across and see my folks. Okay with you?'

She can't hide her puzzlement. He attempts an explanation.

'I'm not good at doing the family thing, Jazz. It's helpful to have a distraction. Visiting with a colleague makes it more casual.'

'Okay, Sonny. I'll come with you.' She heads outside to avoid his gaze.

Sonny is watching through the window as the bus trundles through Kumburapola, even the aromas from Mrs Andrado's parcel of short eats failing to divert his attention. They are on their way together to spend a day and night with Guy Barthelot before travelling inland together to Badulla and Sonny's home.

'What are you looking at?'

'Buggers are here from other newspapers. I recognise a few; come like crows to pick the bones from our story for themselves.'

'An appropriate turn of phrase, no?'

Sonny gives a weak grin.

'We broke the story anyhow. And we are ahead of the game, they still don't know the body was part skeleton.'

After a while Sonny's head drops forward and the air around him stills.

She waits before finally slitting open the food packet, helping herself to a patty, still warm, her mouth filling pleasantly with flaked pieces of fish, onion, and green chillies. After a while there is movement beside her, she feels a hand rummaging through the packets as Sonny reaches for the vadais.

'We must be about halfway there now.' His tone is lighter, his nap has revived him.

'Yes.'

'By the way, don't think I didn't notice the sergeant's admiration. He's got a crush on you.'

'Don't be silly,' says Jazz affecting a nonchalant tone.

'I am right, though. Didn't I say you needed looking after?'

'What about you, Sonny?' she retorts.

'I don't think I'm the sergeant's type.'

'Silly boy. I mean no romantic interests on the horizon?'

Their eyes meet fractionally before sliding away.

'Despite my mother's best efforts, no. Not really.'

Jazz says in a light tone, 'I suppose I'm lucky in that respect. My father is very supportive of what I want to do with my life, without bending to social pressure to marry me off. And then of course, I don't have a mother, Burgher or otherwise, desperate for a wedding and grandchildren.'

'But you have your Aunty in Colombo. Angelo's wife.'

'Yes, she tries to influence me, but since I have been back from England, she has been a little wary of me. Apparently, I question everything, which she says is very draining.'

'Maybe that has contributed to your uncle's decision to keep you on the East Coast for a while? A chastisement for having enjoyed living in Colombo on your own terms?'

She nods agreement.

At the point where the bus terminates a mile or two outside Kalmunai, Guy Barthelot is waiting beside his car. Sonny steps forward, hand outstretched. 'This is very good of you, Mr Barthelot.'

'Guy, please. I'm sure you are both working too hard, it will be my pleasure to give you a little break.'

'Good to see you, Daddy.'

'And you, daughter.'

Jazz looks through the window with pleasure as the town begins to reveal itself as they nudge towards the centre.

'Place has got bigger since I was here,' Sonny comments.

'Yes,' says Guy, 'it will never be as big as Batticaloa but it's still a substantial settlement.'

Jazz looks out at her hometown with pride; the uneven rows of streets, shops, schools, a government hospital, several churches, a cluster of white Government bungalows and a college and somewhere close by out of view, the ocean.

A bullock has broken free from its loaded cart and comes charging into the road directly in front of them. It stops, looking around with wild eyes. The cart owner comes forward with a stick, shouting angrily as a group of children gather, pointing and laughing, kicking the scattered coconuts that have fallen from the cart.

Once the bullock is under control, Guy drives on towards an ornate mosque in the distance, its spires glinting in a momentary ray of sunlight. They leave the main street, turning into a lane of bungalows with small square front gardens and shutters at the windows.

'Nearly there.'

'Is this the house where you were born?'

Jazz smiles. 'No. Daddy eventually left the forestry work behind and took a desk job with a forestry conservation company. He has a very nice bungalow now.'

Guy parks the car and leads the way up a neat pathway, opening the front door into a tiled hallway filled with potted plants on wooden stands. 'Go and get washed up. Then we can sit.'

'Okay. I'll show Sonny where he's sleeping, then we'll come join you.'

'The bungalow has indoor plumbing and guest quarters at the back', Jazz says to Sonny, proud of her father's achievements.

'I'm sure it will be very comfortable.'

She goes into what her father always insists is her room and opens the almirah.

She puts on a fresh dress and checks her appearance carefully in the mirror, deciding to pile her hair up to keep her neck cool. Making her way out to the covered outdoor area, she pauses as she hears her father and Sonny talking in low voices, ice clinking against glass.

'She is quite a girl, my daughter,' her father is saying.

'She is very bright. I'm sure you are proud of her.'

Her stomach flutters. He is probably just being polite to his host.

'I can take no credit for her success. Circumstances meant that I was unable to be a proper parent. What I try my best to do for her these days, is support her decision to follow a career, rather than try and marry her off like so many of my friends and acquaintances are doing with their daughters. But then I think this behaviour tends to stem from the woman of the house, which sadly we lack. I think Jacintha has told you of our sadness?'

'Yes, she mentioned her mother passing away and how she went to live with the Croziers.'

'Yes, indeed. And now all these years later, my younger brother is your boss. I'm sure you must be in the good books having made a scoop with the body in the lake.'

'Yes,' says Sonny in what Jazz considers a doubting tone.

'You don't sound convinced.'

'No. I er....' Sonny takes a deep, confessional breath. 'Life is a bit of a mess for me at the moment. I think your brother would like to get rid of me. It's my own fault, I know. I drink too much, lose my focus.'

Her father sounds concerned. 'You are such a young man to be feeling like this, Sonny. Surely it was not always this way? I mean is it the pressure to be top dog, or what?'

'I...I can't really say. Sometimes I can scarcely equate the sad figure looming out at me in the mirror each morning as I shave, with the young gun I was when I first arrived in Colombo.'

'And yet by your own admission, you still rise each morning, make yourself presentable and turn up for work. Not the mark of someone who is lost. Don't put yourself down so much, you have merely taken a detour. I bet you can still find your way onto the right path.'

She enters then, not looking at Sonny as she helps herself to a glass of wood apple juice which she knows her father's house-keeper, Rookie has prepared especially for her. As she sips she can feel him sneaking glances at her and she thinks with dismay that maybe she has over dressed.

'You are looking lovely, Jacintha, I have always liked you in that frock, like a flash of orange sun before it dips for the night.'

'Thank you, Daddy.' She catches Sonny nodding in agreement and feels warmth spreading across her face. She takes herself in hand. 'Where is Rookie? I thought she would be busy in the kitchen.'

'It's her evening off. I had an idea we might go to the Flag Hoisting ceremony. We can get food there and it will be a pleasant way to spend the evening.'

'Oh, yes, let's do that, I haven't been for years. I'll get my things. Sonny is that okay with you?'

'Sure, Jazz anything sounds good.'

He sounds relaxed and she is glad he is comfortable in her home.

15

The tide is going out, the receding waves lightly layering the shoreline with white ruffled hems, sweeping the feet of the crowd heading towards the mosque on the beach.

'The Muslims don't mind others attending their ceremony?' Sonny asks.

'Not at all, as long as everybody is respectful. Today they will be hoisting the temple flag, marking the beginning of twelve days of preaching. As you can see, many have brought their own decorated flags. Hanging them signifies personal participation.'

'I see. Like attending mass and lighting a candle.'

Her mind returns to the small white church in Kumburapola. She still hasn't told Sonny what she had witnessed. She glances across at him glad to see he is happy, enjoying the occasion, content to be part of the lively atmosphere on the beach as the crowd wait for the sun to set.

When the sun meets the ocean there is a sudden silence before the air fills with melodious chanting. A mosque leader steps up to the flag, his hands sprinkled with a paste of thick sandalwood. Murmuring the blessing, the crowd surges forward to touch the anointed flag as it rises into the air. Rose petals rain down from one of the small top windows, perfuming the air with their ashy scent.

Jazz, Guy, and Sonny push their way through lines of people to the evening market, stalls selling trinkets and wooden carvings, drawing in the crowds. As well as Muslims there are other visitors like themselves and a few fair-haired tourists who do not seem to mind being stared at, shyly followed by groups of mesmerised children who want to touch their hair.

The three browse until they look at each other and nod their hunger, joining the meandering queues for food at the tea stalls and eating establishments offering short eats, and rice and curry dishes prepared over an open fire. The aromas sizzle in the evening air.

'I am buying dinner,' Sonny announces firmly, 'I would like to thank you for your hospitality.'

'That's very kind of you, Sonny.' Jazz sees her father glancing across at Sonny with approval and she feels a burst of happiness.

By now hundreds of Muslims are thronging the area, many have travelled great distances to be in attendance on this first night of celebrations. Families are hauling mats to spread out on the beach where they will spend the night in devotional prayer. Children scamper through the crowds, causing mischief, mothers are spreading cloths, unpacking food, calling families to eat. The sounds of drums, tambourines and singing rise harmoniously over the crowd

They have reached the front of a food stall where portions of vegetable rice and fish curry are being parcelled onto plantain leaves and wrapped in sheets of newspaper.

Carrying their food, they find a less crowded place. Her father spreads a cloth onto the sands. The food is good; fiery red chilli heat and pepper corns complementing the grilled fish and sticky rice and for a while they eat in satisfied silence, the beach a wave of heat and flickering flames as people light fires to sit around.

Jazz notices her father has fallen into a light doze. 'Lovely meal, Sonny. Did you enjoy?'

'Yes, food was good. I suppose you have eaten in some fancy places in your time. You have travelled a lot, no?'

'Well, yes. I've done lots of travelling with Aunty and Uncle. They have several places where they stay, the house in Colombo of course, but also the house in Galle where I spent a lot of time as a child, a small hunting lodge in Matale and a flat in Kandy.'

'Do you have a favourite?'

'The house in Galle' she says. 'It's an old Portuguese spice trader's house, and I remember it always seemed that cinnamon and nutmeg scents still lingered in the wooden panels. Uncle was always relaxed there, a different sort of person than he was in Colombo. He used to take me marketing every morning, winding our way through the cobbled streets of the fort to the bazaar, my mouth full of sugar from bol friado, hoping for a chance to go sea bathing and a beach picnic in the afternoon.'

'Do they still have the house?'

'Yes, but some relatives are living in it at the moment. I haven't been there for a long time.'

'And of course, you have your home here, with your father.'

'What about Badulla? Where you grew up? Do you like it?'

He nods.

'You told me your father got sick and had to stop work. Was that on a tea estate?'

'Yes, he was head clerk on a large plantation. We were given a big house with a garden which is where I spent my first fifteen years. Daddy had the use of a vehicle and Mummy had servants to boss, so she was happy enough.'

'So, the good life for you, too.'

Sonny waggles his head and picks up his packet of cigarettes, spinning it around on the sand until the contents spill out. 'Life was all okay until my father started getting headaches which gradually got worse. At first, they thought it was his eyes, but new spectacles made no difference. The aches in his head increased, he had to lie down, he felt sick, sometimes for whole days at a time and he had frequent dizziness. The estate manager arranged for him to have medical tests in Colombo, but they were unable to find anything wrong.

'In the end, he had to leave his job. We needed to find a place to stay and eventually one of my uncles found a small place for us on the edge of the town. Very small place, to my mother's eternal shame.'

'It must have been a comedown for her.'

'I started work and then my father found he was able to work as a gardener in the Grand Hotel without getting headaches, so the family lives in a slightly better place now. But still my mother remembers her glory days.'

'I'm sorry. But I will look forward to meeting your family.'

A thin breeze is blowing across the sea, goosebumps rising on her arms. She gently gives her father a shake.

'Daddy wake up, you'll get a stiff neck.'

Her father surfaces from his nap, blinking gently. 'I was going to ask Sonny, if you're a hunting man? Next time you're here we could take a couple of rifles and bag ourselves a deer.'

'Hey, don't forget me in your plans. You know Uncle has taught me to shoot. What about it, Sonny?'

'No, no...I don't go hunting.'

'Really?'

'I mean I did but I don't enjoy it now.' He pauses. 'When I was a child my Uncle Ferdy would sometimes drive up to our place, load up the car and drive my father away for the weekend. As soon as I was old enough, I joined them. I used to brim over with excitement every time my uncle arrived with a grin in his voice, shouting that the Land Rover was packed and ready, and we would be off in a flash.

'I loved the camaraderie in the emerald heart of the forest, the relief of finding fresh stream water, the first sighting of the deer, the wild boar or the jungle fowl, the reassuring grip of the rifle and the final thrill arising from the trigger pull...'

His voice trails away, his eyes darkening.

'Ah. My dear fellow, I'm sorry, I have been thoughtless. I suppose, with the crimes you have reported, you would feel like that now, about killing.'

Sonny gives Guy a grateful nod. Jazz thinks he's looking pale again.

Back in the bungalow, she prepares cups of Horlicks and roots out the remaining slices of love cake left over from Christmas. Soon they are all yawning.

'Well, I think it's time for my bed.' Sonny capitulates first. Jazz is relieved to see him disappear, anxious that Marlee might arrive unannounced and pounce.

'Sleep well, then. Good night.'

On her way to the tap to rinse the cups, she watches Sonny's departing figure and something very like tenderness washes over her, lapping at her heart. It's a complication she has not anticipated.

PART II

THE GARDEN

16

The leaves of the plantain tree swayed in a sudden puff of wind. Reclining in her chair, the woman mopped her brow with a handkerchief and reached for her drink. She took a long cooling draught, then put the glass down; a few remaining droplets clung to the empty glass, like tears.

She sank back against the padded cushion, her fingers tracing the pattern of tiny kicks in her swelling abdomen. She was limp and a little dizzy. She should not have gone out in the midday heat, but her elderly neighbour had gone to a lot of trouble to get a present for the baby, which was why she had traipsed half a mile up the dusty road and back again.

The parcel was on the grass by her feet, wrapped in paper and ribbon. She wanted to open it but thought she would wait for her husband to come home in the evening when they would be able to open it together.

Her head ached. She placed a palm across her forehead. Perhaps she was a little feverish. Thoughts were swirling around her head like mist, and she struggled to catch hold of them. There was so much to do, but she just couldn't summon the energy.

Her mother was due to arrive next week for the birth. She kept forgetting to ask her husband to fix the overhead fan in the spare bedroom. Space needed to be cleared in the almirah for her mother's belongings. Pillows...her mother liked at least four. She would have to search for spare pillowcases.

In the hallway was a gift from her husband's workmates, a hand-carved cradle with a panel of baby elephants. It needed one final layer of linseed oil before it could be moved into the bedroom.

In the parlour was a pile of newly sewn white cotton sheets waiting to be ironed and folded. She had wanted to dye some of them blue, but her husband had protested, worried in case the baby turned out to be a girl. But she knew it was going to be a boy.

She should finish the list she had started earlier that day, for the servant, Kamala to go marketing. Chillies, yams, and onions. Rambutans. A packet of monkey nuts as a treat for her husband, even though it maddened her when he left the shells scattered over the furniture.

A ripe mango fell from its branch, hitting the ground with a thwack, giving rise to a tiny cloud of dust. The tree belonged to the neighbours but most of the fruit normally landed on their side of the fence. Another one fell and then another. She should have put mats down to catch them when Kamala had pointed them out to her earlier in the day, hanging on the branches ready to drop. If they were not retrieved soon, they would be devoured by the crows.

She didn't move.

The heat was relentless. She shifted in her chair, her cotton dress sticking unpleasantly to her skin. Something moved next to the latrine. Probably a stray dog looking for a bone although she had the impression of something bigger. A deer maybe, lost from its path. The hunters' guns had sounded earlier in the day.

Her head sank low. Adrift in a sea of memories she combed the flotsam and jetsam, retrieving her childhood. She saw herself curled up in Uncle's boat, lying ashore in the shade of the coconut trees, her cousins working alongside mending the sail and she, sky-walking the acres beyond the blue, glimpsed through the palm fronds. Later there would be Aunty's fish curry for supper with hoppers, and an evening walk to the lagoon before bed.

Somebody coughed. The harsh sound of retching, globules of spittle flung to the ground. Her eyes flew open in alarm. She wished she had stayed on the veranda in her usual spot where the deep purple bougainvillea adorned the wall of the bungalow with its gauzy blooms, but her husband had moved her wicker chair out into the shady part of the garden before leaving for work. He had been energised since discovering her pregnancy, reading articles, fussing about her diet. He was always so good to her. She wondered what kind of a father he would be.

She turned her head. A flash of white at the corner of her vision. Maybe a cloud of butterflies. She called out hesitantly. 'Is someone there?'

A figure emerged slowly from the side of the house making its way towards her chair. She frowned, wondering who could be calling at that hour in the ferocious early afternoon heat, pulling herself up with an effort. 'What do you want?'

And then she looked up into the face.

From the notebook of Jazz Barthelot

17

Jazz is awakened by a single scream.

She springs up, ties her robe and races down the corridor where she stops outside the guest bedroom. She hesitates, hand on the doorknob, and then hears a high-pitched yell. She enters. Sonny is groaning, thrashing around in his bed sheets. As she stands over him, he opens his eyes abruptly, looking without seeing.

'Sonny? Are you okay?'

He rasps in a heavy voice, 'just sitting there... why not get up? cold eyes... so terrible.'

He comes out of his trance after several moments. 'Jazz? I... what's going on?' He looks and sounds completely normal.

She has the sense to play down the incident. 'I thought I heard you call out.'

He looks away. 'Sorry. Sometimes I have vivid dreams. An overactive imagination, I suppose. Sorry for disturbing you.'

She catches sight of the hipflask he must have emptied before bed, and frowns. 'Well, we need an early start anyway.' The light is filtering through the shutters, she can hear the sounds of her father's housekeeper, Rookie clattering around in the kitchen.

'I'll get dressed and come,' she hears him say as she leaves the room.

She dresses, gathers a few more items into her case then goes to sit on the veranda. She thinks perhaps Sonny was dreaming about a past case, maybe the Ratnayake Boy. He had seen the crime scene at close quarters, and it must have been horrific. She wonders if in the future she will become similarly affected by her own news reports.

The sounds from the kitchen intensify and she goes in search of a cup of tea. Rookie is making string hoppers, sodhi and coconut sambol with some left-over meat curry for their breakfast. 'Smells good, Rookie.'

'Stop your nibbling there will be nothing left. Go and find your father and I'll bring you some tea.'

Guy is still in his dressing gown in the dining room. He looks up and smiles as she appears beside him.

'Good morning. You're up early. Sleep well?'

She is glad he has not heard Sonny's disturbance.

'Very well. Daddy, it's so kind of you to lend us your car. It would take so long to get to Badulla on the train.'

'You are welcome, my dear daughter. I hope you will have a pleasant visit with Sonny's family'.

'What did your mother say when you told her I would be coming? I hope she wasn't too disappointed that they wouldn't have you all to yourself.'

'I...er...,' says Sonny.

Her head whips round. His face is impassive as he watches the road ahead, hands steady on the wheel, but she can tell by the subtle tilt of his chin that he's amused.

'You haven't told them, have you? Sonny, how could you not have said something?'

'You don't know what my mother is like. It's far better that she hasn't spent five days fussing and fixing in your honour. Much better to turn up with you casually. I did try and explain this to you.'

'Yes, but—'

'Look, I just didn't want them to know, okay? Telling my mother something formally is like making an announcement. I don't want there to be any misunderstandings.'

That stings for some reason. She says at last, 'But every woman likes to be prepared, to have the dust dispersed, the food cupboards groaning, when visitors come.'

'You don't need to worry about that, my homecoming is always the equivalent of the return of the King to Kandy.' He turns his eyes back to the road but not without remarking casually, 'You look nice, by the way, Jazz. New dress?'

'Just something I found hanging,' she says but her heart is gladdened by the compliment. A present from her father a while back, she's wearing dusky pink chiffon, pale as a blush with a tight belt that accentuates her waist.

Around lunch time, Jazz watches the city appear, a white stone Roman Catholic cathedral, a garish flash of yellow temple, the market winding down after a busy morning. Sonny drives to the outskirts, the road flanked by terraced rice paddies that wind upwards into the hills towards the waterfalls, before turning the car off the main road, driving round a cluster of tiny streets and parking beside a small house with a pristine lawn overlooked by a short veranda. A couple of peacocks are pecking by the roadside.

Sonny switches the engine off, glances towards the house and clicks his tongue to scare the birds away. 'They do such terrible damage to the roof if you don't keep them away.'

A woman has flung open the door and is running down the steps with a wide smile on her face. Jazz feels like staying unseen in the back of the car, but Sonny gives her a look and she gets out of the vehicle, hanging back slightly.

'Sonnah boy! He's here! Artie, come, come!' Lily de Roye, face powdered and hair immaculate clutches her son close. Sonny appears to be struggling to breathe but he endures until his father comes walking quickly round the side of the house.

'Lily, you are half strangling the boy. Sonnah boy, it's good to see you.' He gently extricates him from his mother's grip and gives him a quick hug.

His parents notice her at the same time and look at each other in confusion. Sonny clears his throat. 'This is my colleague from the *Courier*, Jacintha Barthelot.' His explanation runs dry.

Jazz steps forward, carrying a box of chocolates. She had planned to buy flowers before they arrived at the house, but there has been no opportunity.

'Hello Mr de Roye, Mrs de Roye.' She makes herself sound meeker, less confident than her normal manner.

'Well,' says Artie de Roye as his wife stares open mouthed, 'this is a surprise, but we are glad to meet you. My dear child, you are very welcome in our house.'

His eyes are sparkling sapphires behind his spectacles. He looks kind. If she is honest, she has not immediately taken to Lily. She scolds herself inwardly for judging them as if they are prospective parents-in-law.

She smiles into Artie's eyes. 'Thank you very much, Mr de Roye.'

Lily de Roye finds her words. 'Well, well, let's all have lunch, plenty to eat.'

Sonny strides ahead and runs up the veranda steps.

'Let me show you where you can wash,' he calls to her. Jazz follows to the side of the house where there is a hut housing a shower and toilet. As she splashes water over her tired face, she can hear Lily de Roye talking to Sonny.

'Jacintha is quite dark… Burgher girl, no?'

'Mummy…' he says in what Jazz knows is a warning tone.

'Sonnah boy, a nice family has come to the town recently, they've come from Colombo for a long stay, a good family, friends of the Crowes, you know. There are two daughters, both very light-skinned girls and the father has a good job in the bank…'

As Jazz approaches, she hears Sonny hissing at his mother as they make their way to the table. 'Mummy, I just came to see you. To be back with the family. I don't want to hear any of this fuss and nonsense.'

Lily's brow darkens but she composes herself as Jazz takes her place quietly beside.

'Good, child, you have come. Sit, sit.'

The scent of freshly cooked chicken curry makes her mouth water. Lily de Roye ladles rice and parripu onto a plate for Jazz and tells her to help herself to the curry.

'So, Miss Barthelot, or shall I call you Jacintha? Yes? Good. Tell me about your family.'

'Mummy…' says Sonny sharply.

His mother serves a plate for him. 'Jacintha won't mind, will you child?'

Jazz gives a potted history of her family circumstances.

'So, Mamma has passed? That is very sad. And now you are working at the newspaper as a reporter, is it? Very unusual.' She makes it sound as if the two facts are connected. Jazz wonders briefly if this could be the case.

'Jacintha has a degree in English,' Sonny says, 'from Reading University in England.'

Jazz can see that Lily would be far more impressed if Sonny pronounced how hot she makes her curries and that she sews all her own clothes, and indeed Lily does seem startled by this piece of information and the conversation comes to an end. Lily turns to her son.

'Eat more,' says Lily to Jazz, 'fill up your plate, you're too skinny.'

Jazz sits quietly taking in her surroundings. The house is small but spotless and very tidy. She remembers Sonny's tale of his childhood in a big house up country on one of the tea estates and thinks how hard it must have been for Lily de Roye to come to terms with such a sharp change in circumstances.

'You have a daughter living here also?' says Jazz.

'Serena, 'says Lily, 'she has gone with my sister, Flora to the Hendricks family at Nuwara Eliya. Alphonse Hendricks, the youngest son is Serena's boyfriend. Alphonse is studying accountancy, a lovely boy.'

'Boyfriend?' Sonny says, 'when did this all happen?'

'Sonnah boy, I have been telling you this for ages, don't you read my letters? The father, Tony Hendricks was Headmaster of Badulla Central School. Recently retired. They have a big place a few miles from here. It's their pearl wedding anniversary this weekend; big party tonight and Daddy and I are invited tomorrow for the lunch party.'

'I see'. He finishes off his second plate and then rises, scraping the chair legs against the floor tiles. 'I think I'll stretch my legs in the garden.'

He looks across at Jazz and she gets to her feet tiredly. His father leads the way outside. When the sound of Lily de Roye supervising the kitchen duties floats from the house, Sonny and his father light cigarettes, sheltered from sight by the shower hut.

'Want one?' Sonny waves his packet at Jazz.

'You are smoking, is it, child?' says Artie looking at her.

'No, no,' she says crossly waving it away, 'well, sometimes I have one when I'm working.'

In the light, Artie's face looks younger. She can see how much Sonny resembles his father. Sensing father and son might want to talk, Jazz walks towards the roses. She can still hear faintly.

'How are you, Dadda?' Sonny asks. 'I'm sorry I haven't been home for a while.'

'I understand, but you are here now. I'm okay, still doing a few hours in the hotel garden, supervising the young gardeners, and planning the beds each season. How is work for you? Ludo tells me you will be staying in the Eastern Province indefinitely.'

'It's a bit tiresome but that's the current plan.'

'The body in the lake is keeping you busy. The story has caused a stir, not quite the newspaper coverage the government would have imagined after all the pomp and glory when the reservoir opened.' He gives a chuckle.

Sonny's voice drops so low she can barely hear. 'Dadda, how is Gail? She wasn't good last time I saw her.'

'She is up and down.' Their voices drop to a low, fierce rumble.

Jazz wonders at all the discussion around Gail's health.

'And Sonnah boy, how are you? I worry for you.'

'I'm fine Dadda. You don't need to worry about me. I look after myself.'

Jazz thinks how untrue this is; somebody does need to worry about him. If she gets a chance, she thinks she might voice some of her worries to Artie de Roye. But Sonny would never forgive her.

'But I do worry, you're my son...'

The voices of the two men sink lower and further indistinct exchanges take place.

'Come, let me show you around the garden.' Lily de Roye

appears at her side and takes her elbow, leaving the men to their discussion.

'I've made up Serena's bed for you and put your bag in the room.'

'Thank you very much, I'm sorry to have caused you extra work.'

'It's no problem. Tell me, is Sonny okay? He never tells us anything of his life. How do you find him? Is he happy?'

She decides on a tactful approach. 'Sonny has been working hard on this new case and having to teach me as well, means more work for him. And sometimes, I think living in Colombo, we all get caught up in the big city and we lose sight of home and our families. I'm sure he isn't unhappy.'

A feline interloper stalks across the lawn, tail flicking, on a rat hunt. They sit for a while in silence, enjoying the planting talents of Artie de Roye; frangipani and jasmine, roses and marigolds spreading scent and colour, a turtle dove cooing in a young jack-fruit tree.

'A man Sonny's age needs a wife to look after him properly in Colombo, no?'

She makes a non-committal noise.

'Ah, here you both are, gossiping out of sight. Mummy, let's go for a walk and have a chat, shall we?'

'Of course, Sonny, of course. I told Aunty May we would call by. Come here, your hair is all mussed up.'

'Come, Jazz,' Sonny says.

'Yes, Jacintha, you must come also. Aunty would be very pleased to meet with you, I'm sure.' Lily de Roye gives her an arch look.

'I'm very tired. I hope you won't mind if I stay here and sit peacefully in this beautiful garden.'

Artie has come up beside her. 'I will stay also. You go, with Sonnah boy, Lily.'

After they have left, he says, 'You don't like fuss, is it?'

'There really isn't any need for it. I hope Sonny's mother hasn't misunderstood anything. I wouldn't want her to be disappointed.'

'My wife is permanently disappointed, please don't worry. But tell me, Sonny has brought you here just for a visit? No other reason?'

Jazz makes vague explanations about a working trip, and she thinks Artie de Roye, the gentle soul, understands. His eyes are awash with love, mingled with something she can't quite identify, whenever they mention Sonny. She wonders at the tension that had been present in the garden, earlier that morning when the two men had been talking. She sits back enjoying the sun.

Lunch had been plain food, but for dinner that night Lily de Roye lays her best white cloth out on the table and festoons it with the plates and bowls used at Christmas and Easter.

'This all looks wonderful. How lucky you are to be spoilt like this, Sonny,' says Jazz with a smile at Lily as she approaches the table.

Lily de Roye says with great pride, 'come, come sit down next to me. I hope you like cashew curry.'

Mindful of this being a special dish, Jazz enthusiastically assures her that she does. Helping herself, she catches Sonny's eye across the table and is pleased when he gives her a relaxed smile. For a moment she can almost imagine they are a courting couple.

It seems as if Lily de Roye has read her mind. 'Sonnah boy, you remember Hugh Melville, one of your classmates? He got married last week and his younger brother will be married next year.'

Sonny nods, his mouth full.

'Yes, yes, it was a big wedding It felt like half the district was there. A lovely day, wasn't it Artie?'

'Yes indeed.'

'You should really try and meet up with Bobby...you must remember him, John and Daphne's son, he's working somewhere in Colombo, isn't he? He is married now. And what about Victor, how is he? Still at the Galle Face? His mother tells me how hard he works. Another promotion soon, perhaps?'

'I saw him for drinks, back in November. He's doing very well.'

'Family is proud, no?'

Jazz relaxes, listening, not knowing any of the people but fascinated to watch Sonny in his home environment.

'And so, what is the latest with this body in the lake? Ludo must be working very hard with this difficult case.'

'Ludo scuttles between Colombo and the Eastern Province, trying to get more leads. No more news, nobody knows who the poor bugger is.'

'Was.'

'But what is all this nonsense; how can somebody not be missing a father or an uncle or a brother? A grandfather? Friend? Neighbour? Nobody can be that solitary.'

After their meal, they move onto the veranda, Sonny and his father smoking constantly, Lily de Roy looking at recipes in a magazine with Jazz. The stars have been up for quite a while and bedtime drinks have been served when Jazz feels her eyes closing.

'Game of cards, Jazz?' Sonny is pouring another arrack, set for the night. When she shakes her head, Artie takes the pack and begins to shuffle. Sonny gives him a small smile. Lily gets up stiffly.

'Jacintha, you are falling asleep. Go to bed, child. I will come also. It's very late.'

Rising from her chair, Jazz realises that Sonny and Artie are picking up their taut conversation from earlier in the day. She can't fathom what it means, but she feels sadness for them.

After breakfast, Lily de Roye walks them to Mass. The bell is ringing as they approach an elegant little church set back from the road, surrounded by trees and shrubs. They follow a stream of worshippers through the open wooden doors, stopping in the porch to dip into the holy water, dampening their brows with the sign of the cross. Lily de Roye leads the way towards her favourite pew.

The smell of incense and the clamour of a low bell announce the arrival of the priest, a pale American with sweat on his brow, processing slowly down the aisle. Jazz, no longer a believer but still a regular attendee at her aunt's bequest, exchanges a look with Sonny to see if he is communing with the Lord. He is looking at the floor, frowning.

'In the name of the Father, the Son, and the Holy Spirit. Let us pray.' The congregation bow their heads, and the Mass begins.

Afterwards, Sonny's mother holds onto him as they walk back to the de Roye house. She shows no sign of letting go. Jazz goes to collect their bags and places them in the car. When Jazz reappears, to her surprise, Lily comes across and pats her arm affectionately. Sonny takes the opportunity to open the door and slip into the driver's seat. Jazz is bending to take her seat in the car next to Sonny when Artie pulls her in for a hug. He whispers fiercely into her ear, 'please Jacintha, take care of Sonnah boy, for me.'

'Of course,' she murmurs, touched, and troubled. She wonders if he has misunderstood their relationship, after all, or maybe there is something else he is worried about, something she can't glean.

Sonny rolls down the window and calls across to where his parents now stand watching from the top of the veranda. 'It's been lovely being back.' He gives his mother a smile. 'You have no idea how much I miss your cooking.'

Artie puts his hands together as if he is praying. 'Goodbye, Sonnah boy, be careful.'

Jazz feels a lash of emotion as they drive away. She stretches out, trying to erase the complicated feelings the visit has brought. For a while they chat, the windows wound down to catch the breeze which lightly whips at their hair. As they pass through endless villages and onto the road, hemmed in on each side by mountains, she closes her eyes and sinks into a light sleep.

18

The murder investigation is currently focussed on trying to identify the fishing net in which the body had been trussed up. Superintendent Ludowyk looks glum; he's back in Kumburapola and the detective work is proceeding at a snail's pace. 'You can report if you like, but it's not much of a story. Still, it will keep the matter alive in people's minds and maybe we will get an identification, even at this late stage.'

Having finished the briefing, they make their way to the office, through the busy market. As they enter, Sonny says, 'Do you think we need a sign, Jazz?'

'A sign? From God? Asking for a clue as to why we have to remain here?'

'We need a sign in the window that tells people we're the *Colombo Courier*. I'm going out to see if I can get one made up. When I was in here the other day, two people came in separately to ask if they could buy some pens. Does it look as if we are selling stationery and whatnot?' He gestures around the office. 'Are you okay to write up that little report?'

'Sure.' It needs only one to write up the few meagre lines of information from the superintendent and Sonny is best kept occupied. She thought he had seemed subdued when they were listening to the superintendent telling them about the fishing net.

Once he has disappeared out onto the street, she sits down at Sonny's typewriter and feeds through a fresh sheet of paper and gets a couple of paragraphs down summing up the scant information.

Detectives in Kumburapola working on the case of the Body in the Lake, are trying to trace where the fisherman's net, wrapped around the body, might have come from. It is thought that the body may have travelled a long distance in the water before surfacing in the Lanka Samudraya, remaining intact due to the strength of the rope.

The net, partly disintegrated, was large, estimated at being between eight and nine feet, similar to those regularly seen being hauled in on beaches all over the island. The nets are produced by various companies and are widely available to buy, although fishermen tend to band together, sharing a single net. The police are currently making enquiries as to whether any fishing communities have previously reported a lost or stolen net. One fisherman interviewed in Batticaloa said that sometimes damaged nets would be left behind on beaches. There are also companies running tours on the island that sell hunting and fishing nets which are aimed at the tourist market.

The police would still like to hear of any man between the ages of 55-70, who has not been seen for over a year.

She has removed the paper and is laying it face down on the desk when Sonny bursts through the door.

'Come, come!'

'What is it?' She is looking around for the key to the door to lock up.

'No time to waste.'

Sonny leads her along the street, treading through the narrow spaces around the back of the market stalls. He stops at a booth selling dusty tins and packets of food. He nods at the owner.

'Look.' He directs her gaze to one of the old style kades selling refreshments, a few wooden mismatched chairs and tables dotted outside. Three men in business suits are seated, talking, and gesticulating wildly.

'Recognise that one in the middle?'

Jazz peers. 'Oh, yes. It's that strange chap from the train. Ray somebody or other.'

'I spotted him a while ago a few streets away going into a shabby looking building with his shiny briefcase. I thought it seemed a bit strange. He works in the bank, so what would he be doing in such an unsavoury place? Anyway, I hung around for a bit, he came out alone looking cross, sat down over there at the table, kept checking his fancy watch, then the other fellows turned up and the next minute the buggers are all shouting and screaming at each other.'

'That does seem strange. Did you hear any of the conversation?'

'Just a few odd words,' says Sonny, 'two of them being 'Dick and Fry.'

'What?'

'Exactly. We need to have a little chat with Ray, I think.'

'You don't think he's dangerous, do you?'

'He's softer than a pint of Milkmaid,' Sonny scoffs, 'look at his stance, he's clearly terrified. I think the poor fool has got himself into something too deep for his small shoes. Remember what he said on the train about a lucrative deal, then quickly closed his trap and didn't say another word?'

'He's on the move,' says Jazz.

Five minutes later they are following him, as alone, he heads through aromatic spice stalls, fabric merchants and past a hardware shop, towards the new crossroads where the bank stands.

'Quick, before he goes in,' says Sonny, rushing up behind him. 'Ray, hey, man!'

Ray Chandimal turns towards them with a quizzical air.

'Do I know you?'

'Sure, we travelled together to Batticaloa a few weeks ago on the train. We sat opposite you.'

Jazz notices that as before, Ray Chandimal barely gives her a look.

'Did I fall asleep? I usually do. I may have had a few drinks. I'm sorry Mr...? I can't quite recall.'

'Sonny de Roye. He holds out his hand. 'Time for a drink, Ray?'

'Well...'

'Only, last time we met, you were keen to tell me about your hush-hush deals.'

'I say, I wouldn't have said anything. Why would I tell you such nonsense?'

'You thought I might be interested.'

'No, I couldn't possibly...'

'Ray. Calm down and let's go and get that drink. I know just the place. Nice and quiet where we can talk. Come on, don't be shy, Jacintha and I just want to get to know you a bit better.'

Ray Chandimal has sweat pouring off his forehead. Sonny takes his elbow and guides their steps into a dead-end lane with fewer kades. They sidle in between the booths to a small shack with a doorway covered by a dingy curtain. Sonny pushes it aside. There is a fan whirring away unsteadily overhead, making a grinding noise. Ray sits down gratefully and puts his face upwards to catch the thinly circulating air. Jazz sits opposite, stony-faced.

Sonny murmurs something to the man behind the tiny wooden bar who brings over an open bottle of arrack and three chipped glasses. Sonny pours generous amounts of liquid into each and clinks his glass to Ray's.

'Cheers.'

Ray looks askance at them but after a few sips he gives a snort of laughter and relaxes back into the chair.

'Well,' says Sonny cheerily, 'what can you tell me?'

'Mr de Roye I must apologise. I was shooting my mouth off like a big shot on the train. It meant nothing.'

'I'm not sure I believe you, Ray but I guess your business is your business. You work for Island Bank, right?'

'I do.'

'I thought that's what you said. Only, when I saw you a while ago, you were coming out of a very different kind of building. A falling-down kind of place. Was that a business meeting? I know places like that, and it didn't look the kind of place I imagine a respectable bank clerk to be working.'

'What? No, no, I was just meeting some business contacts in the building trade.'

'You came out looking nervous. Are you in some kind of trouble?'

Ray suddenly bangs his hand on the table. 'Are you following me? Who the hell are you people?' He gives Jazz a fleeting stare.

'Relax. Look, sorry if we've made a mistake. You gave me your card on the train and so when we spotted you, we thought we'd be friendly, show you a little bit of hospitality.' He takes Ray's business card from his wallet and props it against the bottle.

'That may be true, but you ask a hell of a lot of questions.' Mollified, he gives Sonny a shifty grin. 'Sorry if I'm being paranoid. I'm just a bit overworked.' He swirls the liquid around his glass, then drains it swiftly before rising to his feet. 'Good to meet you again. I hope next time I see you I can find my manners a bit quicker.'

'I'll definitely hope to see you.' Jazz grins to herself at how threatening Sonny sounds. 'Drinks on us again, of course. Maybe in that half-built hotel out on the coastal road, if they ever finish it. Do you know it? The one that they had to halt working on due to defective materials?'

'Me? Why would I know it?'

'I just thought you might.'

'Well, I don't.'

'What about Still Waters? Ever been there? Know any of the Lanka Reservoir Project crowd? What about Dick Fry?'

'I – I'm sorry I really can't help. But look, my lunchtime is over, I must get back to the bank.'

He scurries away after giving Sonny a damp handshake.

'What on earth was that about?'

Sonny grins. 'I don't know exactly but give it a few days and we will definitely be meeting up with Ray Chandimal again. I want to know why he is lying.'

19

When Jazz hands the post office clerk her envelope containing their report about the fishing nets, she is surprised to be handed one with her own name on the front. She is poring over it wondering what it might say, when a man comes up beside her, encroaching on her personal space.

'You are that girl reporter from Colombo?'

She nods.

'Tamil girl?'

She doesn't reply, shocked at his tone.

'If I were you, I would go back to Colombo, very soon. Your sort not welcome around here.' He slopes off looking back and glaring over his shoulder.

'What the hell?' Sonny growls when she returns to the office and tells him of the encounter.

'I thought at first he had taken against me because I'm a reporter but as he asked if I was a Tamil I'm not sure it wasn't something more.'

'If I see him, I will knock his bloody block off.'

Trying to shake off the unpleasant incident she sits down at one of the desks and tears open the envelope. It doesn't take long to read it and she throws it down on the desk with an expression of disgust. 'Well, this is turning out to be a terrible sort of a day.'

'What now, man?'

He glances across at her, bolts through the door and is back minutes later with a hot cup of steaming tea and a bun. Still annoyed, she is nonetheless touched.

'Thank you.'

'What is in the envelope that has annoyed you?'

'For God's sake! Walter wants me to do a feature on the women from Still Waters...how they spend their day...where they buy their clothes and other kinds of banality. I mean, what kind of nonsense is this?'

'It's great to be asked to do a feature, Jazz.'

'I wouldn't call this a feature. It's more like filling a gap. Did you know about this?'

'No.'

'Why didn't Walter ask you to do it?'

'Come on, I think we know why.'

'I just feel as though I'm being sidelined.'

'Think of it as an opportunity. Walter is expecting a few paragraphs to edit but prove him wrong.'

'Okay. You're right.'

'If you time your visit right and get there for lunch, you will get a good feed.'

'You think I should go now?'

'Why not? Otherwise, you will only be sulking about it for days.'

'I don't even know if Peyton will be at the club today.'

'Well, if she isn't, others will be. They will all be bored enough to want to talk to you, and vain enough to be willing to see themselves in print.'

'Fine. I will go. But promise me you won't go meeting up with Ray Chandimal again, without me.'

She spends some time crashing around the office, loosening her temper, until with a sigh she bundles up her notebook, puts on lipstick and sets off to find a taxi.

She wonders briefly how, without Sonny's easy charm, she will gain entry to this elite club, remembering that they had left previously on a sour note. When the car drops her outside, she lingers a while and when a gaggle of women arrive and noticing her, smile politely, she attaches herself to their party and slips inside unchallenged. One of the women booms at her in a jolly voice. 'Are you meeting somebody?'

'I'm Jacintha Barthelot,' she says offering her hand. 'I'm here to do an article for the *Colombo Courier*.'

A couple of ladies flutter around her, while the others stand a little aloof with worried faces. 'Aren't you one of the reporters who wrote about the body in the reservoir?'

'That's right.'

'We thought we recognised you. Maybe you shouldn't really be here, the LRP were angry when you came last time. I don't think they would want us to be talking to you.'

'Oh, well, but nothing was said in the article about Still Waters, I'm sure Miss Barthelot can be here as our guest.'

'Thank you, that is kind,' says Jazz. She stands her ground as the group reshapes itself around her.

'And what is the latest news about the body?'

'The investigation is progressing slowly.'

One of the ladies suddenly exclaims. 'Golly! You're not here about Dick Fry, are you?' There's a startled silence.

'No,' says Jazz firmly, 'actually I am here to do a piece about you ladies.'

The air surrounding the group grows softer. 'Well, what about us?' comes an uncertain voice.

Jazz crosses her fingers that there will be no mention of knitting patterns and recipes. She gives a determined smile. She has made up her mind there must be more to this singular band of women.

'I think your stories must be interesting. How you got here, what you make of the place, how does it compare to back home?'

'Well…that doesn't sound harmful in any way. Come this way, Miss Barthelot, have a drink with us before we lunch. We've got plenty of time for a lovely chat.' A couple of the women detach themselves from the group and head straight into the dining room but the rest surround Jazz enthusiastically, leading the way into a panelled bar.

'Let me get some drinks', she says forcing herself to sound more confident than she feels. She has never purchased an alcoholic drink before, not even during her time in England when she and her friends were often invited to the pub by their fellow male students who always bought the drinks. It's a bit of luck that she has spent so much time with Sonny, recently.

The Tamil behind the bar looks at her impassively. Jazz roves the shelves with her eyes and spots a familiar bottle of gin. 'Hello' she says, 'six glasses of Rockland and a slice. Make them doubles.'

The ladies have given permission for her to take notes and before long she has filled pages of her book with stories of lives lived in London, Glasgow, Toronto, Maine, and Chicago, before Ceylon. One of them, Audrey Rivers, has not been back to the United States for ten years and hopes she will be lucky enough to stay away another ten. Another gentler sort, Joan Mullins, confides she misses her parents and sister and being able to buy 'nice blouses and underwear' from Bourne and Hollingsworth.

All but one had been secretaries before meeting their husbands and had given up working after marriage and children.

'And so how do you spend your time?'

'There are lots of clubs; Bridge of course, the Debating Society. A few go and visit the poorer communities; they bake cakes and pies, and we all donate clothes and toys.'

'Some of us have our children out here. We have ayahs to look after them but a few of us get together between eight and noon and set up a classroom each day. Between us we do a little bit of reading, writing and arithmetic with them and sometimes a little bit of history and geography too. Most of the children will be sent home when they are older to attend school, but we don't want them to arrive knowing absolutely nothing.'

'They say travel broadens the mind. Your children will have learnt many things on their journeys that can't be taught in a classroom.'

'Yes. They have learnt about other cultures and religions, and experienced for themselves different foods, languages, and customs. They've seen birds, animals, and plants that you would normally only read about in books. A worthy education.'

'As for us, we try and read a book each month, don't we girls? I've just finished the latest Daphne du Maurier which was splendid, and I've got an Agatha Christie next, once my husband's finished it. We've amassed a rather hefty library now between us all. We get the books sent from Cargills, of course.'

'Oh, yes, what would we do without Cargills? We can get so many nice things from there,' says the youngest, Alice Rix who Jazz thinks is probably homesick, 'my husband always arranges little treats for me when I'm feeling blue. He knows how I love John West Salmon. And Huntley and Palmers biscuits.'

'Oh, yes,' says Jazz, 'I used to love their tins of assorted biscuits when I was in England.'

'Oh really?' The ladies are interested in Jazz's time spent in

Reading. It takes a little while before she can spin the questions back to them. After discovering the ladies also participate in regular painting and drawing excursions across the region, (Alice and Joan collaborating on a monthly illustrated botany pamphlet) she feels she has enough material.

'Well,' she says finally, 'you must all be getting hungry and I'm sure you are ready for your lunch. Thank you for talking to me, it's been a pleasure.'

She follows slowly behind the group as they wave at her before going in to dine. She's feeling hungry and wishing she had taken up their lunch invitation, when somebody accosts her in the corridor after she has come out of the lavatory.

'Jacintha? How nice to see you again.'

Peyton Emery stands smiling at her, looking chic in a dress with a collar and flared skirt. 'How have you been? Is Sonny not with you?'

'Just me today. I have been talking to some of the wives, I'm doing a feature on their life out here.'

Peyton nods and smiles. 'Have you had lunch? Would you like to join me?'

'Well, I…'

'Please do, I don't like to eat alone, and the others look as though they are already settled in.'

'I will join you. Thank you.'

'Maybe I can give you more information for your article.' She trails off hopefully.

Jazz spends the next hour listening to Peyton talking nonstop about dress patterns and the silk stalls in the market. She grins to herself, enjoying the food, not taking any notes. As soon as Peyton switches onto her favourite family recipes, Jazz rises.

'You're going already? Well, here's an idea, why don't you and Sonny come over to our place for a meal? Shall we say Saturday?'

Here, let me write down the address for you. Come at six and we'll have drinks on the terrace beforehand.'

'Drinks on the terrace,' mutters Jazz as she conveys the invitation to Sonny back in the office, 'she makes out she is living in a mansion.'

'Come on, Jazz, cheer up. It's a night out.'

'You're only interested in the free drinks.'

'Jazz, I understand how you feel, she's the kind of female that tends to alienate other women. My guess is that makes her a bit lonely.'

'That's true.' Jazz thinks about how the other women had politely waved but had made no attempt to come across and chat to Peyton.

'I bet she has a fancy cook who will serve us up something delicious.'

'Have you ever thought of being a food critic, Sonny?' she says in a teasing way.

He grins. 'That is a plan for when I get older. Anyway, I am glad you got some good material from your interviews.'

'I also went to visit the woman who sold me the lotion for my hair. You're right, she is a Vedda, she now lives a few miles away with her Tamil husband and children. I bought you this.' She gives him a small jar of ointment. 'For your headaches.'

'Thank you. I will try it before I go to bed.'

'I visited her to see if she'd had any trouble with that horrible fellow who accosted me on the street. Seems she knows of him. She's discovered I'm a reporter and she asked me if I would be running a story on him.'

'What did you say?'

'I said I hoped that it was just a phase, and he would eventually get bored with throwing insults around. What about you? Did anything happen while I was away?'

'Actually yes. Sergeant Rutnam called in, and by the way you should have seen his face drop to his knees when he saw you were out of the office.'

'Sonny,' she says warningly, 'what did he want?'

'He came to see if we, but mostly you I suspect, would like to take a drive out with him tomorrow, apparently a woman telephoned the police station this morning to say her father has been missing – for about a year.'

20

'The village is a few miles away, so I have brought the car. Come, come.' The sergeant, who has come to pick them up from their office, waggles his head at them, mainly at her, Jazz realises.

'This is very kind of you, Sergeant,' she says.

'My pleasure. I imagine things must be quiet for you at the moment. This could be the breakthrough we are waiting for. We'd better hope so, otherwise you will be sent back to Colombo, no?'

After half an hour the vehicle bounces to a halt into a hamlet, a huddle of shanty huts and a small kade selling fruit and vegetables. Sergeant Rutnam parks up and slamming the door behind him, stands in the middle of the road, surveying the scene. 'She didn't give me an address; I will have to knock and ask the neighbours who this woman might be.'

'Perhaps she will find us. There can't be many people here expecting a visit from an officer in a police vehicle.'

Sonny is right. As they are hovering, an overweight woman dressed in a blue sari arrives beside them, puffing and panting. She wears sunglasses on her head and a pair of heeled sandals.

'Sergeant Rutnam? I've been looking out for you. I'm Mrs Taylor. I'm staying in a guest house halfway between here and Kalmunai.'

'Mrs Taylor, these are journalists from Colombo; are you happy for them to accompany us to your father's house?'

'I don't mind.' The woman's face twists. 'Do you think this is a story for the newspapers?'

'I'm sure it's nothing,' Sonny soothes her.

'Mrs Taylor, when exactly did you last see or hear from your father?'

'Must be well over a year.' She dabs at her eyes with a lace edged handkerchief.

They follow as she walks past the largest dwelling, to a much smaller abode standing a way apart, tattered curtains blowing from dirty windows, the ground alongside covered in weeds. Mrs Taylor pushes the door ajar, and they follow her in. Piles of unopened letters bearing English stamps are scattered on the floor, pushed through the door by the postman over a long period of time.

'These are all from me', says Mrs Taylor softly, 'not a single one opened.' The sergeant gathers them up into a bundle.

'May I?'

'Of course.'

'You have no mother or siblings, Mrs Taylor?'

'My mother died during the war. I have an older sister who emigrated to Canada before the war. We're not really in touch but I did send her a telegram to ask if she had heard anything from Appa and she replied to say she had heard nothing.'

She takes Sergeant Rutnam into the small back bedroom where evidently, she had previously discovered traces of old blood. Jazz and Sonny hang back, watching through the door as Sergeant Rutnam scrapes a blood sample from the floor and measures the sparse blood spatter, muttering and making notes.

'I will have to send this to the laboratory, Mrs Taylor, which may take some time. Do you understand?'

She nods slowly.

They move through the rest of the dwelling, standing in the decaying kitchen area, wrinkling their noses against the traces of food, rotten with age, blobs of congealed cooking fat and outside the back door, a pail of rancid milk with a skin over the top.

'This must be a very different place to where you are living now,' Sonny suggests.

She looks at him. 'Of course it is,' she replies shortly.

'How long have you been gone from Ceylon, Mrs Taylor?' asks Sergeant Rutnam.

'I met my husband, William after the war while he was still stationed in Trincomalee. He was serving in the Royal Navy at the time, although he has since left the service. We married in December 1951 and sailed for London. We have been saving up so that I could come out and bring Appa back for a holiday with us in London.'

'You must have been worried when you didn't hear from him,' says the sergeant.

'Not at first. I didn't expect he would sit down and write me every month so to make it easy, before we left for England, we bought him a pile of postcards and some stamps. I put them in a drawer…oh, here they are. Never been used.' She looks as if she is about to cry.

'Did you speak to the neighbours?'

'Not many people around here, as you can see. We had arranged that for the first few months after I had gone, Appa would go to stay with a cousin in Trinco for a long holiday. I know he wasn't fond of his cousin, she tended to boss him around, but it would have been a change of scenery for him. He always liked the sea, and he would have enjoyed her cooking for him. A couple of months after we settled back in London, I wrote to the cousin to find out how things were, and after a very long while she finally wrote to me to say he had never arrived. She didn't seem very bothered. I assumed that he had just changed his mind.

'At the beginning of this year my husband paid for my passage back in the hope that I would be able to persuade Appa to come back with me. Now I just don't know what to think. That blood in the bedroom...' She dabs her eyes again.

'Do you have a photograph of your father?' asks Sergeant Rutnam.

'I think so. Yes, somewhere in my bag, I have.' She scrabbles around and hands him a small square photograph.

When the sergeant has finished looking and is satisfied, they leave the empty dwelling, glad to be back out on the sunlit road. Mrs Taylor's hired car and driver is parked at the other end of the hamlet. Sergeant Rutnam walks her back and says a few words in a reassuring voice.

'I do hope you're right, Sergeant. And besides', she continues in a tone of some relief, 'it's not as if there's a body or anything...'

Jazz exchanges a cautious look with Sonny.

'How long are you staying in the country, Mrs Taylor?'

'I'm here for another ten days, but I can stay for longer if... you need me to.'

'What about enemies? Can you think of anybody who would wish your father harm?'

'My gosh, of course not, he wouldn't hurt a fly.' Her hand flies up to her face. 'I've just thought...you don't think he could be that person found in the lake, do you? The man in all the newspapers?'

'Well, we can't rule it out, I'm afraid, Mrs Taylor, at this time.'

'Will...will I need to look at the body?'

'Perhaps, but it is not as straightforward as that. I will need to arrange for you to come and have another interview first.'

Sonny and Jazz walk back to the vehicle while the sergeant says a final few words to the poor woman.

'Do you think he's the body in the lake?'

'I don't know what to think.'

'I should make notes then. Write it up?'

'Record the encounter but we will have to wait for any positive identification.'

Sergeant Rutnam has said all he can, and finally they watch as Mrs Taylor is driven away. The sergeant puts his car into gear and begins the drive back to Kumburapola.

'What do you think?' Jazz asks him.

'I am not sure. I don't know how her father would end up getting shot when he rarely left the village. But you can never tell.' His mind wanders. 'That poor fellow lying in the mortuary. Shot and buried like a nameless animal in the woods. Let's hope we find somebody who will claim and give him a decent burial.'

'Sergeant Rutnam,' Jazz asks, feeling contrary, 'what makes you think the man in the mortuary was someone to be pitied? He might have been a terrible kind of person.'

Sergeant Rutnam stares intensely into her eyes, from his rear-view mirror. 'Of course, Jacintha, you are correct. We don't know anything about the victim but as a mark of respect we treat him as an innocent.'

She gives a little shake of her head. A silence fills the car. She thinks the sergeant dislikes being challenged, especially by a woman. After a while Sergeant Rutnam recovers himself. 'Just to remind you both that if you are reporting this visit, could you refrain from mentioning any names at this stage. Just refer to a new lead. Okay?'

'We are aware, thank you Sergeant.'

As they are nearing Kumburapola, Sergeant Rutnam coughs self-importantly before inviting them both out for a meal. 'Must be hungry, no?' His eyes slide to the back of the car surveying Jazz through the mirror, searching for an answering signal.

She immediately declines.

21

February has brought a little less rain to Kumburapola as the monsoon season begins to take its leave of the Eastern Province, but the weather is still overcast on the morning of the Emerys' dinner party. It's the weekend so there is no need for them to go into the office. Mrs Andrado has decided to engage in an unnecessary spring clean of both their rooms, so they sit outside playing cards and smoking.

'I wonder if that body is Mrs Taylor's father,' says Jazz, 'it sounds more than likely.'

'Yes, it does,' says Sonny sounding happier than he has for a while.

Mrs Andrado appears, finished now with her labours, smiling broadly. 'Little snippet of news for you.'

'Tell us,' says Sonny winking at Jazz.

'My neighbour tells me a few journalists booked into the new hotel yesterday. What for, I don't know, wasting money like that.' Mrs Andrado is clearly annoyed that the journalists from the more upmarket Colombo newspapers have snubbed her establishment.

'Anyway, when you were in office yesterday and I was doing my marketing, they came sniffing around here looking for you. My neighbour saw them knocking and decided to tease them and told them you had been called back to Colombo on a story and may not be returning. She says they looked worried. One of the constables said they had been making a nuisance of themselves at the police station, getting in the way and joking around and that sergeant fellow got very annoyed and told them to leave. Then, this morning when I went to buy bread, I heard they had tried to get into Still Waters and had not been allowed in!'

'Ah,' says Sonny. Jazz can tell he is silently crowing that yet again the *Courier* is ahead of the game. He jumps up.

'Room is now ready, Mrs A?'

'Yes, yes, you go on up.'

He takes the stairs two at a time, to his room. Jazz looks at the landlady and gives a shrug.

'And you are going out to dinner tonight?' says Mrs Andrado watching his retreating back.

'Yes, meeting up with friends.'

Sonny reappears.

'You look pleased with yourself.'

'We will get some lunch out,' he says to Mrs Andrado, 'we've got to go to office now.'

'Saturday, no?'

'No rest for the wicked.'

Jazz looks to him for clarification. He puts his finger on his lips and says nothing further until they are safely at their desks.

'Okay, what is with all the secrecy?'

'Easier to talk here. Mrs A hears everything.'

'True.'

'Remember when we were on that building site, the half-built hotel?'

'I remember.'

'I picked this up on-site. Take a look,'

She takes the piece of paper, curled at the edges and peers closely. It bears the remnants of a name, '*F... Moon*' and then '*ild...*' The rest had been torn away. She looks at him blankly and he draws from his pocket, one of the papers he had found hidden outside Dick Fry's room.

'Look,' he says, 'what does that say?' directing her attention to one in particular.

'Full Moon Building Company,' she reads and looks at him. 'Ah, I see what you mean. You think this wrapper from the pallet on the building site, is from the same company?'

'I am sure it is.'

The Emery bungalow nestles in a grove of similar buildings half an hour's drive from the main town. Sonny rents a car from the town's only garage owner, an old Morris Minor which he parks in the driveway alongside Peyton's fancy Opel and a gleaming Cadillac, which Jazz assumes belongs to Bob Emery.

A maid answers their knock. They follow her down a cool hallway, catching a glimpse of a futuristic style kitchen; steel cabinets, a tall refrigerator humming away in the corner and an electric oven with hobs built into the work surface. Everything has been painted and tiled in complementary pastel shades of blue and pale green.

'Very fancy,' says Sonny.

The parlour has armchairs, a bar filled with bottles, and a glass cabinet lit up to highlight a pyramid of crystal glasses, but Peyton appears and beckons them out onto the imposing veranda which is filled with cane furniture. To the side a large square dining table stands, laid with a white cloth, plates, and silver cutlery.

'So glad you could make it! We thought we'd eat outside; it's cooled down a little now the sun has gone down.'

Sonny spreads his arms. 'This is quite a place you have here.'

She inclines her head, graciously accepting the compliment. 'Let me fix you some drinks.' Deftly she produces a bottle of gin, pours a glass for Jazz and a tumbler of whisky for Sonny.

'Sit,' she says, 'you've got a night off, tonight, I hope you're going to make the most of it. Tell me, any further news about the body in the lake?'

Sonny and Jazz give a smile.

'No further developments at present.'

'I see,' says Peyton, 'well, relax and make yourselves at home.' She spreads her arms out at the house and garden arrayed before them. 'We don't own this, of course, these bungalows were specially bought and kitted out for all the Lanka Reservoir Project people and their families, but it's been a marvellous home for us, and we'll miss it when we're gone.'

'I'm sure you will,' says Jazz.

'You should have seen what they expected us to live in when we came over. Nothing more than primitive hovels! No running water for Christ's sake.'

Jazz can't avoid responding with a flash of her eyes, and catching the spark, Peyton's poise falters. It is fortunate that Bob Emery chooses that moment to make his entrance. Like Sonny he is wearing relaxed cotton slacks and a short-sleeved shirt.

'So sorry, I had to take a telephone call. Sonny, Jacintha, I've heard a lot about you. It's good to finally meet.' His tone is measured and down to earth, friendly but not effusive like his expansive wife. Intelligent, Jazz thinks.

Everyone unbends over dinner. While they are having their prawn and melon starters, a servant heads to the end of the garden where there is a fire pit. Sonny watches with interest as a grill attachment is laid over the top and huge slices of beef steak laid on top.

'We thought we'd cook American style tonight; we're having steak and fries with corn on the cob. There are some chillies on the side just in case it's a bit bland for your taste. We get this served to us whenever we visit Peyton's folks in the States. We certainly don't have food that we cook outside like this back in England, but I'm a convert'.

Sonny and Jazz sip their drinks slowly, listening to Bob sharing his first impressions of the country.

'I arrived over here to discover absolute chaos. I nearly turned tail and caught the next plane home! The project had progressed rather quickly from its inception to legal status, to the beginning of the build. A lot of people in charge didn't know what had hit them, what with the speed they were being asked to turn every-thing around. They organised tons of equipment to be used for the irrigation work, scheduled to arrive from all over the world, millions of pounds worth but then as it started to arrive over the weeks and months at Batticaloa they suddenly realised they had nowhere to store anything! Can you imagine that?' He gives a deep rumble of laughter at the memories. 'I remember Dick Fry saying to me, "What the hell have we let ourselves in for, Bob? Are they thinking to pile it all on the backs of elephants to get it to Inginiyagala?"

Bob raises his eyes to the heavens at the memories. 'In the end, Dick and I were diverted from the irrigation planning for a while to take charge of widening the existing road, which was tiny by any standards, so it could be used to transport everything by road. It was quite a job; I can tell you.' He laughs again. Sonny continues to gently press for information and the men fall into a murmur.

Jazz is trying to listen to the conversation, but Peyton touches her arm. 'Jacintha, tell me, when can we expect to see your article about us? Some of the ladies have been asking.'

'I'm working on it. I'm not sure when the article will appear, but I will of course let you know.'

'How long have you been working on the newspaper?'

Relaxed by the gin, Jazz is happy to talk to Peyton about her experiences on the newspaper.

'And do you think you will stay in this country or go abroad eventually?'

Jazz pauses. 'Well, sometimes I think I would like to work elsewhere. I went to university in England, and I liked it there very much.'

'Maybe you would have more chances in journalism over there than here?'

Jazz thinks of her uncle. 'Yes. Maybe I would.'

'Could you really live in such a cold, rainy country? Full of bland food and grey skies?'

'What's this, Jazz?'

She always forgets that Sonny's antennae work with an almost supernatural force.

'Nothing,' she says lightly, relieved when a servant brings a tray of desserts out onto the table too early, without having been asked, and it is clear that Peyton is not amused.

After the meal Sonny asks Bob if there has been any news of Dick Fry. The older man is cutting the end of a cigar. He makes an exclamation. 'Dammit, nearly had my finger off. Sorry, you were saying?'

'Dick Fry,' Sonny prompts gently, 'I understand he's been missing for a while?'

'Well, yes. Actually, the police came and took a statement. I didn't really have much to tell them but apparently, he is now officially a missing person.'

'I realise you worked with him closely. You must be puzzled and concerned about his whereabouts.'

Bob sighs. 'It's an upsetting business. But I wouldn't say we were close, particularly. Oh, we were back at the beginning when we first came over, but this last year or so, I don't think anybody knew what was going on with Dick.'

'What do you mean?'

'The poor chap went completely off the rails. That sounds harsh but there's no other way to describe it. And you know, on long jobs like the Lanka Reservoir Project, when you find yourself far from home in a totally different landscape, new foods, strange customs, it does happen.'

'Are you saying you were no longer friends; you had some kind of falling out? I thought he had just decided to widen his circle and befriend a few local chaps. Why would that stop you from being friends?'

Bob pours them all a generous measure of brandy which burns pleasurably on the way down. 'Let's just say he was doing some things I didn't agree with. At least I had my suspicions. And it was sad to see him falling in with the wrong crowd. He took to gambling you know, and when he couldn't pay his debts…well, I mean I helped him out a couple of times, but he was in such a deep pit, I couldn't do much for him. A while back we had a couple of suspicious looking characters asking for him at the club house. Lord knows how much trouble he's in.'

'Do you think he's left the country to avoid paying his debts?'

'No. He told me a while back that he'd sold his passport to raise money.' Bob sighs again. 'Now listen to me, young fellow, you've made me say more than I wanted. I won't hold that against you, but I don't want to hear any of my words repeated or printed. All this is off-the-record, as you would say, alright?'

'Okay, of course.'

Jazz watches Bob as he pours another hefty glass for himself.

'Have you ever come across Full Moon Building Company?' Sonny asks casually.

Jazz waits for a look of guilt or panic but Bob merely looks puzzled. 'I've never heard of it. Should I? Is it a new company? A firm you are planning to use?'

'I just came across the name, recently, that's all. Is there a particular supplier that is used for the new builds in town? The hospital buildings, the school, and the hotels? I've also heard the names Colombo Strongest Steel and Island Build 53; do you know either of those?'

'I'm not familiar with those either and I know every company we contract, believe me. No, the usual suppliers would be either Stanton's or East Build.'

'Bob!' calls Peyton, loudly, 'let's put a record on. We can all have a dance.'

Sonny and Jazz's eyes meet, and they rise from the table simultaneously.

'It's been a wonderful evening. We can't thank you enough.'

'What, you can't be going already? It's not yet eleven. We haven't even had coffee. Or tea?' There's more brandy.'

'No thank you, Peyton we must be going, I'm afraid.'

'Well, we must do it again.'

'Sonny are you okay to drive?' she hisses anxiously as he fumbles in the driveway for his car keys. The Emerys are standing in the porch, arms around each other. Peyton is slightly giggly, swaying in her husband's arms.

'Of course, I am, I paced myself.'

'It was quite a good night, I thought. What did you make of Bob's reactions? Did you find anything we can follow up, Sonny?'

He grins at her maddeningly in the darkness and drives them back to the guest house.

22

Jazz and Sonny are sitting in the office while he takes her carefully through his instructions. 'Go into the Island Bank just as if you are any other customer. Wait for Ray Chandimal to be free, reintroduce yourself and tell him you are making enquiries about these companies.' He hands her the papers discovered under the eaves.

'What if he refuses to talk to me?'

'Firstly, he can't refuse to talk to a customer. Secondly, he won't wish to make a scene at his place of work so you might get somewhere with him. I think he will feel less threatened if you go and talk to him. I will be waiting outside to see what develops.'

She is still feeling uncomfortable.

'Tell him that you are checking up on building regulations. And that you are also anxious to make contact with Dick Fry.'

'Okay, Sonny, but can you just tell me what exactly is going on?'

'All in good time.'

Ray Chandimal is serving at his counter. Jazz stands in the queue with the folder of papers under her arm. As soon as his position becomes free, she approaches the counter. He looks up and gives her a meaningless smile. 'Good morning, Madam'. Clearly, he doesn't recognise her.

'Good morning, Mr Chandimal. I am making some enquiries on behalf of my firm in Colombo.'

He doesn't bother to ask which firm. His eyes light up. 'Ah, right, Colombo. Yes, we have clients based in Colombo who are planning second offices here. Kumburapola is really going places, you know. Lots of new offices coming soon, shops and houses and hotels.'

'Yes, so I understand,' she says crisply. She listens for five minutes while Ray Chandimal gives her a rundown of all the building developments within the town. Jazz nods politely and then when he has finally finished, she produces Dick Fry's letter-heads, spreading them in front of him.

'Can you tell me about these companies? I believe they have been used in some of the new build, is that correct?'

He runs his eye silently over the documents then meets her gaze with shocked eyes.

'Who the hell are you?' he says, 'Wait…I've seen you before. You were on the train with that pest, Sonny de Roye.'

She smiles thinly.

'I don't know anything about these companies,' he says quietly, 'they are nothing to do with me.'

'Are you quite sure about that?' Jazz says loudly. The other bank clerks look across at them and one or two customers are nudging each other curiously.

'Please,' says Ray Chandimal urgently, 'I must ask you to leave. I am afraid I cannot help with your enquiries today.'

'How about tomorrow?'

He looks at her realising she isn't going to go away. 'Do you know the Green Parrot Tea Boutique?' he says at last.

'I don't, but I am sure I can find it.'

'It's on the edge of the market, next to the place that sells pots and pans. I will meet you there in fifteen minutes. Okay?'

'As you wish.'

She turns away. 'A quarter of an hour,' she says over her shoulder as she heads for the door.

As she walks out onto the humid street, she looks around for Sonny and spots

him at the newspaper stall leafing through a magazine. Realising he doesn't want to make contact she wonders what to do next.

She decides to go on ahead to find the tea place. Turning a corner, her eye detects bright green plumage on a sign over a modern refreshment place. She goes into the shop next door, feigning an interest in copper bottomed pans and utensils. After fifteen minutes with no sign of Ray Chandimal, she enters The Green Parrot and sits down at a table, wondering where he could have got to. With dread she realises that he was never going to keep the appointment and has ducked out somewhere else. She worries that she should have done something differently until there is a commotion at the door of the boutique and standing up, she sees Sonny holding Ray Chandimal's arm tightly, directing him to the table where she is sitting.

'Good work, Jazz. Well, here we all are.'

'Great,' she says brightly, 'I have ordered tea.'

Ray Chandimal snorts. Sonny nudges him into a seat.

'What is this all about? Who the hell are you exactly?'

'I'm Sonny de Roye as you know, and this is my colleague, Jacintha Barthelot. We're from the *Colombo Courier* and we'd like to ask you a few questions.'

'The *Colombo Courier*! I'm not going to answer any of your questions. I have nothing to say that would be of interest to the newspaper.' Ray Chandimal is sweating heavily.

'Well, we think differently.'

Jazz looks at Sonny for clarification. She still has no idea what Ray Chandimal is involved in.

'Why are you hounding me like this? It was the same the last time we met. I will make a complaint to your editor.'

'Do you want me to tell you what I think? Okay. I think you are a common fraudster, and you are everything I hate most about our country, a man only interested in putting money in his own pocket at the expense of the poor.'

'What the bloody hell, man?'

'Let's start with some clarification regarding your partnership with Dick Fry.'

'Keep your damned voice down! Do you want to get us all killed?'

They fall silent as the tea arrives and then Sonny picks up from where he left off.

'Cat got your tongue? How about we have a look at these, firstly?' Sonny takes the folder from Jazz and takes the documents out, fanning them across the table.

'Where did you get those from?' Ray Chandimal sounds subdued.

'When I found them, I thought to myself, why on earth would somebody have original letterheads carefully hidden? And why, when I asked around, had nobody heard of these companies? What could be the reason that new buildings around the new town are not progressing as they should?'

Jazz is following the story, slowly putting together the pieces as the story tumbles out. From his privileged position in the bank, Ray Chandimal has been setting up bank accounts for non-existent companies, in cahoots with Dick Fry.

'Where did you first meet Dick Fry?' Sonny throws the question into the silent void. 'Let me guess. A game of poker?'

Sonny has hit the mark. Ray Chandimal's neck flushes, and

his eye flickers, a give-away tell. Jazz thinks he must be a poor card player.

'You got talking after the game. Dick must have, by that time, begun his losing streak. He discovered you worked in the bank and his desperate mind must have started to turn over. And you…you were just plain greedy. So together you hatched a plan.

'With his success on the Lanka Reservoir Project, Dick was a prestigious name. He was on the board of several building conglomerates. It would have been simplicity itself for him to organise a select band of tradesmen and tell them how he could organise things so that they could all make an easy living.

'You and Dick set up fake companies supplying steel and bricks and probably other building materials too. Set up one or two salesmen, sent them into new and developing Kumburapola to undercut the usual suppliers. Lied about their pedigree, gave them the spin about being used in Colombo and Kandy. Cheaper than the usual companies, they got the deals because Dick Fry, as the experienced one, would have been asked his opinion and he, of course would give them the go-ahead. The building consortiums trusted Dick. They didn't realise he was pulling the wool over their eyes with his recommendations.

'The first order supplied to the construction companies would probably have been of high quality, so as not to alert the developers. Dick probably bought up shipments from the established bricks and steel suppliers and changed the packaging, so it looked as if they came from his fake supply companies. The managers and the site foreman would have been satisfied with the standard of the materials. All further shipments of course, would have been those containing the defective building materials.'

Ray Chandimal attempts a defence.

'Look, we are not as bad as you are making out. The Government Superintendents got behind in their work, which we could not have anticipated, and buildings began to get used before receiving their safety certificates. Nobody was meant to get hurt.'

'What about the time and money wasted? Or the smaller companies who buy up surplus supplies at reduced rates, selling them on to desperate people on the fringes of poverty? These poor people, work two jobs to make a living, in order to build homes for their families, outside the cities and towns. What about their young children sleeping at night, not realising the bricks and the steel above their heads are defective, innocent of the fact that high winds and storms can bring everything crashing down?'

A sudden memory pops into Jazz's head; the cleaning woman, mentioned by Sergeant Rutnam, who had almost died in one of the newly built factories presumably constructed using Dick Fry's defective materials.

'If people choose to build illegally, that's not my fault. And the rest of the greedy developers.'

'Greedy! You're the greedy one,' says Jazz in anger.

'Ray, you are a poor fool,' says Sonny quietly. 'No wonder you were attracted to working in a bank. You care only for money.'

There is a long pause.

'Why has Dick Fry disappeared?' says Jazz.

'Stupid bugger,' says Ray Chandimal bitterly. 'Whatever money he made, and he made plenty, was used to pay back his gambling debts. But then, he started to gamble again once his slate had been cleared, and now he's in debt to the tune of millions of rupees. He's hiding out from the men he owes; they're brothers - very bad people. I don't know if they have...done something to him. I don't know if they yet know of my part in it. But I will have to get out while I can if you are going to put this in the newspapers.'

'My God.' Jazz looks nervously at Sonny.

'Bob told me of this, the other night. Ever since the foreign workers came to this region, a network of gambling dens has sprung up, run by two rather unsavoury brothers from Kandy. They ensnare the lonely men who don't have their families with them during the long stretch working out here.'

Jazz sighs. 'Like Dick Fry.'

'I think you do know where Dick Fry is. You can either tell us or the police. It's up to you, man.'

After a long pause, Ray Chandimal tells them of a place out in the hills on the road to Kalmunai. 'What's going to happen now?' he asks fearfully.

Sonny looks at him grimly. 'Nothing good, Ray. Not as far as you're concerned.'

23

After they finally get to see Sergeant Rutnam and report their findings, it is early in the evening. The sergeant has assured them he will be sending somebody to the bank the following day to interview Ray Chandimal and that the police will be speaking to Dick Fry very soon.

'Right, Jazz. One last place to go.'

'Now? It's getting late.'

'We need access to Dick Fry before the police arrest him.'

'What? You mad fellow! We can't do that it could be dangerous.'

He looks at her and his face instantly softens. 'You are right. I will go alone. I don't want anything to happen to you.'

'No, you won't. Neither of us will go.'

He takes a cigarette and lights one for her, before lighting up himself.

'I understand your apprehension. But this is the job. Getting the story, fleshing out the characters.'

'Even if it's potentially unsafe?'

'It's what I've always done. I've got a plan, I'm not just going to go blundering in. I'm going incognito. He won't have any idea who I am.'

'What if Ray Chandimal has managed to warn him?'

'Ray Chandimal has no loyalty to Dick Fry; he'll be halfway to Colombo by now.'

'But what are you going to say to him when you find him?'

'I need to report my own impressions of the man, before he's in custody. I like to do more than simply typing up notes from police briefings. Look, I know you think I'm a drunken fellow most of the time, but I'm not lazy. I don't want to deliver a second-hand story when I've got a chance to be in on the action. Do you see?'

She understands what he's saying.

'There's just one thing I don't agree with,' she says finally.

'Jazz, you can't stop me.'

'I know I can't. That's why I'm going to come with you.' She sees him glancing at her determined face and hopes he can't read her fear.

Following Ray Chandimal's directions they take the road heading out of the town, Sonny striding ahead leading them into the dwindling light. Once they start to climb into the hills, in the darkness she grabs Sonny's arm. 'Are you okay?'

'Yes and no.'

He comes close to her ear. 'Can you swap your ring around and put it on your wedding finger?'

She is glad of the darkness so that Sonny can't see her sudden flush of embarrassment. She slips the jade ring that had belonged to her mother, onto the finger of the opposite hand. The unfamiliar feel of it adds to her rising tension.

By now they are climbing steeply, following a rocky path. 'Are you sure this is the way?'

'Yes.' Conversation peters out as they walk unevenly through the winding hills, beyond the safety of the outlying villages and hamlets. A cool breeze is playing, and Jazz can feel goosebumps rising along her arms. She is starting to seriously doubt this tale about a hidden cave, told to them by Ray Chandimal, a man they know to be a liar. For all they know, he could be sending them into the path of the dangerous brothers, helping his own cause as well as that of Dick Fry. For a moment she wishes she was safely back in her uncle's house in Colombo. They stop suddenly as they hear a twig snap behind them. They swing around simultaneously, Sonny warning Jazz with a hand on her arm.

'Who in God's name are you?' A halo of light surrounds them, revealing a weathered looking white man, dressed in shorts, a torn shirt and laced hiking boots. It can only be Dick Fry.

'I say! You gave us a fright, man.' Sonny sounds righteously indignant.

'What the hell are you people doing out here? Are you crazy?'

'We were on a bus out on the main road heading to Kumburapola, but it broke down and we foolishly decided we couldn't wait. We thought we could walk it but then my wife got thirsty, so we are in search of a stream.'

Dick Fry's grizzled face remains impassive. 'I've been wandering along these parts, and I've seen no bus stopped by the roadside.'

'It was a long way out. We've been walking for hours. I think we must be lost.'

Dick Fry grunts.

'Thank God, you've found us. We would be grateful for your help.' Jazz gives an impressive gasping cough.

Dick Fry's impatient sigh rents the air, but he says, 'bring your wife this way, I have water.'

Ray Chandimal had been telling the truth she thinks, as they follow Dick Fry higher still, to an overhang in the hills where there is a concealed entrance to a cave.

'You live out here?' Sonny asks him innocently.

'I'm camping out, for a while. I enjoy the peace and quiet.'

'Ah, I see you're a hunter,' states Sonny, spotting a rifle leaning against the cave wall.

'Here you are.' Dick Fry hands Jazz a tin mug filled with spring water. She drinks obediently and hands it to Sonny.

'You know you really shouldn't be here. I've been alone out here for quite a few weeks and not seen a soul, and then suddenly you materialise from thin air. I find that very disconcerting if you must know. I don't like strangers.'

Jazz's heart is racing. He sounds so suspicious, on his guard. Ray Chandimal must have chosen to come out earlier in the day to deliver a warning, after all. Why the hell could Sonny not have done the easy thing and let the police take care of it? But observing the loneliness in Dick Fry's eyes, the guilt behind the greying beard, she understands the journalistic need to record it all.

Her gaze sweeps the candlelit cave, taking in the single enamel camping plate and the grimy sleeping bag. She wonders how long he can hope to evade the criminal brothers who are searching for him.

'Where is your accent from? American?'

'You ask a lot of questions.' Dick Fry gives a bitter laugh. 'Giving you answers won't help you and it certainly won't help me. Then again, maybe I can't imagine what would help me now.' He makes a gesture for them to sit, and they sink captive on the dusty floor of the cave as he ranges restlessly around his makeshift home.

'I'm from Canada since you ask. A very different kind of place.'

'Do you miss it?'

'I guess I do. When I arrived here, I was seduced by this island of yours. The cool forests, the warm oceans. The opportunities...'

'The arrack,' says Sonny.

Dick looks at him with sly hope as Sonny slowly withdraws a bottle from his bag. Dick Fry gives a deep sigh as he holds out his hand and takes the bottle, caressing it gently.

'The coconut temptress. You take one little dip and before you know it, it comes in waves that flow over your head, stopping you from thinking.' He takes a long drink, coming up for breath and then another.

Jazz and Sonny sit silently watching.

Dick Fry drinks his fill, snorts, and places the bottle at his feet, then takes up his rifle.

'Has somebody sent you out here to find me? Was it that swine Ranil? Or his brother, Chelliah?'

'What? Who? Look, I'm sorry but I have no idea what you are talking about. We are just lost and trying to get to the town.'

Dick Fry grunts, looking closely at Jazz.

'Do you really expect me to believe that? I don't know what I was thinking, talking to you people. Talking does no good.' He pauses. 'Being out here alone for a while, you get to wondering what is real. Maybe it's impossible to tell anymore.' He takes a final swig from the bottle of arrack. 'Right. I've had enough of talking. Up you get.'

Jazz looks fearfully across at Sonny. He tries to smile reassuringly but she can tell that like hers, his heart is pounding. They scramble to their feet. Brandishing his rifle, Dick Fry leads them in low torchlight towards the back of the cave. The cave opens out into a rocky corridor. They move on, ducking when it gets low, sometimes the corridor opening out into cavernous spaces before narrowing again.

It's a place where bodies will never be found. Jazz swallows. She holds out her hand searchingly and Sonny, groping in the dark finds it and holds on tightly as they move through the deep heart of the hills.

After about a mile of groping and ducking their way through a dense network of caves, she spots a faint light up ahead. Suddenly they are out in the fresh night air, the stars out by now, a pale sliver of moon hanging low on the horizon.

She blinks in surprise.

Dick Fry shows his teeth in the wavering torchlight. 'Here we are. Just down there is the main road leading into Kumburapola. I didn't want you stumbling out on the hillside on your own, there are leopards out here, so I took you on a little short cut.

'Sorry if I seemed out of sorts, back there, I've got a lot on my mind. You seem like two lovely young people, and I wish you a happier life than I've managed to live. Anyway, I'm going to make tracks back now.' He pauses. 'I'd appreciate it if you didn't mention this to anyone. I like to be private.' He turns away. 'Good night. Be safe.'

They stumble onto the main road, walking fast, not daring to look back. Neither speak for some time, their breathy gasps betraying their pent-up fear.

'Jazz, I'm sorry. I shouldn't have put you in that position.'

'I thought he was going to kill us.'

'At one point, so did I. I wish he'd given us back the arrack, we could both do with a shot.' He manages a smile. 'I'm not even sure we were in any danger, now I look back on it.'

'Maybe so, but I'm glad to get away from him.' She looks at him. 'What is it?'

'I don't know. I feel sorry for the fellow.'

'Well, he is a criminal.'

'Of course, he is,' Sonny agrees, 'he was vulnerable; his crimes committed out of desperation. I can imagine how that could happen to a man.'

'But Sonny, the punishment must in the end, fit the crime, no?'

'Yes, Jazz, of course.'

With the lights of Kumburapola glittering ahead, they fall into silence. It is only when they reach the comfort and safety of the guest house, that Jazz realises they are still holding hands.

24

The police take Dick Fry in for questioning the next day. Having waited outside the police station all afternoon for news, Sergeant Rutnam finally advises them that Dick Fry has been formally arrested and charged with manslaughter and fraud. Of Ray Chandimal there is unfortunately no sign.

'Manslaughter?' Jazz is puzzled.

'Two people in separate incidents have died in accidents related to faulty building work.'

Once the Dick Fry story breaks a couple of days later, Mrs Andrado is crowing as she buys up copies of the *Courier* bearing the Dick Fry headline. She has a mock scowl on her face, but Jazz senses her delight to have played a small part in the drama.

'Well, really, I cannot believe this of Mr Fry! Hiding out like a beast in a cave! And this is a respectable establishment. Just think: all that time I was harbouring a criminal. And in your room, Sonny, he plotted and planned his wicked mischief. Ai, this had better not drive away business.'

'I think you may find people coming to have a look who will see what a wonderful place you have here.'

The landlady disappears, happily anticipating future streams of guests beating a path to her door.

They are lounging on the veranda after an early dinner. Jazz is looking through her notebook which reads like a map of her emotions: the ominous feel of the reservoir; the last resting place of the unknown body, the threatening encounter with Dick Fry, and the long walk back through the night when she and Sonny had held hands.

It is this last thought which holds her captive, not knowing whether the incident has even registered with him. He has never spoken about any girls he might be seeing away from the office, but he's so secretive she can't be sure.

She must have been holding her breath, it comes out in a soft, prolonged sigh. Sonny looks up from his restless card shuffling. 'Everything okay?'

'Yes. Of course.'

'A lot of strange things have happened; we need to get back to normality.'

She finds it hard remembering what normal is. Sonny sounds as if he might be hankering for something long ago lost. 'I mean, especially after the Dick Fry incident we need this time to sit and take stock'. He gives an awkward cough and lowers his voice. 'I... I've been meaning to mention...the night we went to see Dick Fry...I hope I didn't make a fool of myself clutching onto your hand like that. I hope I didn't offend you.'

She looks across at him, but he doesn't meet her eyes. She looks up at the sound of a vehicle. 'I wonder who that could be? Quite late for a visitor.'

Moments later, Sonny is looking across as his brother-in-law, Bernard Alvis steps onto the veranda. He jumps up and greets him with a firm handshake.

'Hey man, good to see you.'

'I got your address from your boss in Colombo.'

'Everything okay? Its rather late for a visit.'

Bernard glances across at Jazz.

'Sorry, let me introduce my colleague, Jacintha Barthelot.'

'Pleased to meet you.'

'Likewise.'

'Sonny, let's take a walk.'

Sonny lays his cards down and follows Bernard out of the guest house into the darkness. Jazz scribbles in her notebook, idly structuring her notes into the semblance of a story, wondering all the time what drama is currently playing out in Sonny's life.

The men return within the hour, Bernard looking calmer, Sonny noticeably rattled.

'Jazz,' he says shortly, 'fancy a trip?'

'Now? To where?'

'We've been invited to Gail and Bernard's place for the weekend.'

Bernard gives her a small smile.

'Well, if you are sure I won't be in the way.'

'Of course you won't. Come, come let's grab a bag and go. Bernard, we'll see you in the car.'

Jazz jumps into the back of the car and makes herself comfortable while Bernard and Sonny converse sporadically in tones so low she cannot hear them. When Sonny shakes her awake, she can tell immediately they have arrived on the coast, the smothering air tinged with salt, filling her nostrils. Bernard has parked the car and Sonny is holding the door open for her.

'We're here. Wake up sleepy head.'

It's long past midnight. Bernard leads the way quietly, 'Come, come.' Jazz follows him on tiptoe past a cluster of bedrooms at the back of the house and is shown into a pleasant room. The bed is comfortable when she sinks down into cool sheets. She just has time to wonder where Sonny is sleeping before her eyes close.

She is awoken by noise and movement at sunrise. She gets out of bed, finds her robe, and turns to find two small girls in star patterned night dresses have crept in, and are now standing in front of her. Sonny appears at the door. 'Hey, you monkeys, I told you not to wake her.' There is a lot of giggling. 'Okay, girls, say hello to Jacintha and sorry for waking her.'

She smiles at them. 'Hello. Who have we got here?'

'This is Marjorie in the yellow and Millie in pink.' One of them tugs at Sonny and whispers in his ear. He gives a serious nod.

'It's true! She really is a princess!' The girls lisp adorably, bounding around the room. 'Play time!'

Sonny retreats, chuckling. Jazz nods and smiles and allows Millie and Marjorie to march her into their bedroom. Passing through, she catches the sound of murmuring, Gail and Bernard talking in another room, she assumes. Sonny has disappeared but catching the scent of cigarette smoke she knows he can't be far away.

Considering the early hour, the girls are flying around like demons. Roughly pushing her down onto a chair, they begin smoothing her hair with a toy brush. One of them has a gentle touch but the other soon grows bored and begins to rummage in a cupboard, throwing things onto the floor wildly, clearly seeking something.

'Cut,' says one of them gravely and squeals with delight when the other advances brandishing a real pair of scissors.

'Um, I'm not sure you should be playing with those...' says Jazz, her voice rising a notch.

To her relief, a woman, presumably Gail appears in the doorway looking cross. 'Give those back to me! Where did you get scissors from, I told you not to take things from the cupboard! Come on and get dressed, your breakfast is ready.'

'I...thank you.' Jazz feels foolish at not being able to control a couple of small children. Gail looks at her appraisingly and Jazz feels she is making the same assessment.

'Good morning, I'm Gail. I see you have met my daughters.'

'They are very sweet.' They exchange careful smiles.

'I'm afraid they are obsessed with hair at the moment, it seems to be the latest craze.'

Jazz feels the need to apologise. 'I'm sorry to have just turned up like this. I think your husband and Sonny thought it would be a nice surprise. You have been feeling under the weather, no? I hope you are better today.'

Gail has a cool manner. She is dressed plainly in a shift dress, her hair in a long plait, face scrubbed clean. 'I'm up and down all the time. It's no matter. Come and meet our Joey boy, he's a lot calmer than his crazy sisters.'

She leads Jazz to a door. 'Sonny is with him,' she says, 'go on through.' She disappears down the corridor to deal with her daughters.

The room is full of wooden toys, cars, tanks, aeroplanes, and other mechanical wonders on neat rows of shelving. Her eyes travel to the bed where a boy is sitting with his back to her, facing Sonny who is telling him a story and making him laugh.

'Come, come', Sonny is saying, 'get up and have something to eat. Are you hungry? Let's get you dressed. What do you want to wear today, Joey?'

She must have made a noise. Sonny looks up, a shadow falling across his face. 'Ah, hello again, Jazz. Joe, this lady is Jazz. You remember I was telling you about her.'

'Hello, I'm Joe,' the boy says turning to face her.

Jazz stiffens as he turns in her direction with blank eyes. Her eyes roam the room for clues, finding a small white stick propped against the wall next to the bed. 'Hello…' she stammers.

Standing stock still in the doorway, she feels moisture gathering in her eyes. She is aware of Bernard arriving beside her. He touches her elbow gently. 'Come sit.' He leads her into the parlour where she takes a seat feeling foolish.

'I'm so sorry, Bernard. I just…'

He turns to her with a sigh. 'Sonny didn't tell you, did he?'

'I had no idea.'

'If you're not expecting it, then it's a shock.'

'I hope I haven't upset Joe.'

'He will be fine. He likes meeting new people.'

'Has he…has he always been blind?'

'From birth. As a baby he lit the room up with his smile. So carefree and happy in his cot or lying on a blanket in the garden. Content, you know? Poor fellow didn't know any different. After a while, we began to notice that when we came near, he didn't seem to pay us much attention. We saw his eyes remained unfocussed. He didn't follow any of our movements, even close up. He didn't seem to want to move around, showed no signs of crawling.

'We made a joke about it, how we were getting a few months more of an easy life. But we were worried. We took him to the local doctor who didn't seem to know what to do, and he sent us to Colombo, where after a lot of tests they eventually told us that he was blind. Just one of those unexplainable things, they said.'

She sits silently, processing her feelings. Sonny's nephew is blind.

'I don't know why Sonny has never mentioned it. Not even when he invited me here.'

'I don't know either but well, you know Sonny, master of his own moods.'

He pauses. 'A few years ago, things seemed to get too much for my wife. For some reason she began to blame herself. I suppose all mothers feel that if something is wrong with a child, they should have been able to prevent it, or be able to solve the aftermath. She suffers from her nerves; in case you find her behaviour a little strange. She has episodes. When she's depressed, she lies silent in her bed for days, face against the wall, eyes closed to all. She takes pills which are quite strong. Even when she is not feeling blue, she is subdued.'

He rises slowly from his seat, for a moment looking like a much older man. 'I must leave now. Although it's Saturday I have to go into office for a few hours. Enjoy your day.'

She remains sitting and, on a whim, helps herself to one of Sonny's cigarettes from the packet on the table. Feeling calmer she heads into the kitchen where a noisy breakfast is taking place.

'Ah, there you are,' says Gail. Sonny avoids her eye.

'I was just chatting to Bernard before he left.'

'Sit, eat.'

'This looks a lovely spread.' She has the words but not the appetite.

Afterwards when Gail has taken the children out into the garden, Jazz throws Sonny's packet of Peacocks across the table.

'I wondered where they were.' He lights one up, offers it to her and she shakes her head. 'I get the sense you are annoyed with me. For not telling you about Joe.'

'Isn't that something I should be annoyed about? Or maybe it's to be expected from you. That is how you operate, giving away as little as possible.'

'Don't be like that, Jazz. I brought you along, didn't I? I do want you to know me better. To...share stuff about myself. It's just that there are some things you don't know. That I can't talk about.'

'And Joe is one of those things?' She's puzzled.

'It's complicated.'

'Sonny, Jacintha, come. Let's take the children out somewhere.'

They walk to the mangroves where the lighthouse fringed by

palms looms against the sky, birds taking flight with the sun on their wings. Holding the boy between them, Jazz and Sonny encourage Joe to dip his toes in the water, laughing as the waters tickle his feet. The twins are surprisingly gentle with their brother, although easily bored. They soon race away to play chase.

In the afternoon, amid laughter and clattering, Gail bakes a cake with the twins.

'They love it in the kitchen. All the stirring and whatnot,' says Sonny.

'Although it's probably not as much fun for Gail. More like hard work.'

Jazz has drawn Joe onto her lap and is reading to him from a book that has been left on the table by one of the twins, a treasury of children's tales. She does her best to ensure her voice is conveying the actions, achingly aware that he cannot see the beautiful illustrations. She turns the page to a story about a knight and a dragon and presently to her surprise, Joe leans in under her arm and tilts his face up to hers, capturing the rhythm of her breath while she reads the words.

At the end of the story, he slides slowly from her lap. He stands, turning his head to one side and then the other, listening, before tapping his way over to the windowpane.

'Aunty, glass is crying! Listen!'

She hasn't even realised that it is raining softly. 'It's okay, Joe, it's just rain drops.' She puts an arm around him and together they listen to the rain until the gentle drizzle abates as quickly as it had arrived. When she looks up, she catches Sonny gazing at her with an unreadable expression on his face.

In a side room off the kitchen, Gail calls to her. 'Come and see my painting studio, Jacintha.'

She places Joe in Sonny's lap and joins Gail in what had previously been the pantry.

'It was remodelled just before Christmas. Bernard arranged it as a surprise. Of course, kitchen is now very crowded, but Bernard has applied for permission to make further enlargements. He is so good; he thinks of everything.'

The studio houses a table against one side of the wall, covered with brushes, paints, jars, chalks and pencils and old bits of rag. An easel stands in the centre, its canvas covered with a cloth. Jazz watches Gail kneel, delving into the stacks of canvasses that lean against the remaining wall space, pulling out pictures and explaining them.

'This is my favourite, the twins last year at Vesak.'

Jazz gazes at the midnight blue canvas, a huge moon rising high, the girls carrying their paper lanterns aloft amid the celebrating crowds. Gail has caught their energy and sense of fun, Marjorie with a serious pull to her mouth, her eyes filled with mirth, Millie pure mischief, mouth reaching upwards in a wide smile, her curls seeming to bounce across her forehead with their own force of energy.

'You are good for him,' says Gail suddenly. 'Sonny, I mean. I just hope you can last the course.'

She is so flustered she can think of nothing to say.

25

'Walk with me, Jazz? I'm not ready yet for my bed.'

It's the early hours of Sunday morning. The adults have been drinking, playing cards, and talking for several hours, enjoying the peaceful interlude that only occurs when children are tucked up in their beds. Gail and Bernard have turned in for the night and Jazz had assumed she would soon be doing the same.

'Okay,' she agrees.

They walk briskly past the police station and the Hindu temple, the clouds hanging above the mellow town obscuring the light. They reach the Kallady Bridge.

'Shall we?'

They step onto the iron structure, taking slow steps until they reach the middle when they stop to look across the darkening lagoon. Somewhere beyond, in the mangrove swamps and sea grass, an aquatic bird gives a guttural grunt.

'I haven't been here since my school days,' says Jazz, 'in my last year, a crowd of us would sometimes sneak out of the dorm and come out here.'

'What, to meet with boys? Smoke and sip a little bit of arrack?'

'No, not at all. Well, some girls did, but my crowd wasn't like that. We used to borrow a boat and row out to the lagoon to listen for the singing fish.'

'Did you ever hear them?'

'Never. You need a full moon, and we were just never lucky enough. If they even exist.'

'I wonder if they do exist. I'd like to think they do.'

'You don't think it's just a legend?'

'I hope it's not.'

'I suppose it could be true. Lots of the fishing boys used to say they'd heard sounds.'

They fall silent, gazing into the inky darkness of the water below. After a while Sonny turns his head.

'I watched you today with Joe. You're good with him.'

'He's a lovely boy, no?'

Sonny nods. 'I remember coming here with Joe for the first time. It was hot and quiet, not many people around. The sky was clear blue; cranes and crows skimming low across the water. Gail handed me Joe to hold. I hadn't had a look in with my mother grabbing him every spare moment, and the parades of aunties all staking their claim. I remember whispering to him that when he was a bigger boy, I would come for him one night and show him the stars and listen to the singing fish.

'We were so happy and eager to share in Joe's future. We could never have guessed how soon his future was going to be taken away from him, and that all he had in front of him was eternal darkness.'

'Oh, Sonny. So sad for the boy.'

'Daddy more than anyone has always wanted to believe there must be a miracle cure somewhere. Just after Joe's third birthday, I got a call from him when I was at work. He was so excitable on the phone I could barely make out what he was saying. Eventually I managed to get from him that he had been at home listening to an interview on the radio, with a doctor who was visiting Colombo from England, who specialised in helping the blind to see again.

'The next day, Daddy travelled to the city on the first train out that morning. In his jacket pocket was the piece of paper on which he had written down the name of the clinic. I met him off the train and we walked for ages, trying to find this place. After hours we found it and it looked quiet, like they were about to close for the day. I was hanging around outside having a smoke, but Daddy walked straight in and managed to grab hold of this doctor who agreed to see him. He wasn't in there for long and when he came out, he looked as if he had aged ten years.

'Daddy had misunderstood. He had only caught part of the radio programme; what the doctor had said was that he was able to work with people who had become blind, but not those who had been born blind. All his hopes raised for nothing.'

'I say. That must have been so very sad for your father.'

'Very sad.' She hears something in his voice.

'There's something else I would like to tell you. Nobody knows this outside the family.'

'Okay.'

'Joe's blindness…it came about as a result of a curse, when he was still in the womb.' His voice trembles.

She exhales. 'My God, Sonny.' She doesn't know what to say. 'You hear of these things of course, but…'

'Like me, you prefer to think we are living in a progressive society. Skyscrapers, cars, aviation, penicillin. But what is the use of such things when the whole damned country is stitched into place by superstition and magic; facing the east when you eat a meal will bring good luck, evil will come to you if you see a woman coming towards you bearing a chatty, bathing on a Wednesday will bring riches.'

She struggles to bring some logic to the conversation. 'Children can be born with afflictions, can't they? Damage at birth? A shortcoming inherited from a parent?'

'The doctors were unable to give a reason,' says Sonny.

'I see. But who cursed him? Why? And how do you know this?'

'I know. I have seen it with my own eyes. I will tell you more, one day. You will have to take my word for it, now.'

She is grateful he has revealed so much, but still he hides the very heart of the trouble. Jazz feels tiredness engulfing her.

He lights two cigarettes, and they puff in silence. 'Remember,' Sonny says, 'not a word to anybody.'

'Of course not.'

'Thank you.'

'Well,' says Sonny after a while as they retrace their steps back to Gail and Bernard's place, 'thanks for coming this weekend. It has lifted Gail's spirits. Bernard thought she was heading for another episode when he came to see me. Sometimes she just needs a distraction.'

'Well, I'm glad you invited me. And I'm happy the crisis has been averted.'

'Thanks, Jazz.' His voice is distant in the darkness.

'For what?'

'For enduring the family. But mainly for being a good listener.'

'Isn't that the trait of being a good journalist?' She yawns.

'Do you know what the other essential quality is for being a good reporter?'

'Having enough cigarettes?'

'This is serious, Jazz. Think.'

'Oh, I don't know, Sonny. How about you tell me when I'm more awake?'

They are walking up the veranda steps.

She almost misses his soft murmur.

'I'll tell you anyway: you have to get into the habit of asking the right questions at the right time.'

26

Jazz is finishing her piece on the women of Still Waters when somebody raps on the door of the office before entering. She turns, thinking it's Sonny who's been to make a telephone call to Walter from the post office. She comes face to face with Sergeant Rutnam. She takes a step back.

'Good afternoon, Sergeant,' she says formally, 'how are things?'

'Nothing much to report on the dead man, I'm afraid. We have got nowhere with tracing the fishing net.'

'I didn't think you would,' Sonny says cheerily, returning just in time.

The sergeant tries to hide his disappointment at Sonny's entrance. 'There will be something to tell in the weeks to come, some analysis of the bullet. We will keep you informed of developments at the appropriate time.'

The look on Sonny's face tells Jazz that he will be picking up the telephone to Superintendent Ludowyk as soon as he can. The sergeant's next words cause them both to react.

'I have come to tell you that there has been a development in the Dick Fry case. A body has been found in a canal in Colombo.'

There is a silence. Jazz marvels at the symmetry of her short but intense career.

'Superintendent Ludowyk would like to see you both in Colombo, regarding this matter.'

'Righto, Sergeant,' says Sonny, 'we will get the train this evening and we'll be back in Colombo by dawn.'

The train should have set them down on the platform in Colombo at around five thirty but there had been a delay, longer than usual at Gal Oya Junction and it is now six fifteen in the morning. The city is just uncoiling itself from the night.

'I'm going straight to office. Why don't you go home first and freshen up?'

She turns to him. During the long journey she had been fascinated as Sonny became once again the jaunty reporter at home in his surroundings, his eyes bright, his energy levels rising as each mile took them further away from the Eastern Province.

'I'm fine Sonny. I will come to office also.'

They swing their steps towards Chatham Street. The food stalls are open for business and as they approach the office, Sonny declares himself hungry. They buy strong plain tea and cinnamon buns, consuming them by the side of the road, watching the parking spaces fill up with dark coloured Austins and Morris Minors, the pavements beginning to resound with the hurrying strides of businessmen.

They enjoy a couple of cigarettes and then make their way into the double doors through the foyer of the office block that houses the newspaper.

It is seven a.m. when they reach their desks. Walter is already in his glass domain. Jazz wonders if he ever leaves his post. She can't imagine his energy being subdued in the domestic sphere. He looks up at their movement, gives a double-take, and beckons them in.

'What is this? Sit, sit, tell me everything.'

As Jazz sinks down, she thinks she will never be able to get up again, her bones ache so.

'What is the latest news from Eastern Province? I'm beginning to think your uncle was right to implement a base in Kumburapola. Quite aside from the body in the lake scoop, everybody is talking now about Dick Fry. The Board is very pleased with both of you.'

They make non-committal noises. From outside Walter's office comes the sound of something breaking. Their heads swivel, taking in Pearl, scarlet-faced on her hands and knees picking up the pieces of a broken cup.

'You have given her a heart attack, Sonny, turning up like this without a word to any of us. She has been like an elephant at a dry well, since you've been gone.'

Sonny grins tiredly at Jazz.

'So, what are you both doing back here? I think your uncle may have something to say about this,' says Walter with a frown at Jazz.

'We've had an official summons from Superintendent Ludowyk. There's been a development.'

'The body in the lake? That's great. Another big headline.'

'I believe this is connected to Dick Fry. Believe it or not, another body has been found here in one of the canals, apparently.'

Walter roars, his fleshy stomach heaving with laughter. 'Trouble always finds you, Sonny de Roye. So, you are off to the police station? Come back with the news and we can get something out in tomorrow's edition.'

'We'll come back and do a late shift if that's okay with you. We've been travelling all night.'

'Hey, Sonny, you're back!' Suresh Kandasamy jumps up from his desk, scattering papers all over the floor as they leave Walter's office. Sonny embraces him.

'How are you, man? Still overworked?'

'Of course. And you are still underworked no doubt?'

'You know me so well.'

Suresh checks his watch. 'Damn, I've got to get going, I have an interview in half an hour with the Minister of Trade and Commerce. Are you staying in office all day?'

'Be back later.'

'We can catch up then. Great to have you back. You too, Jacintha.'

'Great to be back.'

Out on the street Jazz totters with sudden tiredness. She has forgotten how noisy the streets of Colombo are and her thoughts are spiralling: the dead man in the lake, the strange meeting with Dick Fry and now another body also dead in the water.

'You okay, Jazz? Lack of sleep catching up with you? Let's go and see the superintendent – the quicker we see what he has to say, the quicker we can get to our beds.'

'Come in, come in.' Superintendent Ludowyk is looking flustered. 'Everything happening at once, always the same. Sit, sit, how are you Sonnah boy? And Jacintha? You are both well I think, maybe a little sleepy looking. Well, I'll get straight to the point. Body found yesterday afternoon in the canal near Wellawatte, somebody spotted it floating beside the mill.'

'Any idea who it is?'

'We are pretty certain it is your man, Ray Chandimal.'

'Oh.' Jazz feels dismay, as if it were their actions and not his own life choices, that have sent him to his watery grave.

'The fellow has an elderly mother unable to come down and identify him. No other family apparently, so the mother says, although she seems very confused.'

'You want us to identify the body?'

'His wallet was found in the mud on the banks of the canal. The mother's description will help but you saw him only recently I believe?'

They nod.

'Then that will confirm what we suspect. Shall we?'

On their way to the morgue Jazz asks, 'Did he drown?'

'He was already dead when he hit the water. A knife wound in his back.'

Jazz waits outside while Sonny goes through to where the body is ready to receive its final visitor. When they come back, he nods brusquely. 'It's him'.

'So, now we have confirmation, take me through again exactly what happened in Kumburapola, what was said, and who you think might have done this to him.'

The interview lasts an hour. The superintendent is very thorough, making notes of everything they tell him, including the names of the brothers that Dick Fry had mentioned in the cave. 'I have heard these names before. Seems they are at the heart of a lot of trouble. Let's hope we can apprehend them before they wreak any more. Thank you both for your help; it's a shame this stupid bugger ended up this way, but when you're running with the pack, you can be sure they will turn on you eventually.'

As the superintendent is wrapping things up, Sonny changes focus.

'Are you able to confirm something Sergeant Rutnam mentioned before we came back? Something about testing the bullet that killed the man in the reservoir?'

Superintendent Ludowyk leans back in his chair. 'Well, Sonny, I will tell you but please wait a few more days until I give you the nod. Anyhow, to satisfy your reporter's nose, I will tell you that it looks likely that fragments found within the bullet contain pieces of silver.'

'Oh.' Jazz is trying to keep up. 'What does that mean, exactly?'

'Silver is not part of the bullet's makeup, you understand? So therefore, we need to discover what its presence could mean.'

'I see.' Jazz is blinking hard, trying to stay awake. Sonny has not said a word. The superintendent orders one of his constables to drive them home.

'You are going out again? But you only just came back.'

Jazz has slept for several hours straight; she had not even removed her clothing before falling asleep. Now, arisen from her creased sheets, her fatigue washed away under a long cool shower, she presents herself in front of her aunt who is seated outside in the shade with a book and a cold drink. Her aunt places a bookmark across her page and looks at her closely.

'You still look very tired, Jacintha. I don't think you should be going off and running around the city. Sit, sit, and tell me all about it. I'll get Bimali to bring a little food.'

'I have to be back at office by five o' clock. We have a report to write on the man found in the canal, part of a story we have been working on.'

Her aunt rings for the servant girl who brings a plate of mutton rolls and noodles with green chillies. Jazz is suddenly ravenous.

'I thought Uncle said you would be having a day off today after your travels?'

'Well, there have been unexpected developments. I don't mind, I'm enjoying it.'

'Well, you must go about your business, I suppose. Your uncle is very pleased with you and Mr de Roye. Circulation has increased significantly which has put him in a good position to be able to borrow money from the bank for the expansion. It's all systems go now, huge changes afoot.'

Jazz pauses for thought. She hopes expansion will not change things too much. She assumes that everyone will keep their job if the newspaper is expanding. The main thing is that Sonny is back in favour, which is a source of great relief.

'You must ask Mr de Roye to dinner one evening. You know, Jacintha, it is not proper that you are working and travelling around alone with this fellow. I have not even met with him. Uncle and I were very unhappy that you should have gone across to the East Coast with him, but Walter was insistent.'

'It's just work, Aunty.'

'Not everybody will see it that way. I think your uncle is sometimes a little scared of Walter.'

'Most people are.'

'Whatever Walter's opinion, I think you are giving the wrong impression of yourself.'

Jazz wills herself to keep calm. 'Aunty, I'm doing a job. And I think I am giving a good impression of myself as a hardworking, responsible employee.'

'Jacintha, you know what I mean. It is not respectable behaviour.'

They don't speak for a few moments.

'Well, I am just grateful that we hear from the landlady as to how things are with you. Otherwise, I would be sitting here worrying myself to death.'

'The landlady? Mrs Andrado?'

'She posts a card every once in a while, at your uncle's insistence, just letting us know how you are getting on so far away from us.'

Jazz immediately closes the conversation and lapses into silence. When her aunt is preoccupied, she tips the remainder of her meal into a cloth napkin to bring to Sonny, and in an act of quiet rebellion decides to walk to work rather than be chauffeured into the office.

27

It has been agreed with Walter that Jazz and Sonny can spend a few days in Colombo before heading back to Kumburapola. On Saturday night, Sonny manages to persuade Suresh away from his desk at the *Courier* to dine in the Grand Oriental Hotel on York Street. Jazz is invited to join them.

Worried about what her aunt and uncle will think, she concocts a tale of a birthday dinner for one of the work crowd and makes sure to mention the names of a few female colleagues to give the impression of a party. As she sits on the terrace over-looking the harbour where the clientele is mostly a mixture of tourists, businessmen from abroad and a few well-heeled Colombo residents, she hopes she will not be caught out.

Suresh had arrived first and ordered gin for Jazz and whisky for himself and Sonny. They clink glasses together, which Jazz knows is just the start of the evening. She had been surprised and pleased when Sonny had asked her along. She did not have much of a chance to get to know Suresh before she was sent to the Eastern Province and has a vague impression of him working the Economics and Politics desk by himself and always being frantic.

'It's good to be back in the city. Let's drink to home. Cheers.'

'Cheers.

'When was the last time I managed to drag you out?' Sonny asks Suresh, 'we haven't gone out and had any fun for ages. This is long overdue.'

'Too long ago to remember.'

'You know what your problem is, you work too hard, you bugger. You should be more like me.'

'Well, maybe you should be more like me.' Suresh winks at Jazz. 'I've got five stories simultaneously on the go, ministers asking me to interview them...that's the kind of work ethic which stops me from being sent to the Eastern Province. Whereas you...'

Sonny grimaces. 'Yes, yes, of course you are right.'

'I mean the East Coast of all places? What the hell are you doing there, man? The Dick Fry story is done. The Body in the Lake affair has stalled. Why does Angelo Crozier envisage the need for you to stay?'

'Exactly,' Sonny says gloomily. 'What was it you said about the Eastern Province when we were on the train out, Jazz? A place of devils?' She nods.

Suresh jumps in. 'I agree with you, Jacintha, I witnessed something as a child in Trinco and even to this day, if I think too much about it, I have to sleep with the light on.'

'We have come for a night out, not to tell each other scary stories,' says Sonny, irritably.

'Perhaps we should change the subject', suggests Jazz, newly mindful of Sonny's sensitivity regarding the supernatural, but Suresh is intent.

'I must have been about six years old. I had a school friend, a bit of a wild fellow, he used to let out all the goats from the neighbours' back yards, steal fruit from trees, and one time he poured a whole scoop of pepper and a mound of chillies into the curry that had been simmering on the fire all day. The family had a lot of sickness that night, as you can imagine.

'He was great fun, but the parents didn't know what to do with him half the time as he simply couldn't take instruction or obey rules. As he got older, he got harder to control. His mother told mine she feared what he might become.

'One day, we came home to his house after school to play, to discover his parents had called in a holy man. They were waiting in the parlour. The mother told me to turn around and go home but I wanted to see what was going on, so I peeked in through the window from outside.

'His father, normally a lovely, laughing man, on instructions from the holy man tied his son to a chair in the kitchen and put a rag in his mouth to stop him making a noise. The holy man poured some brew or other onto the fire which flared up with abnormally large flames.

'The holy man went into a trance and started chanting and the next minute I saw

strange shapes moving within the flames...they were like fire people...devils I suppose you might say. One of the figures became more solid and passed into the room and stood in front of my friend, putting his hands either side of his small head and massaging it fiercely. I could see my friend's face in agony, unable to scream. The figure suddenly disappeared, and the fire died down. When my friend was untied, he fell to the floor, jabbering nonsense, as if all his sense had been taken away. From that day on, he was a simpleton who never left the house.

'The family moved away from the village soon after, and nobody has heard from them again. To this day, I still don't like to look into the flames when there is a fire burning.'

'I don't know how the parents could have allowed such a thing,' mutters Jazz in disgust. She looks across at Sonny worriedly, but he doesn't meet her eyes instead jumping up in a burst of wild laughter, dragging hard on his cigarette, showering Suresh with flaking ash. 'Suresh, stop this nonsense. We are safe in our modern city now, away from such things.'

'I will drink to that.'

They order more gin and whisky. Suresh who, Jazz thinks, clearly needs to go out more often, is now regaling them with the latest whispers from the government. 'Poor Dudley; never has there been a more reluctant Prime Minister. He's like a man who has answered the call to lead because it's his duty; he does it entirely without pleasure. A nice fellow but he has no real leadership qualities. The country needs to see more forward thinking at the helm.'

'The predicted Rice Crisis.' Sonny pulls a face. 'I thought these were just rumours. Government has made no statements.'

'Not yet. But it could well happen, we can't afford to be flippant. A low price for our rubber exports, and high import price for rice, spells economic depression for Ceylon.'

Sonny groans. 'Yes, yes, I helped you out on your article, remember?'

'Actually, I helped him out,' says Jazz slurring slightly, 'it was the first thing I ever wrote in the office. You know Suresh, you should be proud of us; we can now actually tell you all about rice, Sonny also, he's quite the expert.' Jazz gives a performance recalling Sonny's interview, mostly about rice, at Still Waters.

'And so, what is the rest of the town like?'

Sonny makes a face. 'Very strange place, half- built, secluded from other towns. One foot trembling on the brink of the new age, one placed firmly in the past.'

'Not just Kumburapola that's the whole bloody country.'

They drink another toast. A young waiter appears at the table with platters of food, setting down half a dozen steaming dishes in front of them.

'We surely didn't order all this,' Jazz says heaping rice and various curries onto their plates. They eat, savouring the delicately spiced fish patties, prawns in coconut milk, dry lime pickle, dhal, and vegetable rice.

There is a smattering of applause as a crooner and a pianist take their places, beginning a smoky jazz medley. The mellifluous tones of the singer rise into the air, smoke wreathes across the tables and Jazz realises she is pleasantly drunk. She glances over at Sonny who is half asleep in his chair, looking peaceful.

She exchanges a grin with Suresh.

'So, Jacintha, while you were in the Eastern Province, did you get any sense of racial tension?'

She thinks of her encounter on the street with the angry anti-Tamil fellow. 'There's certainly something simmering under the surface. You're our Politics and Economics Editor, what's your view? Do you think the Lanka Reservoir Project was designed to be anti-Tamil?'

He seems surprised at her vehemence, but of course he is unaware of her Tamil heritage.

'The project has been viewed certainly as a positive thing for the Sinhalese, not necessarily as a negative action towards the Tamils. But of course, it can be argued that's just semantics. I believe it was well-intentioned. Tamils and Sinhalese were included in decisions to balance their different interests.'

'But I think you can understand that from the Tamil point of view it's a huge blow for them. The area was predominantly and historically theirs before the colonisation took place and now, they've had an influx of Sinhalese invited to farm in the most fertile parts, while the Tamils have been reapportioned the lower basins with less irrigation. I wonder if there has ever been a colonisation scheme, even on a small scale, in a Sinhalese area?'

'I can't recall any,' says Suresh slowly. 'So, you think this is a deliberate attempt to lessen Tamil rights in the area, by taking away the continuity of the region and reducing their communal voice? That's interesting. There are far more Tamils in the north of the country of course; I wonder if the government would have dared initiate the same sort of scheme there?'

They rest their voices, hoarse now from shouting over the music, allowing themselves to lose their thoughts in the soulful piano notes. Presently Sonny opens his eyes and orders another round.

'When are you headed back to Kumburapola?' Suresh asks presently.

'Within a few days,' Jazz says through a haze of gin, thoughts of work seeming far away.

'I say.' Suresh pauses, giving a nervous laugh. 'I will miss you though, both of you, of course. Office is dull without you.'

She knows she is now the wrong side of tipsy, but she could swear this last remark is aimed at her alone. She thinks it best to pretend not to have heard him, but she sees Sonny give Suresh a hard stare. The evening is winding down, the music has finished, cloths are being removed from tables, and empty dishes and glasses spirited away.

'We should be going.' Sonny's good mood seems to have evaporated at the thought of having to leave Colombo once more. He rises from the table, straightening his collar, frowning slightly.

They make their way out onto the street and walk as far as the residential area close to Wesley College, pleasant surroundings to walk through in the warm night air. Strolling down Karlsruhe Gardens past the college, they shake their heads in mock disapproval at a huddle of older schoolboys who are standing smoking off premises illicitly, keeping an anxious eye out for prefects on the prowl after lights out in the dormitories.

Sonny shouts out a couple of silly remarks and they turn their startled faces in his direction.

'Young buggers.'

'I don't suppose we were any different. I bet you were a terror.'

'He still is.' They stop at a junction on the main road; Sonny is heading back to Darley Road, about a mile away while Suresh will have to wait for the last bus out to the new Bambalapitiya flats overlooking the Indian Ocean, where he shares a place with two Burgher friends.

At Sonny's whistle a taxi draws up and he opens the door for Jazz.

'Want to share?' she asks but he shakes his head. 'Night air will do me good.'

From the back window she watches Sonny and Suresh clap each other on the back before going their separate ways. Later that night, as she lays on her pillow waiting for sleep, it's the image of Sonny she can't remove from her memory, standing alone on the pavement looking after Suresh with a look on his face, as if his friend's steps receding into the night were like the slow withdrawing of comfort.

28

Expecting to be handed train tickets back to the Eastern Province, Jazz and Sonny are called into Walter's office at the beginning of the working week.

'I need you to stay a while longer and work alongside Suresh.'

'How so?' asks Sonny exchanging an elated grin with Jazz.

'There is something big brewing that Suresh wants to spend a little time on. Several of his sources have begun mentioning Marxists active in the capital who are stirring up unrest. I find this incredible; Ceylon is not a nation that has ever been on strike before, but Suresh feels there could be something in it in the months ahead.

'You will focus on Suresh's less important leads, just keep them on the boil until he can attend to them. A temporary measure,' he concludes, 'don't get too comfortable back in the city.'

Jazz finds her workload is suddenly hectic; interviews with minor politicians, charts, and graphs to plot, long hours of research upstairs in the library where she pores over articles and information until her eyes ache. Although Sonny is also given research to undertake, he seems to be out much of the time, drinking with his reporter buddies, Jazz suspects. She hopes her uncle is unaware.

Sonny comes looking for her in the archives one afternoon, as she is making notes.

'Hello,' he says softly.

She looks up startled. 'Hello. Have you come to help?'

He gives her a grin. 'Got something on at the moment. I came to ask if you are free tomorrow night? The superintendent has invited us for dinner.'

'Oh. That's nice of him.'

'You will come?'

'I will come.'

'Great. I will get a taxi and pick you up at eight.'

'How have you been, Sonny?'

'Fine.' He pauses. 'A little less late-night drinking.'

'Really?'

'I'm trying, anyhow.'

'Jacintha, I have those files you asked for...' The archivist, Deepa comes over hesitantly, wary of interrupting.

'Ah, well you seem busy so I will leave you to your work. See you tomorrow night.' He disappears down the stairs before she can ask him anything further.

'Something to drink to round off the evening? A whisky? What about you, Jacintha?'

Superintendent Ludowyk and his wife Barbara occupy a well-appointed house in Mount Lavinia, not far from the Zoological Gardens. The couple employ an excellent cook and Jazz is feeling decidedly full when they sit down with the superintendent after dinner.

'Just some water for me, please.'

'I'll take a glass of whisky, please, Aunty.'

Barbara fusses, bringing glasses and a jug of water before leaving them to business matters, seated in comfortable chairs in the study.

'Time has flown since that poor bugger came to be floating in the reservoir,' Ludo says, leaning back against a floral cushion, his wife's addition to the otherwise masculine room. They are seated in the centre of the room between walls of law books and a leather-bound set of Greek and French Classics. Jazz also notices with amusement a pristine copy of *Crime and Punishment*, in between a copy of Shakespeare's plays and a collection of Romantic poetry. Perhaps the superintendent is saving it for his retirement.

'The time has gone by quickly,' Jazz and Sonny agree.

'But what's with you, Sonnah boy? Being stuck out on the East Coast?'

'I'm not really sure. I just do what I'm told.'

He roars. 'Good one, Sonny.'

'It's like a promotion, Superintendent, as far as Sonny is concerned. He gets to take on the responsibility of running the office out there.'

A quieter chuckle this time. 'Cigar?' He opens a wooden box containing rows of fat brown Havanas and pushes it towards Sonny.

Sonny is immensely pleased. The blue smoke drifts above them causing a pleasant aroma. Through the window, Jazz catches the glow of fireflies, circling in the far secluded corner of the garden.

'So,' the superintendent says, 'A couple of things to brief you on. A while ago now, you accompanied Sergeant Rutnam to interview Mrs Taylor?'

'That's right. Everything seems to point to her father being the body in the lake, no?'

'Actually, that is incorrect. Yesterday evening Mrs Taylor rang to say she has found her father very much alive and well and living with a Tamil woman in Batticaloa.'

Jazz blinks in surprise.

'The poor bugger hadn't known how to tell his daughter about his new life, thinking she would be ashamed of this new arrangement, so the stupid fellow just slunk away without a word to anyone.'

'So, he is not the body in the lake.'

'No,' says Sonny quietly. His hand irreversibly creeps towards the whisky decanter.

'I suppose for that old man, it seems like he got something he deserved.' She remembers the old man's house, the scraps of life left behind in the soured remains of food, the carpet of dead flies and beetles, the rancid milk. The blood. 'It's never too late to start a new life.'

'What's that?'

'I was just saying it was nice for him to find a happy ending for himself. His daughters left for pastures new, so he must have been very lonely.'

'It seems all I hear about these days is people tearing up roots and starting afresh. Friends on the force, family members, all heading for something new.'

'Something better,' says Jazz, unexpectedly.

Sonny raises an eyebrow. The superintendent stares at her. 'Ah yes, you have been over to England yourself. As have I. When I was young, I went to London to study at the Hendon Police College.'

'Do you wish you had stayed?'

'It was not the life for me.'

'I think though, our Burgher generation does not have as much to look forward to in this country as you did,' says Jazz, looking at Sonny to back her up. He is staring at a spot on the ceiling.

'So, now what?' she asks, bringing them back to their original topic. 'What is the next step for the body in the lake? You mentioned a while back, silver fragments in the bullet?'

Sonny says sharply, 'Jazz, I don't think Uncle wants to talk about that now.'

She blushes, annoyed that she seems to have miscalculated. She had been expecting Sonny to raise the subject and thought it would be fun to get in first. But Sonny seems almost angry.

'Not at all, Jacintha,' says the superintendent rescuing her, 'This is my second piece of news for you.'

Refusing to look at Sonny, she reaches for her notebook, a new one.

'The test results have confirmed that the unknown substance found in the bullet is definitely silver. And so, we have to ask ourselves how this could be?'

Jazz remains quiet. Sonny is trying to reach her with his eyes, but she keeps her gaze on the superintendent.

'While we try and work that problem out, you can please publish these findings in your latest report and let's get people wondering, fishing through their memories. Where was this man standing when he was shot? Was he carrying some kind of shield to protect himself from the shooter? Maybe this will be the breakthrough we have been waiting for.'

When Jazz has finished making her notes she looks up and finally meets Sonny's eye. He is pale, a little perspiration on his brow. She thinks he must have taken too much food and drink but then she looks closely and sees something in his face that makes her think otherwise.

She stands briskly. 'It's been such a lovely evening. Thank you so much for the dinner and for keeping us updated. Come on Sonny, we can stroll back, take our time.'

'She's got you organised, Sonnah boy. It is something that is needed, eh?'

Sonny mumbles his goodbyes and kisses Barbara briskly on the cheek as they are leaving. 'Sonny, the cook can give you leftovers if you wait a moment.'

'It's okay, Aunty, I...I should get going. Busy day tomorrow.'

Jazz takes him by the arm and walks him into the night. As they pass down the road, Sonny mutters, 'I'm sorry. I was a bit of a pig to you.'

'And now you are a lost lamb. What is wrong?'

'Ah...Jazz, the question should be, what is right?' He bursts into wild laughter. She tentatively joins in, and he seems to gather himself after a couple of cigarettes.

'It was a good night, no?' says Jazz relieved he is looking more like his normal self.

'An evening of good food, great company, and some revelations,' he says, suddenly revitalised. 'Speaking of which,' he continues, 'I never did tell you the proper story of Joe's curse, did I?'

'Oh, but you don't have to, it's really none of my business.'

'You are far too polite; I can see the writer in you is dying to know. Don't think I don't see you, Jazz. You are on your sixth... no seventh notebook since I have known you. You must be writing down more than just the plain facts.'

'It's just something I do.'

'It's fine, I'm merely making an observation. You see things, I see things, that's our job. But I guessed a while ago, you are spinning fiction from the facts, no?'

She nods.

'But don't forget that facts can be a hundred times more potent than fiction.'

'I'm not sure I agree with that.'

'Listen then, I'll tell you something that will make you change your mind.'

'Is this connected to Joe being cursed?'

'It is.' He takes a breath. 'If I told you that my father and I had visited a Hindu temple deep within a forest where nobody goes, what would you say? And that we had met a swami there who showed us the curse within a single teardrop of sacred oil?'

As he continues to speak, a door opens in her mind. It's not the Ratnayake case that has sent Sonny spiralling, he has not lost his way as a response to the accumulation of crimes and horrors he has written about. It's about the family; Joe, Gail, his father. She closes her eyes and listens, connecting the threads.

Once again, they find themselves holding hands in the darkness. Much later, back at her uncle and aunt's place, she fills her notebook before going to sleep with troubled dreams.

29

She arrives at the office on Monday morning to find Walter banging the telephone down in a huff. He sees her enter and strides over.

'Leave Suresh's stuff today. I've got something more important for you to do. Come into my office in five minutes, okay?'

'Okay.' She looks around for Sonny.

'Sonny just telephoned; I don't know what the hell is up with him, but he sounds terrible.'

'Oh.' With her heart racing, she seats herself at her desk, thinking about what could be wrong. It's possible something has snagged in Sonny's mind after unburdening himself to her. He must be suffering with the pressure of the thoughts he carries around in his head. She wonders if she should go round to his place after work, but something tells her he would not appreciate it.

When Sonny has still not made an appearance two days later, she grows increasingly worried and struggles to keep her mind on her work. Finally, she breaks for lunch and leaves the office, feeling the need to walk. As she wanders haphazardly, not sure where to go, somebody gives a low whistle from the other side of the road. Startled, she looks up to see Sonny staring across at her, teetering close to the roadside. For a second, she has the impression he is about to step out blindly into the road. She shouts a warning, and he pulls back as she makes her way to him.

'What the hell? You nearly got yourself killed.' She pays him closer attention. 'How are you feeling? Maybe you shouldn't be out if you're ill.'

He shrugs. 'I'm not feeling too bad now. My buddy, Victor is leaving for Canada tomorrow. This is my last chance to see him before he goes.' He pauses. 'Come with me, Jazz.'

'I think I'd better, just to be on the safe side.'

'I'm okay. Really.' He doesn't meet her eyes.

Sonny leads them to the spot where the Galle Face Hotel stares wistfully across the green to the Indian Ocean. Passing the colonnaded entrance where well-heeled guests are gliding in and out, they duck around the side of the building to the back of the kitchens.

'So, this is your friend who you came to Colombo with, the chap who works in hotels?'

'That's right. Victor has been working here at the Galle Face Hotel for a few years, now. Oh, and here's the bugger himself.'

A man with a friendly face, in a spotless suit and tie appears holding food packets. He raises his eyebrows at the sight of Jazz.

'Meet Jacintha. My partner-in-crime.'

'Aha, so this is Jazz. I've heard a lot about you.' His face falls.

Jazz follows his gaze to the food parcels, wrapped in newspaper, one of them enfolded in a sheet from the previous day's edition of the *Courier*. A headline, 'THE SILVER BULLET', with both hers and Sonny's name underneath, now smeared with food seeping through the newsprint.

'I apologise,' says Victor. Sonny glares at him.

'My first by-line. I worked so hard on that.' Her voice falters but she can't keep up the pretence. Meeting Victor's eye she bursts into peals of laughter.

'I've been lying in my sick bed, I haven't even read it yet,' Sonny grumbles. Victor and Jazz are still laughing.

Sonny turns to her. 'It's a great headline, Jazz. I'm proud of you.'

'Did you know Walter was going to ask me?'

'It was my idea.'

Her heart swells. 'Well, thank you for the opportunity.' She grins at him, and he gives a tired smile.

'You see, that's what happens when you go out late night drinking,' says Victor sternly to Sonny, 'you literally lose the plot.' He turns to Jazz. 'Seriously, though, congratulations, it's a great achievement.'

He turns his attention to Sonny and his face creases. 'You okay, man? In all honesty, you don't look so good.'

'I'm just hungry.'

They stroll towards the water's edge and sit against a wall. Sonny splits open one of the packets revealing beads of rice and trails of golden sauce, the fragrant scents of chicken curry seeping into the air. Victor pushes a packet towards her, and she opens it; hoppers and katta sambol. Her eyes tear up as she takes a hit of chilli.

'It's delicious. Thank you.'

'Left over from the breakfast buffet. I like to make sure that my old buddy here is not going hungry. Enjoy.'

'Victor is one of the under-managers here.' There is affectionate pride in Sonny's voice which quickly changes to a more sombre tone. 'Not for much longer though. He's hitting the big time.'

'Ah yes, congratulations, I heard you are off to Canada.'

'Yes. I've got a work placement for six months in a hotel in

Toronto. I'm confident it will become a permanent position.' He checks his watch.

'I'd better be going, last shift before I clock off forever. I know you hate goodbyes, Sonny but what else can we do?'

The two embrace. Sonny breaks free remembering something. 'Man, I need a final favour. A table at the restaurant tomorrow night? Around six?'

'Shouldn't be a problem. Six is early, hardly anybody in. Are you sure you don't want a later time?'

'Quite sure.' Sonny gives a grimace. 'My parents want me to formally meet Serena's boyfriend.'

'Wait, Serena has a boyfriend? Who is the fellow?'

'Alphonse Hendricks.'

'The Hendricks family, huh? They're a big deal. She's still a bit young, no?'

Sonny waggles his head. 'Serena is just like Mummy, knows her own mind and nothing will change it. Alphonse telephoned me yesterday, he wants to get to know me, so he says. He's here to sit an exam or something. Apparently, the usual accommodation he has when he's in Colombo is being refurbished, so he's taken a suite here.' Sonny gestures at the hotel. 'I really can't stand to go but Mummy telephoned to the office after he had called and was very insistent.'

'If you're dreading the evening, take somebody along for company. Why not ask somebody from office? It would make it less awkward.'

Sonny brightens. 'You're right. I'll get Suresh to come along. You too, Jazz.'

She prays that she won't start blushing, keeping her voice low and ordinary. 'I will come.'

~

Al Hendricks is a smooth young man. Smart suit, polished shoes, Brylcreemed hair; a dream son-in-law. There is something about the eyes that causes Jazz to pause. She watches Sonny straightening his fraying collar inside his suit jacket and running his fingers hastily through his hair. He still looks unwell, purple shadows under his eyes, his cheeks almost concave.

She hangs back while Sonny introduces himself. Suresh is supposed to be there too, but she imagines he has become embroiled with something or another, last minute as he always does.

'Good to meet you, Al.'

'You too, Mr de Roye.'

The two men exchange a handshake. 'Call me Sonny. By the way, this is Jacintha, my colleague.'

After another polite handshake Sonny leads them to their reserved table. A waiter takes their drinks order which Sonny attends to. The first band of the evening is starting up. 'You like music?' Al asks Sonny, watching his toes tapping to the jazz rhythms.

'Of course. What about you?'

'I like music, but this is just a horrible noise.'

Jazz and Sonny exchange a look.

'My passion is to go to the pictures. I saw *Singing in the Rain* four times when it came out last year. Have you seen it?'

Sonny and Jazz shake their heads.

Double shots of whisky arrive in heavy glass tumblers with a small ice bucket and tongs, a glass of juice for Jazz. 'Two more after these,' Sonny says swiftly as the waiter departs with a bow. 'So now, why don't you tell me about yourself.'

'I'm in my final year at university.'

'Ah yes. What is it you study?'

'Accountancy. I also did a Business Diploma in my spare time during the university holidays.'

'It sounds as though you are all set to have a successful career. But you must let me know if I can introduce you to people here in Colombo, I know a lot of people in the city.'

'I have employment lined up for when I leave, I will be joining a firm of accountants here in Colombo; Lamb and Da Silva, do you know them?'

'Yes, I know them, a high-ranking firm, no?'

'Top firm in the country. The accountancy firms do a sweep of final year undergraduates to cream off the best potential employees for the summer intake. I had quite a few offers.' Jazz tries to look interested, but she is finding Al Hendricks heavy going.

'Yes,' Al continues, 'I had my pick, but I chose Lamb and Da Silva as they have offices in Canada and America and will also be expanding into Europe, in a couple of years.'

'I see. You want to go abroad?'

'I'd like to go to America. I have family in Chicago.'

'And how does Serena feel about you working abroad?'

'I…well, we would obviously hope to be married by then and she will be coming with me.'

'Oh. I see. Is this official? I mean, have you asked her?'

'I have asked her, and also your father's permission which he granted on condition I come and see you first and tell you in person.'

'Well, that's wonderful. Congratulations.'

Jazz watches as Sonny empties his fourth shot in a very short space of time. The back of his throat must be burning. She imagines he has a headache brewing at the thought of the engagement party and the prolonged family gatherings in the build up to the wedding, not to mention the big day itself.

Al is still talking. Her mind wanders, thinking of what it would be like to plan a wedding, find dress patterns, organise the flowers and the cake. She supposes when it comes to her turn, she will have to do all that kind of thing with her Aunt Ada. She tries for a moment to imagine such an occasion, but her mind remains blank. Perhaps she will be one of those women who never find love.

She gestures discreetly to Sonny that he needs to wipe his face, he is starting to perspire a little. She sees Al looking at him with distaste.

Al is addressing Sonny impatiently. 'Serena and your mother are already making plans. They have written to you. Your father has also tried to ring you a few times.'

'Well, I'm in the middle of a big case,' Sonny says, slurring his words.

'Yes, we've seen the newspaper reports. Your mother is very proud of you.' Al's tone is doubtful as Sonny drains his fifth glass in a flash, already looking to summon the waiter for a refill.

'You know, Sonny,' says Al, 'I am very fond of your parents. I mean to take care of them as soon as I am able.'

'Oh?'

'Your mother once told me about the big house and the servants you used to have. It must have hit them hard when they had to leave. And of course, the place they live in now is very basic by their previous standards.'

'I suppose it is.'

'I'm looking at plots of land at the moment, big enough to build two properties on.'

'In Badulla?'

'Yes, in Badulla. My folks are nearby, so it makes sense. When Serena and I go abroad, we will want our own house to come back to, whenever we visit. And we will build your parents a nice modern house next door, with indoor plumbing, so they can keep an eye on our place when we are away.'

'I see. You have thought of everything.'

'Of course. That's what we do for family, right, Sonny?'

Across the foyer, coming through the double doors, a vision appears; Suresh, who unaccountably has changed into a smarter suit and even more oddly, a bow tie, as if he is part of an orchestra, Jazz thinks. Or on a date. He approaches her with an aching look on his face and her heart plummets.

Sonny rounds on him. 'Why Suresh, how fine you look. I'm glad you could make it. More drinks all round!' Sonny shouts. 'We should have a bottle of champagne to toast my sister's engagement!'

Al looks scornfully at Sonny before meeting Jazz's eyes.

She takes command. 'No', she says firmly, 'Sonny, we'll order some lemonade. Or would you prefer tea?'

Suresh has quickly summed up the situation. 'My gosh, he's had far too much to drink, hasn't he? And probably on an empty stomach,' he says to her in a low voice. 'I'll go and order some food.' Jazz watches him, grateful for his understanding.

A silence falls over the table until food and soft drinks arrive. Jazz persuades Sonny to drink several glasses of lemonade with the food, while Suresh chats mindlessly with Al Hendricks.

After a while, Sonny looks across at her stricken face and says in a small voice, 'I'm sorry, Jazz.' He sounds more coherent.

'Oh, Sonny,' she says.

They shift away from Al Hendricks and Suresh.

Sonny puts a hand to her cheek. 'I've made you cry. Your tiger eyes are full. I should have had lunch today, but I forgot. I actually haven't had any food since we saw Victor yesterday. I got used to us being together in Kumburapola, I felt safe with you. I am a hopeless fellow. Look at my shirt sleeves, I still haven't managed to find my cufflinks. Remember? The night in the DBU when I stabbed you with the pins?'

'Oh, Sonny,' she says again. 'I don't know how to help you.'

'Don't cry for me,' he says and then can't remember the rest of his sentence. He drinks more lemonade, then absent-mindedly consumes the final two portions of prawns which Al Hendricks has been eyeing up.

'I must apologise to you, Al,' Sonny says turning back to his guest, holding out his hand, 'I have ruined your evening. I'm not usually like this, I'm feeling under the weather, it's best I leave.'

'It was only what I expected,' says Al in measured tones, ignoring his outstretched hand, 'I've heard about your drinking and Serena also mentioned something about you not coming home for Christmas, preferring all sorts of crazy antics in Colombo.' He meets Sonny's gaze with a cool look, then turns back to his conversation with Suresh, who has the grace to look awkward.

Sonny rises and Jazz follows him, waving goodbye to Suresh, ignoring Al Hendricks. They stand uncertainly in the foyer.

'Is it my imagination,' she whispers, 'or is your soon-to-be-brother-in-law a little bit of a shit?'

Sonny gives a snort.

'You see how you journalist fellows have corrupted me in just a couple of months?' She stands on tiptoe, brushing her lips against his cheek, a touch as delicate as a baby's whisper.

A gentle car horn makes her look up. 'Uncle's chauffeur is waiting outside. Would you like a lift?'

'I er...no. I'm going to walk down the Galle Face maidan. Gather my thoughts.'

'No visiting any bars on the way home, do you hear me?'

'I hear you.' He walks with her through the foyer doors before turning his steps along the road briskly.

Through the car window the moonstruck sea is coldly silver. A lone figure stands on the shore, a breeze cooling his forehead as he spits out the remnants of the evening. She thinks it might be Sonny, but she can't be sure; all her thoughts these days seem to be hurtling along that same, single track.

30

'This is nice. All three of us eating together and catching up on our news.' Ada Crozier gives a contented sigh.

'Yes, Aunty. I'm glad we found time to do this before I head back to Kumburapola. Things have been hectic.'

Angelo and Ada Crozier exchange glances. 'Your uncle has something to tell you.'

'Oh, what is it, Uncle?'

Angelo Crozier clears his throat. 'Things have changed, and you will now be staying in Colombo. Walter will be having you in for a chat tomorrow. I thought you would like to know in advance.'

Jazz processes her thoughts as she chews her food without enjoyment, wondering what is behind her uncle's decision. 'So, what, the office in the East will be closed down now?'

Angelo Crozier helps himself to another portion of rice and curry. 'Sonny can manage it by himself. He will come backwards and forwards depending on what stories he picks up. I will be hiring a reporter to cover the courts here in Colombo, directly reporting to Sonny of course.'

'Oh, but Uncle—'

'Your time on the crime desk has come to an end. It has been far longer than the six weeks you were originally given.'

'But the Body in the Lake story is not finished. I'd really like to see the whole thing through,' she says at last, 'especially as I wrote the last article.'

Angelo is silent for a while. Jazz avoids Ada's sharp eyes.

'Well, okay,' says her uncle finally, 'if anything more should come of this investigation, I will tell Walter to allow you to work on it also. But things have gone very quiet on that front, no? Walter thinks the presence of the silver bullet has put Superintendent Ludowyk almost more at a loss now, than when he started.'

Jazz is forced to nod agreement. She helps herself to fruit salad. 'When will Sonny have to leave?' she asks, keeping her voice light.

'Fellow should be there by now. He left this morning.'

Her heart stops. She forces herself to smile, aware that she is being watched closely. She casually chatters for the next half an hour. 'And now I will go and write some letters before bed,' she says finally.

'Writing to anyone in particular?'

'Just Marlee. She is coming into the city to stay with her godmother, and we are arranging to meet.'

'Well, goodnight. Sleep well.'

Her uncle also rises.

'I've got a little work to do before bed, Ada. Don't wait up,' she hears him saying. Jazz forces herself not to rush up the stairs, anxious not to reveal the depth of her hurt regarding Sonny's silent departure. Alone in her room she tries to reason with herself. Sonny has not said anything about his feelings towards her, nor even if he has any. It is not as though there is what the aunties would call an 'understanding' between them. But she had been sure there was something.

She stares out of the window, her life in Colombo stretching before her, empty of its magic now that Sonny is so far away. She suddenly sees her journalistic ambitions have all been tied up with Sonny. She can't imagine enjoying the job half as much if he is not by her side.

She is aware of her aunt and uncle downstairs, no doubt discussing her. She should never have asked her uncle for the opportunity at the *Courier*, it is only now she can see the price tag, her freedom, is much too high.

She sits and thinks for a long time before opening her notebook, seeking solace in her writing.

'Jacintha!' calls an unfamiliar voice from the parlour. It has been three long weeks at the *Courier*, and things have gone from bad to worse. Walter had officially taken her off the Crime Desk, having thanked her for all her hard work. After saying that her feature on the Women at Still Waters had been excellent, he cemented the praise by informing her that as a result she was now to concentrate on Women's Features, while helping out on other desks from time to time.

It may have been her imagination, but he had seemed ill at ease during the conversation. She had got the impression that her uncle had had a hand in the new arrangement.

She concentrates now on entering the room where she knows her aunt is waiting for her, having informed her at breakfast that some old friends would be paying a visit that evening so she should not be late home from work. She had noted that her uncle had not been given the same speech.

· · ·

Gloria Hepponstall's smile is fronted by a slash of alarmingly red lipstick. 'Ah, here she is, come on in darling. Look at her, with her briefcase. Last time I saw you, you were playing with your dollies and now you are like a man, out working all day.'

Her aunt comes forward with a glass of something fruity. Jazz thinks for the first time, she can understand why people turn to alcohol.

'Do you remember the Hepponstalls, we used to holiday with them in Galle?'

Jazz nods and smiles.

'Sadly, Cristy passed away a few years ago. It's just me and Donny now.'

She sees a male pair of legs rising from one of the armchairs. Her mood drops. Don Hepponstall, the son, comes forward to shake her hand, slicked-back hair, a gold signet ring glinting on his little finger, aftershave oozing from his smooth skin.

'Jacintha! It's been a long time. Too long.' She thinks he has been watching too many films. His accent has changed since childhood, only faint traces of a native accent clinging to his perfect vowels. 'Shall we?'

He leads her back to the armchairs. 'How are you?' she says with the faintest of sighs.

Removed from his mother and her aunt they begin to chat.

'Aunty tells me you went to university in England. I too made this journey. We have something in common already.' Don is charmless, his conversation punctuated at regular intervals by winks and intense stares, a light house blinking desperately across an empty ocean. Their university experiences in England give them a common bond but she finds herself running out of things to say, once Don has put forward his contempt for the cold English weather and the bland food. He gives a theatrical shudder. 'I am glad to be back in the sunshine with hot curries for every meal. And so, you are now working as a reporter, isn't it? This is bold behaviour! Tell me, what stories have you been working on?'

She begins to relay the story of the body in the lake.

'Ah, yes, of course I have read about this. I say, that doesn't seem a very suitable story for you to be covering.'

Jazz is summoning an appropriate response, but then stops, fascinated as he quickly turns the preferred topic of conversation, himself, back on track. She soon stops listening about his job in the rubber industry, thinking instead of Sonny's good humour and energy, and how his presence would blast the staid mood in the room into smithereens.

'...of course, I had not been at the company long before they put me in charge of the entire section. They had to; I know so much more than the other fellows. They resent me but what can I do? You can't turn down a promotion.'

'Children, dinner is served. You have been chatting so hard, you must be hungry.'

Jazz picks at her food, her appetite punctured by the constant lip-sticked smiles from the opposite side of the table.

'Jacintha, you must be tired, no, going out to office every day?'

'I'm not tired, I enjoy it.' Jazz feels her aunt's cool eye resting on her. 'I suppose I am a little tired. I actually have some work to do before tomorrow. I hope you don't mind.'

She stands.

'Ada, you must speak to Angelo, working this girl too hard, she will lose all her good looks before she is thirty, no?'

'It's been lovely to see you all again.'

'See you again, soon darling. You must come for dinner. Donny will come in the car and pick you up.' As she leaves the room, Jazz feels Don Hepponstall's eyes glued to her departing figure, like a threat.

Marlee did not have as much free time as Jazz had been expecting, and only manages to meet up with her on the afternoon before she has to catch the train back home. They are wandering through Victoria Park, an oasis of calm and greenery in the city, keeping in the shade of the jacaranda trees hanging heavy with vivid purple flowers.

'Jazz, you seem moody today.'

'I'm sorry. I think I'm just a little tired.'

'Yes, you seem as if you are wilting. And nothing to do with this heat.'

'Well, I do feel a little bit low at the moment. Wait until you hear…Aunt Ada has been match making.'

Jazz has been longing for the chance to talk to her friend about the awful dinner party, but once she has finished her story, Marlee stares at her.

'But what was wrong with him? The Hepponstalls are a good family, no?'

'Didn't you hear anything I just said? But anyway, that's not really the point. I don't want Aunty getting busy on my behalf.'

'Time to get married before you get too old, and nobody will want you.' She gives a sly smile. 'Or is there somebody else you would like to marry?' She looks around. "I'm disappointed, you know; I thought you would bring the famous Sonny along.'

Jazz's temper flares. 'Stop your talk about Sonny. We don't work together any longer, he's gone back to the East Coast and I'm here.'

'Ah, so that is what has dragged your face to meet your feet.'

Jazz can barely believe the level of insensitivity from her closest friend. 'Something is going on with you, isn't it?'

Marlee looks suddenly shy.

'You've met somebody.'

'Mama's friend, Candy has a nephew, Peter. We were introduced last month.'

'You didn't tell me.'

'You've been so busy.'

'Is it serious?'

'Very.'

'You haven't known him for long.'

'I had my horoscope cast and was told it's a good time to be thinking about marriage.'

'Will he make you happy?'

'He is a bit older than me, it's true but he wants a wife and to be settled and I want to be a mother.' She pauses. 'I'm not clever like you, Jazz.'

Later, Jazz wonders if her friend had meant it as a rebuke.

31

February slips into March and the middle of the month sees the arrival of Medin Full Moon Poya day to the island. The *Courier* crowd has plans to enjoy the national holiday weekend together, deciding to meet for a picnic.

Waves of colour are flowing beside the Beira Lake where hundreds of people having made their offerings, are spilling out from the Buddhist temple. Marooned between huge family groups, Jazz, in a panic, thinks she is never going to find her friends. Mostly she is agitated because Sonny, home for the weekend, will be with them.

She wanders, perspiration gathering on her brow. The crowd surge forward, pulling her along in the slipstream; cries and raised chatter increasing as the temple elephant is brought in, to lay down a lotus flower as an offering.

She thinks that maybe she is getting what she deserves. She should have gone with her aunt and uncle to a lunch party, but she had braved her aunt's wrath and refused. Ada Crozier had pressed her lips together as if she had guessed how desperately Jazz longed to be with Sonny. She had not been able to meet her aunt's knowing eye as she had left the house, a little rouge rubbed into her cheeks, her lips a lightly daubed peach. She knows she is pushing boundaries, but she doesn't care.

After fifteen minutes of wandering, she chances upon Shyam and his wife together with Ganesh, Douglas, and Suresh, free and easy away from the reporters' room, unpacking food in a tiny speck of grass beside the lake. They wave her over.

'So many people, it's such a crowd! We've been looking for you for ages. We thought we'd sit here since it's such a good spot. We have seen Sonny; he has gone to find you.' Suresh motions to her eagerly to sit beside him, but she pays no attention, her heart leaping at his words.

'Where did he go?'

'Back towards the temple, I think he said.'

'I will go and find him.'

She discovers him quite suddenly, sitting motionless on a patch of grass. He is not asleep but there is a stillness about him.

'I've found you.'

Their eyes lock.

'I've been looking everywhere for you. Sit.'

She sinks down close to him. She hasn't seen him for a month but it's as though they have never been apart.

'How are you? Surviving the east?'

'I still hate it but…I'm getting on with things.'

'Things? Drinking? Cards?'

He chuckles. 'I'm trying to be good, Jazz.'

'Any interesting stories brewing?'

'Yes. This will be of interest to you, actually. Remember you told me you had been roughly spoken to on the street by a peculiar Sinhalese fellow? The story is that he had been running a campaign against Tamils in the region.'

'That is horrible.'

'Fellow's name is Herbie Gunasekera. Your favourite sergeant describes him as a terrorist.'

Jazz has the urge to laugh. It is not a term generally bandied around.

'No laughing, I am deadly serious. Sergeant Rutnam formally interviewed him about bad things that had been happening to the Tamils in the town.'

'What kind of things?'

'For over a year, Tamils have been suffering what the police described as orchestrated attacks, and it was all conducted by Herbie. He was paid to do it by a wealthy Sinhalese businessman, who wanted the Tamils out of Kumburapola.'

'This business fellow played on Herbie's simple nature and encouraged him to recruit a gang. He pulled the strings, but it was Herbie who committed the crimes. As well as the abuse and threats, he also led the gang to break into Tamil premises.'

'He was very intimidating, so I'm not really surprised to hear all this.'

'Initially, the Tamils didn't want to draw attention to themselves by complaining, but then somebody's child got hurt accidentally when rocks were thrown through the windows of a house. Some of the Tamils got together and finally reported the incidents to the police. As soon as the investigation was underway, the businessman disappeared from the area, leaving Herbie to take the rap. Stupid fellow was identified by one of his victims.'

'He could go to prison if they make a case against him, no?'

'That's not the best bit of the story. Apparently, his mother who his father had told him had died when he was a baby, turned up in the town looking for him. And guess what? Drum roll...she is a Tamil.'

'What? The Tamil hater is a Tamil?'

'Raised by his Sinhalese father who had thrown the mother

out not long after Herbie was born. He had no idea of his mixed heritage.'

'Sad when you think about it. So that is your next story?'

'Yes.'

'I'm glad you have been keeping busy without me there to keep an eye on you.'

'I've missed your eyes on me though, Jazz.' They look away from each other.

'Well, anyway, what is happening with the body in the lake? Still nothing new? Have you spoken with the superintendent?'

'The superintendent is fed up with the case. He thinks it's... dead in the water.' Sonny gives a weak grin.

'The silver fragments didn't lead to anything?'

'No.'

After a while, Jazz points towards the temple. 'I love this place. I remember the first time I came, just an ordinary morning. I had just come back from England, I wanted to get out of Uncle's house and have some breathing space. I wandered all through the temple complex and at one point found myself alone in the Vihara. Confronted with the calmness of the Buddha, I was overcome by an extraordinary wave of well-being, as if my soul had been cleansed and handed back to me, white and pure. For the rest of that day, I walked with a feeling of knowing who I was for the first time.'

'Nice, Jazz,' he says softly.

'I like to think of it as my single moment of transcendence, all the more sacred because I had not been seeking it.'

He becomes brisker. 'So, what have you been doing all this time? Working on anything good? I saw something you did about a bakery competition.' He gives a wry grin. 'Your uncle has taken you away from the big stories and wants fashion and cookery instead. Watch out, your tiger eyes are flashing again.'

'It's ridiculous. I think I am stuck doing Women's Features for ever, because guess what, I am the only woman. I have been asked to follow the story of our country's first national beauty pageant; apparently, Ceylon has plans to send the winner to represent us in the Miss Universe Contest.'

'What the hell kind of nonsense is that? Such a waste of your brain.'

She suddenly spots Suresh marching into the foreground with a determined look on his face. 'Where are you people, come on you'll miss all the food.'

'Come on.' Sonny holds his hand out to pull her up. 'We can talk some more, later.'

They have eaten and drunk. Scraps of food lie around waiting for the crows to pounce. Jazz gathers up the food wrappings and shoves them back into the basket so as not to attract vermin. Shyam has brought a ball along, and he and Suresh, Sonny and Ganesh are enjoying a kick around, difficult though it is, with the crowds that are packed in around the lake.

Jazz abandons the basket and goes down to the edge of the lake where Douglas, not a sporty lad, is sitting with an empty bottle of peach juice. He gives a hiccup and a shy laugh when she approaches.

'Hello, Douglas. Are you enjoying the day?'

'Yes, thank you.'

She sees now that he is writing a note on a small scrap of paper.

'I hope I'm not interrupting you?'

'Well…no, not really. This is just something I like to do. My mother used to do this with us when we were small. We would write down something we were worried about and float it out into the ocean. She said it released us from having to think about it all the time.'

'I never heard that before, I like the idea very much. Does it work?'

He grins at her. 'Yes, it works.' He hesitates. 'I don't have that much on my mind, would you…I mean would you like to write something instead?'

She may as well. He hands her the scrap of paper and wanders off to join the others, giving her some privacy.

She sits with the paper, wondering, and worrying. When she has it clear in her mind, she begins to write. As she is folding her completed note and placing it into the bottle, a shadow falls. She looks up at Sonny.

'May I join you?'

She waggles her head. He sits, eyeing her curiously.

'What's that you're doing?'

'Something Douglas suggested. Floating my worries away.'

Flustered before him, she rushes the launch and the bottle spins on the water uselessly, going nowhere.

'Here, give it to me.' Sonny reaches with a stick and draws the bottle back to the bank. With a deft movement the bottle glides away. 'Hopefully, that will float down one of the canals to reach the sea.'

'That would be good.'

'What is it you are worrying about, exactly?'

'I…' She hesitates. 'I've been thinking about my options. I can't see I have a place here. Aunty is trying to marry me off, while Uncle is trying to kill my career before it's even started.'

'But what can be done?'

'Maybe I should try my luck elsewhere. I could ask my journalist friend in England if there are any jobs going.' She pauses. 'For both of us.'

He looks at her uncertainly.

She feels a rush of disappointment. She had hoped he might want to leave with her, but he seems unaware of the role she has cast him in. She sees him calculating, his eyes working and thinks maybe he has a plan after all, but then he jumps to his feet.

'Got somewhere to be, Jazz.'

'Oh, but...'

She can't bear to watch him leave. When eventually she looks back, he is a diminishing figure hurrying from the lake. She returns to where the others have finished their game and have flopped back onto the grass and is dismayed to see Pearl standing there with a grim face. 'Why has Sonny hurried away in such a rush? What did you say to him?'

The woman is screeching at her. Everybody is looking at them. The rest of the *Courier* crowd stirs uneasily. 'You drove him away! Chasing him all over the place today! Did you think nobody would notice? And now you have ruined it for the rest of us.'

When eventually Pearl stalks away, Suresh hands her a spotless white handkerchief. She hasn't even realised she is crying. 'It's just shock,' she mutters. He looks at her with such kindness in his eyes, she cries even harder.

32

On Monday she wakes with a headache and stays in bed until the afternoon. Feeling

better towards the end of the day, she gets her uncle's driver to drop her at the office.

'Want me to wait, Miss?'

'That's okay, Ajit, I can make my own way back. I don't know how long I will be.'

She makes her way upstairs, relieved that there is no sign of Pearl. Suresh looks up and raises his eyebrows.

'How are you feeling?'

'Better. I just stopped by to get something from my desk. Oh', she says casually 'I have a message to deliver for Sonny. Is he still in Colombo or has he gone back?'

'Sonny? He popped in briefly, but he's gone for the day. I think he's in the city for a few more days, yet.'

'Do you have Sonny's address? I really need to give him this message.' She fiddles with the pencils on her desk.

She can see that Suresh doesn't want her going to Sonny's

place alone. 'I've nearly finished up here, how about we go there together in about half an hour.'

'I need to go now.'

'Oh. Okay, Jazz.'

She frowns. She likes people to ask permission before shortening her name. Suresh has heard Sonny calling her Jazz and assumes he can do the same.

He is writing on a sheet of paper. 'Here you are. I say, how about meeting up later this evening? We could go to the pictures if you like, the Savoy is showing *High Noon?*' He falters in the face of her agitation.

'Thank you, Suresh, some other time maybe.' She avoids his eye as she rushes from the office. She doesn't know if she needs to be in such a rush, but rather than join the long queue of people for the bus, she takes a taxi.

~

'Sonny? Are you there? Sonny! Answer the door!'

She waits a considerable amount of time until finally a heavily bearded man with clouded eyes opens the door, blinking at her.

'Is Sonny in?'

The stranger opens the door wide, gives an exaggerated bow and ushers her inside.

The room is small, a mattress in one corner against the wall, a cupboard, a desk and chair in front of the single window and a sink with dishes and cups waiting to be washed. Amidst a muddle of books and papers is the Remington. Memories of their time working together flood back.

The room is filled with the sweet, cloying smell of ganja.

'Sonny?'

He is seated in a dark corner on some cushions, very still and quiet. His head jerks up at the sound of her voice.

'Jazz? You are here?'

'I'm here.'

'Why, Jazz? Have you come to fetch me? Am I late for work?'

She stares at him. He is stoned.

'It's five o'clock in the afternoon.'

'That's okay then. Hey, Mateo this is Jazz.'

'Hello, Jazz. I'm glad you're here.'

'That's nice of you. Have we met?'

'No, we haven't but I feel like I know you, we have spent the last two hours talking about you.'

'You have?'

She has no idea what to think. When Mateo hands her a newly rolled joint, it seems easier just to take it. She sinks down onto the floor, close to where Sonny is lolling. Nobody speaks as they pass it round. After a while Jazz can hear something.

'There are bells ringing. A beautiful sound.'

'Maybe they are wedding bells,' says Mateo.

Jazz laughs uproariously. 'More like a warning bell of some kind.'

They look around puzzled as the noise persists.

'The tolling of the death knell. That's what it is. Of course.' Sonny's tone is flat.

Mateo leaps up suddenly. 'Shit! The telephone!' He rushes out in a flap. For some reason he puts Jazz in mind of a jungle fowl. She laughs aloud to herself, for quite some time.

'Who is that chap?' she asks Sonny after a while.

'Mateo'

'And Mateo is...?

'He's a musician. He manages a band. They all live upstairs in the attic room. They travel all over. They're from Mexico, or somewhere like that. It's their telephone.'

The mention of travel awakens in her a dim memory of why she has come.

'Sonny? I need to talk to you more about my plan to go to England. What do you think?'

He blinks at her. 'You are so independent, why do you need my opinion?'

'I just thought you might have one. You have opinions on everything.'

He is silent for so long she is sure he has fallen asleep. She thinks about getting up and leaving.

'I need to tell you something, Jazz.'

They hear Mateo clattering down the stairs. 'Sonny! Hey buddy, it's your father on the telephone.'

'Who?'

'Your father. He's crying, you should speak with him.'

Sonny closes his eyes.

'I can't.' He sits still and silent.

'Shall I talk to him, for you?' Jazz hesitates to involve herself and yet she cannot bear to think of Artie de Roye channelling his grief down an empty telephone line.

Sonny speaks from the depths of his trance. 'Yes. Good idea.'

She rises feeling dizzy and takes the stairs carefully. The telephone receiver dangles from its cord halfway down the wall.

'Hello? Uncle? This is Jacintha speaking.'

'Jacintha? Oh…oh…hello. How are you?'

'Are you okay? Mateo said you were upset.'

'I need…I need to talk to Sonnah boy, you know? Can you get him for me?' His voice is a torrent of pleading.

'He's not feeling well, he's fallen asleep now.'

'You see he needs to come and see Gail, right away…'

'Is something wrong?'

'Child, everything is wrong, you know?'

She doesn't know.

'Gail is hysterical, I don't know what to tell Bernard.'

'Well…does she need her pills changing? Sometimes you can be on the same medication for too long.'

'I need Sonny. Wait one minute please…'

She can hear him opening the booth of the telephone box and shouting to somebody. He must be in a post office, she realises.

'Just get him to come to Gail's place. Can you do that, child?'

'I will try.'

'Tell him Gail is…'

The line goes dead. Sonny is asleep when she returns to his room. Mateo is sipping beer. He offers her a bottle, and parched, she takes it.

'Troubles in the home?'

'It sounds like it. His sister is unwell.'

'Yeah, Sonny told me about her. The artist, right? My aunt went crazy after she had children. She either spoke all the time for days on end and nothing made any sense, or otherwise sat in silence with a face full of misery. I said to Sonny that he can't do anything to help her. But the way he talks, it's like his family owns his soul.'

Jazz sighs.

'This sister, she's got the blind boy, right?'

'Joe. His name is Joe.'

'Man, I can't get my head around what it must be like to live in a world of darkness like he does.'

Sonny stirs and mumbles. 'I would do anything for that boy. Joe. Poor Joe.'

Mateo clambers unsteadily to his feet. 'Gotta go, man. Nice to meet you, Jazz.'

'You, too.' She waits until the slap of his sandals fades away on the stairs. Sonny has woken properly and is drinking a bottle of beer thirstily.

'Sonny, listen. You still haven't told me what you think about me going away.' She waits, feeling her boldness rise. 'Would you consider coming? We could both try and find jobs.'

'A man can go away, but he will still find himself in the same head space. Same burdens. Same heartache.' He is lying on his back staring at the peeling paper on the ceiling. He motions at it with his hands flapping. 'Does that look like a flock of doves, to you?'

'Maybe.'

'Doves bring peace, isn't it? I would like some peace.'

Silence falls. Jazz closes her eyes.

'Maybe I should go to England. See the sights...' says Sonny '...the grey Atlantic, turn right for London town...I remember you told me your favourite thing about springtime in England, was the lambs bleating for their woolly mothers.'

'That's right. If you come to England, you will see them also.'

'When I was a child, Daddy gave me a Sunday Missal. I never read it, I just liked to look at the pearly front cover with an angel tending a sheep, shining white with innocence. The lamb of God who takes away the sins of the world.' His eyes are roaming the ceiling as if searching for the celestial meadow that might reveal his fleecy future.

'My gosh, you really are high.' She gives a deliberate pause, shakes her hair out and sits up. 'So am I'. She looks around, half expecting to see the gecko scurrying down the wall as it had done on the night before she and Sonny had met.

Their eyes lock. The air between them thrums.

'Come here, Jazz. Let's not talk about what might or might not happen. Not tonight.' She doesn't hesitate. She unbuttons her dress and slips it over her head, then lays down beside him.

Much later they fall asleep in each other's arms.

33

She arrives in the office the next morning, full of nervous tension, wondering how she could possibly be her normal self around Sonny after the events of the previous night.

She had awoken in Sonny's room at some time after ten, horrified at being out so late without having given her aunt and uncle prior warning. And as for what had taken place...Hurriedly retrieving her clothing from the floor, she had dressed and scribbled a note for Sonny, reminding him that he needed to telephone his father, leaving him sleeping like the dead.

She disappears to the lavatory a couple of times during the morning, to powder her nose and comb her hair. On one of these occasions, Pearl comes in to wash her hands and silently meets her eyes in the mirror with such scorn, she wilts inside.

When Sonny has still not made an appearance by lunchtime she wonders if she should call round and see if he is feeling the effects of the previous night. It would be good for them to have a sober discussion about the future, try and come up with a plan that would get them both to England. She's gathering her things together when Walter comes out of his office and has a short noisy conversation with Suresh, about Sonny. She sits down again heavily.

Sonny has already departed for the Eastern Province, on the early morning train.

She looks so pale, that Walter passing her by, looks at her closely and then tells her to go home.

'Jacintha? You are home early.'

Home early, home late. Whatever she does is noteworthy, it seems. Still, she goes in and chats a while, assuring her aunt she is perfectly fine, making sure the household is ignorant of her nocturnal sin.

Excusing herself eventually she heads into the hall on her way upstairs, when she sees a bulky envelope addressed to her, with English postage stamps. She recognises Vera's writing. Snatching it eagerly she heads upstairs where she reads it, lolling on her bed and then reads it again slowly, standing at her bedroom window, the smoke from her illicit cigarette curling across the lawn.

My dear Jazz,

How are you, pet? Your last letter seemed a tad gloomy, but fear not, I bring exciting news, at least I hope you will think it exciting!

Firstly, thank you so much for sending me your article, The Silver Bullet, which as you will see in a moment, was a pure piece of divine luck...but let me explain properly...

Jazz reads slowly, dragging fiercely on her cigarette as she digests the contents of the letter. One of Vera's few female colleagues on the *Manchester Guardian* has long been questioning the lack of women's input, and has been trying to persuade her editor that the newspaper needs to have a dedicated women's page. At a recent dinner party, she had met one of the women Jazz had interviewed at Still Waters, who had since returned home to the north of England. The woman from Still Waters had told her how impressive Jazz's article was and had also mentioned that Jazz had been to Reading University. Vera's colleague had suddenly realised that Vera and Jazz must know each other.

...the upshot is my colleague showed her editor The Still Waters piece and The Silver Bullet and has managed to persuade her editor to see you with a view to working on women's features! Do give it some thought, Jazz. I know you seem to be doing well over there, but this could be a big break for you.

She puts the letter down, thinking of how Vera had initially only been hired to do secretarial work on the newspaper, occasionally being asked to write articles when the subject particularly concerned women, until finally becoming a reporter in her own right.

Could she really expect to walk into this role? That evening, she runs out of cigarettes and is forced to ask the maid, Bimali, if she can spare some of hers.

~

It is not a permanent job offer but she wants to take the gamble. It seems like too good an opportunity to waste. The following day, she plans to telephone her father from the post office at lunch time, to talk things over in privacy with him, but then the telephone on her desk starts to purr. She looks at it without enthusiasm as she picks up the receiver.

'Hello, Jazz? Can you hear me?'

'Oh! Sonny...yes, I can hear you.' Her heart is hammering.

'I...I meant to call you when I arrived back, but things have been busy here.' He pauses. There is a long silence. 'Anyway, we can talk properly when you arrive.'

'What do you mean?'

'The young woman with the potions and whatnot, you know the Vedda woman? She came into office yesterday looking for you. She said she needs to talk to you urgently.'

'Why? What has happened?'

'I couldn't understand most of what she said but I gather it is connected to the murder.'

'The body in the lake? Seems unlikely.'

'I know. I'm just passing on a message. I'm sure it's nothing but...'

'I will talk to Walter and send you a telegram if I'm coming, okay?'

'Okay. It's good to hear your voice Jazz.'

She says goodbye and puts the receiver down. Her mind is spinning, unsure if there is much point in continuing to report on the case when her future seems to lie elsewhere. Curious nonetheless, as to what the Vedda woman might have to say, she goes and knocks on Walter's office door. He can be the one to decide.

'My goodness, you are a sight for sore eyes, my girl.' A day later, Mrs Andrado greets her in the hallway of the guest house with a wide smile. 'Sonny is naughty not to have told me you were coming.'

'Sonny doesn't know. It's a surprise. Is my room still free? I'm sorry I should have let you know I was coming.'

'Soon, soon, come, everything is still in place for you. Sonny is at office. Will you be joining him?'

'I think I'll go straight to bed, I've travelled straight through and I'm exhausted.'

'Why not have a little food first? Come, come, I will serve you now.'

'Well, okay. Thank you'

The landlady clatters about, bringing plates and dishes to the table. 'You know, after you and Sonny returned to Colombo, a reporter came with a photographer from another newspaper to do a pictorial report. My best room appearing on the front page! Luckily enough I had whitewashed the walls and windows, so it looked very nice.'

Jazz helps herself to a plate of crab curry with some brinjal pickle on the side.

'You are looking thinner and not very happy. Maybe you will come to your senses one day, but it will be when you are old and grey, and it will be too late. Sonny also, is not looking his best. Aio, too much work and no play, it's too bad for the both of you.'

She jumps at the sound of his voice in the hall. The landlady goes to greet him, delighted to be able to tell him of the surprise. Jazz has time to wipe her mouth and steady her breathing before he comes onto the veranda.

He sees her and is rooted to the spot. 'My goodness, this is unexpected! I wasn't sure if Walter would allow you to come.'

'I have an agreement with my uncle that I can work on the body in the lake if anything new arises,' she says with a small smile.

'May I sit with you?'

'Of course.' He's speaking as if they are at a nineteenth century banquet. She wonders if they will ever be able to be natural around each other again.

'Sonny, will I serve you now?' Mrs Andrado is hovering with intent.

'I won't have anything, thank you. I'm not hungry.'

Jazz and Mrs Andrado exchange surprised looks. The landlady takes the dishes away, coming back with two glasses of arrack. 'You look as though you need these.'

When she is out of earshot, Sonny becomes more like his recognisable self. 'How are you, Jazz? I mean, after...'

'I am okay.' They look at each other uncertainly. She thinks too much time has elapsed for that conversation. She sharpens her tone. 'Actually, this is a good opportunity to tell you my news.'

His face flickers as she tells him of the possible job offer in Manchester.

'I see. You are definitely going, is it?' he says finally.

'I am definitely going.'

'Have you told Walter? What about your uncle?'

'I told my uncle as soon as I received the letter. There was little he could do really; he could see my mind was made up. I left a letter on Walter's desk, giving notice, before I caught the train.'

'And your father?'

'Daddy is happy for me. He has always wanted me to be independent, after all. He is already planning to visit and making lists of the places he wants to see.'

'What will happen if you don't get the job?'

'Then I will find another one.'

Sonny is looking at her like a beaten dog.

She feels her anger brewing. 'Don't look at me like that. I've tried a few times to talk to you about how restless I've been feeling.'

'I...yes, but...'

'I gave you plenty of opportunity to say something, whether you would like me to stay or if you would like to come with me, but there has just been a deafening wall of silence. I actually think I deserved more of a conversation, especially after...well, you know.' She pauses. 'But here we are. Finally, we know where we stand.'

A veil falls over his eyes and his tone becomes brisk, business-like. 'You are right Jazz, it's good to clear things up. I really wish you the best and hope you get the job; it would be well deserved. We must all have a jolly party before you leave. See you off in style.'

They stare at each other in hollow silence, until Jazz, unable to bear the tension, bids him goodnight and bolts to her room.

⁓

After breakfast the next morning, they walk together as far as the corner. The mood is still uneasy between them. 'By the way,' says Jazz suddenly, 'Did you ring your father? What was wrong with Gail? You know, the phone call that evening?

'Ah, yes. That matter. Gail was having one of her episodes and Daddy was very worried.'

'Why did he think you could do anything? I mean if Bernard was there what was the point of ringing you?'

'Daddy gets upset. Feels responsible in some way.'

'But why is your father responsible for Gail's depression?'

She looks at him. His face is closed.

'Anyhow, not your concern.'

'Right,' says Jazz furious by now, 'I'm going to visit the Vedda woman.'

'Want me to come with you?'

'No, I don't.' She walks along the street with her head held high until she is sure Sonny is out of sight before sitting down on a half-built wall, sobbing until she feels empty. All the trust she and Sonny have built up is leaching into the wide empty space between them. All the things he has told her; the temple in the forest, the curse, his nephew's blindness, his sister's fragile state of mind.

She wonders now if there may be more he is keeping from her, things that he thinks he should protect her from and that this could be the root cause of their misunderstandings. Overwhelmed she wishes she could talk to Marlee; Marlee who is probably too busy now making plans for her new life.

She dries her eyes and sets her mind to business. The Vedda

woman is serving a customer but when the transaction is complete, she breaks away to smile at Jazz, speaking in a torrent of Tamil.

'Slow down,' urges Jazz, 'yes, I did get your message. Let me get my notebook out.' She is ushered into the back of the little shop and is invited to sit on the only chair.

'Okay. So, tell me what this is about.'

'I told you I am a Vedda but now living away from my tribe. I still go and see them, let the children see their grandparents. My family were not happy that I left but they understood I wanted to make my own way. Now I have a family they realise there are more opportunities for my sons, this way. My in-laws are not so happy to have a Vedda daughter-in-law.' She makes a face.

'Maybe they just need more time.'

The Vedda woman shrugs. 'My story for you is this: a while ago I was back visiting my family. It was the time of year when the tribe have a hunting ceremony, asking the gods to bring them good fortune and good hunting. There is a part of the ceremony where a bowl is used, and I noticed they had a different bowl, made from some kind of metal, replacing the coconut shell they always use.

'When I asked my father about this, he told me a couple of the Veddas had been walking through the forest and had found it.'

'Okay,' says Jazz, puzzled.

'The tribe rarely read newspapers or hear the radio, but I have seen the reports in your newspaper of the bullet with silver inside. Don't you see,' says the Vedda woman growing excited, 'the bowl could be the silver item you are all looking for, no?'

'I'm confused,' Jazz says, 'why would it be?'

'Sorry, sorry, I have got things in the wrong order. The bowl has a bullet hole in the side.'

PART III

PIECES OF SILVER

34

She had the vague notion that there were bullets in existence made of silver, mainly, she had to admit, from books and films about vampires and were-wolves. When it was explained that the presence of silver in the bullet found in the dead man, was not normal, she felt idiotic; as if she were really showing her naivety. It was a good feeling therefore, to have a moment of triumph when the Vedda woman, who would only talk to her and her alone, finally communicated the existence of a silver bowl with a bullet hole.

Something tangible in this baffling case, at long last.

In the heavy silence that fell as the Vedda woman finished her tale, she took her time, not wanting to overreact at this surprising piece of information. It was an eerie feeling, like the quiet that falls upon the land after the roar of the tsunami, or the thundering crash of a waterfall.

From the notebook of Jazz Barthelot

35

Jazz bursts through the door of the office, ready for action. Sonny looks up in surprise at her change in demeanour. She tells him exactly what the Vedda woman has said, darting around, anxious to make a start, but when she finally slows and looks closely at Sonny there is something unfathomable in his eyes.

'What? Shall we make a plan?'

'A plan?' He is speaking slowly.

'To go and find this bowl with the bullet hole?'

'If it even is a bullet hole, which I doubt.' He looks at her. 'What you're telling me is that you want to go and visit a Vedda tribe and demand to inspect one of their ceremonial bowls? The people whose name is evoked by parents as a threat whenever their children are misbehaving?'

'Obviously not quite like that.' She is deflated, hurt even. 'The Vedda woman, her name is Hendi, is going to draw a map for us when she has finished her work for the day. I did ask if she would come with us, but she said she didn't want to get further involved. Not all the Veddas are happy with her for leaving.'

'You've got everything organised then? You are really going?'

'Yes of course. Sonny we are fortunate to have this lead, no? It will be a great story.'

'This is all kinds of nonsense. Even if it is a bowl with a bullet hole, how do you suppose it could be anything to do with our dead body? The sergeant said the silver has probably come from some kind of shield or identity badge. A bowl makes no sense.'

She can't understand why he is so ready to dismiss the Vedda woman's information. She looks at him calculating. 'Okay, I can see you have made up your mind. I will go and inform Sergeant Rutnam and he can deal with it. I'm sure he would allow me to accompany him, given that he does seem to have a little crush on me. I'll go across to the police station now.'

'Hang on.' Sonny jumps to his feet. 'Let me think about this some more.'

He leaves the office and steps outside, leaning against the wall, perfectly still. When he returns, his tone is calm although his eyes are troubled. 'Okay, I'm sorry. You've done well. You are right. We should go.'

'I'm glad you agree. Hendi was quite insistent that we should be the ones to talk to the Veddas, rather than the police who can sometimes be less, shall we say, sensitive in some instances.'

'Okay. I'll go and find us a decent car, and let Walter know where we are going. Jazz you go and get provisions that might be useful – packs of cigarettes, a couple of bottles of arrack. Use your initiative.'

'I hope we don't miss Hendi while we are doing our chores.'

'Well, go by and see her when you have finished and see if she has the map ready for us. If we can, we should leave tonight and try to reach the settlement by daylight.'

~

The Veddas populate several areas of the island; Hendi's people are forest dwellers, living in the region where the Gal Oya runs partly through. They reach Gonagolla in the early hours of the morning and stop the car for some short eats that the landlady had given them a few hours earlier when she had seen them making their unusual nocturnal preparations.

'Where are you rushing off to at this late hour? Can't it wait until the morning?'

'Don't worry we will be back by tomorrow evening.'

Jazz was certain Sonny had sounded more confident than he felt.

They drive deeper into the region of the thick tropical forest within the Uva province, the borrowed jeep eating up mile after mile of forest tract, Sonny checking the map the Vedda woman had given them, every now and then. After two hours, he draws onto the side of the road and kills the engine.

'We can't go any further?'

'We have made good time, and it seems we are now very close to the Vedda settlement. We can wait here until morning, get a bit of sleep.'

A jackal howls in the distance, the crepuscular language of the forest softly resonating in a chorus of snorts, shrieks, and snuffles. 'If you need to do a number one, I'll come with you. There's a rifle on the floor at the back.'

'Thanks. I'm okay for now.'

She turns away from him and wraps herself in one of the blankets they have brought with them, but she is restless.

'What is it?'

'I hate the way everything closes in on you in the dark.' She can sense bats and nightjars waking, vipers uncurling themselves to slither through the grass, leopards stretching their powerful limbs ready for the prowl. 'I hope you are a good shot, Sonny.'

He grunts. Seconds later she is asleep.

The harsh cawing of crows swooping low across the tree line, cuts through the dawn rising softly pink across the Uva province. Jazz wakes from a few hours of broken sleep groaning softly. Sonny is up, smoking outside the jeep as she clambers out into the day.

'Good morning. Did you get any sleep, Sonny?'

'Yes, I did. Feeling good.' He turns. 'Do you hear that?'

She listens, her ears eventually picking up the rush of running water against rock, yards from where they are parked.

'Bathe your face, it will refresh you.'

She pushes her way through trees and bushes to a platform of rock under a small trickle of waterfall. The water is icy as it drips steadily onto her upturned face, and she gasps as her tiredness is washed away. A movement in the near distance causes her to pause. A loose-haired woman is standing with her back to her around the bend in the river, washing a pile of sarongs, patiently laying them out on a flat stone to dry in the rising heat. Every now and again the woman raises her face up to the sun as if seeking benediction.

'The village must be close by. Righto,' says Sonny when she tells him what she has seen, 'let's go'.

Her adrenalin is rising as they continue their journey on foot, Sonny using the map to follow a twisting path half a mile into the interior, fighting their way through overhanging bushes and branches, stumbling over huge, knotted roots in the ground, until the land opens up into a rough clearing where a number of huts huddle together. Jazz blinks, myths and legends crowding into her mind. She forces herself to focus on what is in front of her; small dwellings made of wattle and daub with an opening at the front of each one, topped by roofs made of grass and leaves, all the walls without windows.

A few dogs appear and growl softly, and she feels the weight of a dozen pairs of curious eyes gazing upon them, assessing the danger.

She glances over at Sonny. 'What should we do?'

He gives a shrug. 'We wait.'

They expect somebody to come forth from the dwellings. Instead, a man slides with ease down one of the trees at the side of the compound and comes striding towards them. 'I am Suddu,' he says in Tamil. 'What do you want?'

Jazz steps forward, her heart racing. Hendi had written a note on the back of the map explaining their purpose, which she now offers to the Vedda. He reads it and frowns slightly, looking them up and down.

'Come', he says finally. He raises his voice. A woman appears from a hut nodding and motioning them forward. After further dialogue between the couple who Jazz assume to be husband and wife, two small children come forth from the interior of the hut, running into the compound, giggling, turning to stare. Jazz and Sonny enter the dwelling.

The sparsely furnished room, set on a floor of packed earth, acts as both living and sleeping quarters for the family. A wooden table is piled with clothing, plates and dishes, a collection of tools stashed underneath. Sleeping mats made from grass are folded neatly in the corner. There are two long seats made of mud with some woven coverings; Suddu's wife bows shyly, clasping her hands together in a traditional gesture. She waves them into seats and after placing small cups of tea in front of them, she leaves.

'So, you are friends of Hendi. How is she?' enquires Suddu after they have drunk their tea.

'She is well. You might know she has a stall selling her herbal cures. They are very popular, she is talented.'

'She learnt everything she knows from living here.' He gestures proudly around the settlement. 'She must think well of you, if she trusted you to come here.' The Vedda pauses. 'Hendi has written that you are here because of the sacred bowl?'

'Yes.' Jazz knows she has to proceed gently. 'Hendi says the bowl has a bullet hole?'

'It does. It seems the gods wanted us to find this for a reason. Our hunting has never been so good since it came into our possession.' It is said firmly but without menace.

Jazz translates for Sonny, and they look at each other.

'Change the subject, ask him about himself,' Sonny suggests, 'ask him what he was doing halfway up the tree.'

Suddu smiles when Jazz asks him, and the conversation becomes looser. It appears that when the Veddas have enjoyed a successful hunt, to preserve the meat, they seal it with honey, wrap it in cloth and store it in the tree hollow.

'Suddu was checking how much meat they have left; they have been eking it out for the last fortnight. With supplies so low he will soon be planning another hunting expedition.' Jazz pauses. 'He says they don't hunt as often as we might imagine.'

With the contentious subject of the silver bowl put to one side, Suddu seems happy to tell his story. Originally a Coastal Vedda from Trincomalee, after his parents died and having no siblings, he took to wandering. He worked as a fisherman for a while and then, still restless, ventured inland. He stayed for a year with a Tamil family and eventually he married the daughter. When his first son was born, Suddu found that he was missing the Vedda lifestyle, so he joined this settlement.'

'It must be a very different lifestyle for your wife,' Jazz says. The Vedda grins waggling his head. Apparently, Suddu and his family now enjoy the best of both worlds; his wife goes on regular visits to her parents, their oldest two children attend school daily, leaving the settlement at the first light of dawn and returning in darkness. This trend is catching on and more of the

Vedda settlers are also starting to also send their children to be educated.

'But' says Suddu, 'there is another, smaller Vedda settlement who do not like the way we are living. They are worried that by embracing some of the modern ways of life, our traditions will be lost. But if we stay buried deep within our communities, I do not think we will endure. Our two settlements were originally one but in recent years we have become fractured which saddens both communities.'

At a look from Sonny, Jazz brings up the subject of the Lanka Reservoir Project. Suddu gives a rueful nod. 'Yes, we have had new families come to us as a result. A lot of forest land was taken away from us because of that reservoir.' His voice rises. 'The redevelopment has been a catastrophe for us. The forest has always been considered ancestral land. What gives government the right to take it all away? Where is it written down that they can do such a thing?'

'Where was it written that they could not?' says Sonny sadly.

A silence falls. Suddu seems to have fallen into a light sleep.

Jazz and Sonny leave silently, lighting cigarettes outside the hut. Suddu's wife sits cross-legged preparing a pile of yams. Nearby a pot of brinjals and chillies is bubbling over the fire. 'Food,' she says giving them an easy smile, 'eat soon.'

She motions hesitantly to Sonny's packet of Peacocks in his shirt pocket. He smiles and offers her a cigarette which she places carefully amongst her dry pots and pans. When he donates the entire packet, she smiles at him in delight.

'Let's take a walk,' says Sonny. They stroll in silence around the perimeter of the village. Jazz peers across at the tree which they now know to be the village larder. She wonders how long it will be before the villagers succumb to modern living. Just beyond she can see where the villagers have cultivated a chena beyond the back of the huts where a crop of maize is growing.

She remembers from her history books that the Veddas had worn very little clothing in bygone days; today the men and women are dressed in clothes and sarongs; the children kicking a ball around are dressed in western style dresses and shorts. A pair of bicycles lean against one of the huts. It seems the twentieth century is encroaching, after all.

'You are doing well,' Sonny says, 'I am proud of you.'

'You are?' She doesn't look at him, but she is pleased. 'It's going to be difficult to make headway with this bowl, no?'

'Maybe, maybe not. Let's see what the mood is when Suddu wakes up.'

To their relief, Suddu is awake and smiling as they approach his hut. Suddu's wife motions for them to sit inside where the children sit shyly. During the meal the children laugh and talk and point at them. Suddu reprimands them sternly.

'It's okay,' says Jazz, 'we're not offended.'

After the meal Suddu turns to Jazz. She listens in surprise then turns to Sonny. 'He is going to take us to the nearby hamlet he mentioned earlier, just beyond that line of trees. He says we have to meet the man who found the bowl.'

36

The sun is high when they arrive at the small tribal community. Suddu leads the way to where a Vedda is seated in the shadow of his hut. 'This is my friend, Gajendra,' says Suddu. The Vedda jumps to his feet at their approach, letting forth a stream of angry words. His Tamil is not fluent and Jazz struggles to understand all parts of the conversation. Suddu holds out his hands in a conciliatory gesture, speaking softly.

'He is nervous of you. He has heard that you are here to steal his bowl.'

'We have no intention of stealing,' says Jazz, her voice shaking.

'Gajendra and I are good friends, even though the ways we have each chosen to live, are sometimes different. He trusts my judgement in bringing you here. You will have to convince him that it is the right thing to give up the bowl.'

After a while, Gajendra's hostility dissipates, and he gestures for them to come into his home. Once they are seated Jazz turns to Gajendra and asks him in a gentle voice, if he will tell them how he came to find the bowl.

He takes his time before replying haltingly in his broken

Tamil. He and his father-in-law had been on a hunting expedition for wild boar. His father-in-law had been armed with the traditional bow and arrow, but Gajendra had recently bartered with a local farmer for a rifle, which he had taken with him, keen to try it out.

He and his father-in-law were not on good terms, but they had been elected to hunt that day. The hunt did not go well and soon the two men were arguing. In a rage, Gajendra had snatched the bow and hurled it towards the riverbank. Immediately remorseful he had scrambled alongside the teeming river down the steep banks where the weapon had landed. As he bent to retrieve it, his eye was caught by something gleaming. Curious, he dug it out and found it was a small bowl. He took it back to his father-in-law to show him. Wiping it clean of mud, they discovered the hole and Gajendra immediately realised it had come from a bullet.

'I realised that this bowl was something we were led to by our ancestors; something to bring us the good fortune we need during our hunting. We brought it back to the community and we have been using it during our ceremonies ever since.'

'Can you remember where you found the bowl?'

Gajendra shakes his head. 'I used to know these forests like the back of my hand, but we have had a lot of flooding in the region, mudslides and illegal tree felling every so often. I did go back a little while ago, but I could not find my way as the landscape has changed.'

'Shame,' murmurs Jazz glancing at Sonny. He nods tightly.

'Now, you will tell me your story. Why is the bowl so important to you in the outside world?'

Choosing her words carefully, Jazz explains about the dead man in the lake.

'And you think this bowl belonged to him? If he is dead, he will have no further need of it.'

'That is true,' Jazz agrees, 'however, he has been unlawfully killed and currently lies unclaimed and unburied. This bowl could be the key to identifying him and bringing justice to whoever killed him.'

'I see.' Gajendra stares into the distance for a long time. Finally, he meets Jazz's eye and nods. 'I accept your explanation. I will give it to you.'

She gives him a smile, looking around his home. 'Thank you, we are grateful. Is it here?'

Suddu answers. 'As Gajendra found it, the bowl belongs to him, but it is kept in the shaman's hut. He is the one to use it during our ceremonies.' He pauses. There is a long discussion between the two Veddas which Jazz cannot understand. Finally, Suddu says, 'Come. We will go and see him.'

Jazz knows the role of a shaman is to act as the mouthpiece for the spirits and feels nervous as they approach Suddu's settlement. Sonny is also looking uncomfortable; his face looks pale, his eyes dull.

When they arrive back, Suddu and Gajendra immediately disappear, presumably visiting the shaman. Jazz and Sonny sit silently in the shade, smoking incessant cigarettes. Jazz nudges Sonny when she sees Suddu once more approaching. He has a serious look on his face.

'Everything is arranged. The shaman has to perform one final ceremony before we can allow you to have it. This will take place tonight. You are both required to attend.'

They have been told that it is the Vedda custom, Kiri Koraha, to call upon the spirits of their ancestors, the Nae Yakka. In the cool of the evening, the edges of the forest are black, the stars slowly becoming bright in the sky. They sit amidst the gathering circle of Veddas. Suddu says to them softly, 'this is a rare thing for outsiders to witness.'

'We feel very privileged. Isn't that right, Sonny?'

Sonny nods briefly.

'I don't know what to expect from this ceremony.'

'You will see shortly.'

A low sound begins and a group of men with drums who have been resting in the shadow of the trees, now make their way into the centre of the circle and begin to play a slow, rhythmic beat.

The drummers circle around a pedestal made from tied tree branches. Jazz nudges Sonny when she sees a small silver bowl on top, unusually decorated with distinctive curves and lines.

The drumbeats intensify. All the Veddas are now standing, slapping their hands against their thighs to the rhythm. Several more figures carrying branches bearing green shoots, approach the pedestal singing, their voices going from a soft chant to a harsh shriek.

When two Veddas come forward, holding the arms of a third man between them, Jazz feels her heartbeat accelerating. They halt their steps, giving the third man a little push so that he is standing beside the pedestal.

Jazz and Sonny exchange a glance. Gajendra. He stands with his head bowed, his body rocking from side to side. In his hands he holds a coconut shell. The elders are standing behind him in a semi-circle, drumming and chanting in low pitched voices. An old man, the shaman steps forward and begins to keen stanzas so ancient, they could have originated from the dawn of time. Presently his head rolls back, and he begins to speak in a voice not his own.

Jazz begins to shiver. Beside her, Sonny takes her hand. The dancing, the chanting, the spirit voice, and the drumming seem to last for hours, sounds that Jazz is sure will stay with her for the rest of her life. She grips onto Sonny tightly.

Suddu whispers in her ear. 'The spirit has been appeased. The bowl is yours.' She has momentarily been in a place deep within herself and has lost sight of the everyday world. Now she sees it is the coconut shell in place on the pedestal.

The crowd are dancing and clapping.

'Please come with me,' Suddu instructs her. She gets up and follows him, turning to make sure Sonny is behind. But he has disappeared. When they reach Suddu's hut, Gajendra is waiting, holding the bowl which is wrapped in a cloth.

'For you,' he says gravely with a small bow.

She takes it gently from him and holds onto it tightly. 'Thank you for your help and understanding. You have done the right thing.'

They bow to her briefly, before disappearing back to the festivities. Jazz takes bottles of arrack from her bag and leaves them in the hut together with assorted packets of cigarettes. Then she goes to find Sonny.

He is sitting, smoking in the jeep. 'Ready to go?'

As the miles between the vehicle and the Vedda village lengthen, Jazz lets out a sigh.

'I haven't even looked at the bowl. I feel I don't want to.'

'Then don't.'

'Will you look at it?'

He snorts. 'No. Let's just get back, get some sleep and then hand this in at the police station.'

'I feel we should check that they have given it to us, and not some old coconut shell.'

'Would we go back if they have done so?'

They look at each other, breaking out in a burst of hysterical laughter. Jazz lifts the cloth briefly and sees a flash of silver. She nods at Sonny.

'I don't know what I was expecting but that was stranger than anything I could have imagined,' says Jazz finally.

'A story to be told,' Sonny says all humour gone, his voice flat.

'Are you okay? I thought you would be pleased to have the story. Another great headline. The bowl looks very distinctive, no? It is bound to jog somebody's memory. I just can't work out how a silver bowl is part of the narrative.'

'That's not our job, remember?'

She glances across at his drawn face as he concentrates on the dark road. Slowly, she feels herself drifting into sleep. She tries to fight it but when she next opens her eyes, they are back in Kumburapola, the bowl safe on her lap.

37

Jazz sits on the veranda enjoying the feeling of the sun warming her bones. Beside her, on the table, the covered bowl seems to emit a malignant energy. She thinks it must be her overstimulated imagination; the Veddas had seemed such peaceful people.

After Sonny appears, groaning and stretching, they leave immediately for the police station, where to their surprise they find the superintendent in attendance.

'Ah, it's you two. Come in and tell me what you have been up to, you have that look upon your face, Sonnah boy, that I know only too well.'

'No, Uncle, this one is all down to Jazz. She was given the tip off and did all the organising.'

'And what, you were just the muscle?' Superintendent Ludowyk gives his usual bellow.

'Well, let us see what all the fuss is about.'

Jazz hands over the bowl without ceremony, feeling lighter of heart once she has relinquished it.

'What have we here?' mutters the superintendent as he uses the cloth carefully to uncover the item, 'I say!' He glances up at them, eyes wide with surprise, turning the thin, delicate bowl around and around, prodding the bullet hole carefully. 'Sergeant!' he calls. 'Come quick.'

'Ai, what is this? My gosh, let me bring something to put it in.'

'Yes, yes, I will be taking this back to Colombo immediately.'

The superintendent grills them about their trip to the Veddas, listening keenly.

'We will have to send some constables in to take statements.'

'I still have the map in my bag, I can let you have it.'

'Sonnah boy, this is going to be another exclusive for you, no? I say, the Veddas...' He is energised by the find.

'Actually, it was Jazz who supplied the lead. It's her story.' She mouths her thanks as he looks at her. She wishes she and Sonny had not clicked back into their old, easy manner with each other; it is time for her to start making her arrangements to leave.

Jazz looks at the superintendent. 'Would it be possible to have a lift back with you? I also need to leave today.'

'Of course, I would welcome the company. But what about you, Sonnah boy?'

'Not me.'

'He is holding the fort at office,' says Jazz loyally.

'Very well, Jacintha, I will pick you up in an hour from the Lanka Welcome Guest House.'

'Better hurry,' she says to Sonny as they leave the police station.

'Yes.'

'You know,' she says, 'it sounds crazy but...there was something about that bowl I didn't like. A strange feeling.' She waits and hopes for his expected dose of acidity.

'I know Jazz. I felt the same way.'

'You did?'

'Totally. Something evil.' He refuses to meet her eye, but she can see his hands shaking as he lights his cigarette. 'Jazz, I am glad we are not angry with each other anymore.'

'So am I.'

'I will see you back in Colombo, before you leave?'

'Of course you will. Weren't you the one who promised me a jolly good party?' She ends things on a deliberately light note.

∾

She watches through the window as Kumburapola recedes forever from her view. Mrs Andrado had cried when they had said goodbye, telling her she was the daughter she had never had. 'Please take care of yourself. And I will keep an eye on Sonny. I still remember the darkness I saw when I looked into both your palms. I have never been wrong, you know.'

She looks along the bustling streets, realising that much of the building work has slowed down since she and Sonny first arrived in the town, obviously connected to the Dick Fry fiasco. She thinks this is a good thing; in her opinion the place is not quite ready for the intrusive arrival of the western world.

It is the people that matter, Burghers, Muslims, Sinhalese, and Tamils sharing the streets, the frenetic energy that comes from the mingling of cultures and the sharing of dreams. It is what she loves most about her country.

And yet she is leaving it all behind.

The superintendent is saying something. 'While I was in Kumburapola, I took the opportunity to visit Sonny's sister, Gail. You have met her, I think?'

'Yes.'

'The visit was not at all satisfactory. In fact, it was rather strange.'

'What do you mean?'

'I hadn't told her I was coming, it just so happened I had a few hours on my hands so I thought I would take the opportunity. I began to realise it wasn't such a good idea, when I heard raised voices as I approached.'

'That must have been awkward.'

He nods agreement. 'I was unsure, but I knocked. I had such a surprise when Artie opened the door, looking pale and drawn, his expression shocked when he saw me. I felt such a foolish bugger at that moment. The poor fellow tried to collect himself and look pleased to see me; we are the oldest of friends and yet at that moment, I felt like a stranger. I say,' he breaks off, 'you don't happen to have a cigarette do you?'

'Of course, Superintendent.' She lights one up and passes it to him. She notices his hand trembling slightly on the steering wheel.

'Things were definitely not right in that house. I looked around trying to work out who had been shouting. Artie, my dear friend, would not look me in the eye. I waited to see what would transpire and after a while Artie explained that Gail was currently ill and in bed and that Gail's mother had taken the children home with her to Badulla for a few days.'

Jazz says, 'Superintendent, I don't know if you are aware that Gail is on medication for depression? She suffers with her nerves. As I understand it, the tablets can only do so much to stabilise her and then it all starts up again, she gets out of control, and they have to put her on different medication.'

The superintendent makes an exclamation. 'I have known Gail her entire life, and yet this is the first I am hearing of it.'

'I suppose it's because such things can be seen as a stigma. The family would want to protect Gail.'

He grunts. 'And then there's all this nonsense between Sonny and his father! I believe they both think this is not a visible thing but to my mind they are not fooling anybody.'

'I agree with you. It is very sad because they obviously care for each other very much. There is something getting in the way.'

'I am the boy's godfather and Artie's best friend, and it pains me to see them like this. '

'Have you asked Artie about it?'

'Have you asked Sonny?'

They look at each other. Jazz reaches for the cigarettes again.

'You have only known Sonny a few months and yet something tells me you know him better than most. And yet, I am sad for you because you don't know the real Sonny, the young man who came blazing into the city and set the *Colombo Courier* alight. I thought after the Ratnayake case, he would be rolling in clover. But something changed.'

'Something happened.' She almost whispers it to herself.

'He has been damaged in some way; by who or what I do not know.'

She stops talking then, fighting the lump in her throat.

After a while the superintendent says, 'I say, I hope you don't mind if we make a little detour.'

She looks across in surprise. 'To where, exactly?'

'You will see. Somewhere interesting. Not too much out of the way.'

After a few more miles the superintendent brings the jeep to a halt in a deep area of forest. Along its borders Jazz sees signs of trees having been felled, the area markedly thinned, a sign that the redevelopment of the region is encroaching.

'Where are we?' She stands outside the vehicle. She can hear sounds of rushing water nearby.

'Follow me,' says Ludo leading the way through rutted terrain, mud, and damp grass, through a grove of tall trees until they have passed through the forest into a clearing to a great waterfall. He has to shout to be heard over its roar.

'So, here we are in Makara. The Dragon's Mouth. Maybe where the dead man's journey began.'

Her spirits drop. On the brink of a new life, she longs to put the body in the lake behind her. She smiles at him tiredly. 'How can you be sure?'

'We have had soil analysis back that suggests this is the area where he was buried. Think of a tiny stream beginning in Badulla, in those cloudy hills, growing wider, faster, at some point in its path the dead man's body, having broken free from its grave, would have wound its way down, following the path of the river until it came hurtling down in that thunder crash of water, ending up on the edge of the Lanka Reservoir. But of course, it is still by no means clear as to where precisely the body entered the water. Or why.'

'Perhaps we may never know,' Jazz says.

'Oddly enough, I have been here before, with Sonny. I brought him here when he was a little boy, a fact which I reminded him of at the beginning of the case.'

'Really?' Her voice comes out low and troubled. 'What a strange coincidence, Superintendent.'

There are sounds of guns going off in the distance. The sudden noise makes them both jump.

'Just hunters,' says the superintendent after a moment.

'Another cigarette?'

'Please.'

'It was Sonny's seventh birthday, and he was supposed to have a family celebration, but Gail was very poorly with a fever and Artie and Lily were flapping around like crows, caring for her. The home was no place for a birthday; Lily had hired a nurse, and everyone was fussing around Gail. I think they thought she might... well she was very ill.'

'The girl has really suffered with her health.'

'Sonny's father called me in a bit of a state. In those days I was an inspector in the Uva Province. I came and took Sonny back home to us for a few days. Barbara and I had recently got married and we were renting a house, so it was no trouble to have him to stay.

'I took him out for the morning while Barbara prepared food and cake for the little fellow. I had his birthday present wrapped in the back of the car; I had remembered how Sonny used to love going out in his uncle's fishing boat, so I had bought him a very fancy toy yacht.

'After we pulled up and got out of the car, I gave him the wrapped packed. How Sonny's face lit up when he opened it! I remember the boat had an orange sail. We set the boat loose on the water and she sailed very well. We almost lost her a couple of times, but we followed her path along the twisting water's edge for hours. I think I gave him a good birthday.'

'I wonder what happened to the boat?'

'Childhood always gets lost at some point,' he says softly.

The great roar of the waterfall fills their ears. He shakes himself as if from a dream. 'Well, let's get back into the car. I need to get back to arrange tests for that bowl.'

'Thank you for bringing me here.'

'You are welcome. I thought you would like to see the place where Sonny, I believe, was truly happy.'

'Thank you. I appreciate it. Superintendent, I don't know if you are aware that I am leaving shortly for England? I want to take this opportunity to thank you for all your help.'

'Not easy being a female reporter in Ceylon?'

'Not easy being my uncle's niece in Ceylon.' She hesitates. The superintendent's car has the same peaceful feeling she had enjoyed as a child in the confessional box.

'I really thought my uncle was giving me a good chance when he put me on the newspaper, but I see now he was humouring me. He probably thought I wouldn't make such a good job of it but since I am doing well, he doesn't know quite what to make of me.'

'I wouldn't be too hard on your uncle. I think, from what I have seen and heard, your aunty has a lot of influence.'

'Yes.'

He turns to her with his brow creased.

'And what of you and Sonny?'

'Sonny is too tangled up to think straight. I can't get him to focus on the future; his, mine…ours.'

'Perhaps it would be best if you took him with you.'

'He won't come.'

'Maybe he has got himself into something so deep, he can't drag himself back out?'

She watches the waterfall receding as they head out of the forest to the main road. She shivers slightly. 'Whatever it is, please take care of him when I have gone.'

He gives her a sad smile. 'I always do.'

38

Analysis of the bowl has proved it to be a match for the fragments of silver found in the bullet, but the police are unable to come up with any theories as to why a person would have been carrying such a thing at the point of being murdered. An expert pronounces the bowl as being valuable: clearly robbery had not been a motive for the killing.

It had been her last story before leaving the *Courier*. The article now lies in her clippings collection, along with her filled notebooks, now totalling almost a dozen. Her hand pauses as she places them into her travel trunk, wondering if she wants to start her new life with such gloomy vestiges of the past. And yet the thought of her notebooks makes her heart skip a beat, as if she has not finished with them yet.

'What are you dreaming about child? Is everything packed and ready?'

Guy Barthelot had arrived the week before, to share Jazz's final days in Colombo. They have walked and talked for hours, almost as if she needed to augment her stored memories, making sure she has enough to last until they meet again.

In an hour's time her aunt and uncle will be throwing open their doors for a lavish leaving party. It is very thoughtful of them, but she cannot imagine who will be attending. She assumes the *Courier* crowd have been invited, among them, maybe Sonny.

Her father taps his wristwatch. 'Time for you to get ready.' She gives a sigh. He pinches her arm. 'Go along child. The evening will be fine.'

Her aunt has bought her a new dress without consultation; a pink affair with cascading frills. She looks at it with loathing but as she has won the war, she feels able to surrender this final battle. She puts it on and allows Bimali to dress her hair. From downstairs she hears music from the grand piano in the large entrance hall and remembers that her aunt has hired a musician. Huge vases of flowers have been artfully displayed all over the house. As Jazz descends the stairs to greet her guests she almost laughs at the fact that it feels like a wedding party. Again, she tries not to think of Sonny.

After two hours she finally realises that the party is for her aunt and uncle, not her, the guests standing around with glasses of champagne and whisky while her aunt basks in the glory of having such an impressive niece.

'Yes,' Jazz hears her saying very loudly, more than once, 'it is a very good newspaper, one of the top English publications. Yes we are very proud of her.'

Don Hepponstall and his mother are prowling somewhere but so far she has skilfully avoided having to speak to them.

Her father comes up and gives her a nudge. 'Come come, let's get some air.'

They take their place on Jazz's favourite seat in the garden. 'It's a shame Marlee couldn't make it,' she says, 'have you seen anything of her?'

He looks awkward, clearing his throat, glancing at his watch.

'Well, she is probably very busy with all her wedding arrangements and whatnot. She told me she would be writing to you.'

'I see.'

'You will make plenty of new friends in England,' he says, 'Vera will introduce you to her friends, and there will be your new colleagues too.' He pauses. 'Speaking of colleagues, what has happened with Sonny? I got the impression that the two of you were quite close. I suppose I thought he might be a reason for you to stay.'

She looks into the distance. 'What gave you that impression?'

'You only have to see the two of you together to know there is something there. But then again, maybe it is my mistake. I saw what I wanted to see, perhaps.'

Jazz, remembering Sonny's empty promise about a party, says in a brittle voice, 'well, he is clearly not here, so maybe we were not such good friends after all. But I wonder why the others didn't come? Suresh and Douglas and Shyam. Walter. It seems strange.'

'Perhaps Aunty and Uncle wanted to keep you to themselves as you are leaving soon.'

'Perhaps.' She swallows. Although she had stayed at the newspaper a mere five months, she had thought she had made friends there.

'Jacintha!'

At first she doesn't hear the voice calling.

'Jacintha!'

She looks around. 'I had better go Daddy, they are calling me in. I suppose Aunty has organised a terrible cake or something.'

'Are you sure you want to go inside?' Her father points to the side of the garden where the fence stops just before the front door. Suresh is standing there, casually dressed, grinning at her.

She runs across to him. 'My gosh, I am glad to see you, but you are so late!'

'I'm not late, you are.'

'What?' She doesn't understand.

'You are late for your own party. Soon, soon come.'

She looks at her father who seems to know what is happening. 'Go, child, be with your friends.'

'But I can't just leave!'

'I will explain things to Angelo. Don't worry. Go and have fun.'

She looks down in dismay at the frilly dress.

'Bimali has left you some clothing in the kitchen. Quick now.'

Moments later, she is wearing her favourite understated dress and Suresh is pulling her along the street to where a taxi is impatiently tooting the horn.

'Where are we going?'

'Surprise.'

She is certainly surprised when they pull up outside a toddy shack. 'Don't worry', Suresh says, 'it's not as bad on the inside. It's very new in fact.'

She walks in and finds a brightly lit interior, modern chairs and tables and a long polished wooden bar. All the *Courier* crowd including Walter, Deepa the archivist, Douglas and even Pearl, are standing underneath a 'Good Luck' banner with a table of drinks to the side and another laden with food.

'You took your time!' says Walter thrusting a drink in her hand.

'I went into the house,' says Suresh a little out of breath, 'walked into every room, but no sign of her. Then I came out again wondering what to do and found her in the garden in a dress that looked like one of those fancy desserts from the Elephant House.' Everybody roars with laughter.

'The dress sounds terrible,' says a familiar voice in her ear and she looks up to see Marlee grinning at her and holding onto the arm of a good-looking older man. 'But you are looking very nice now, Jazz.'

'You came!'

'Of course, I came. Sonny contacted me through your father. He organised for us all to bypass the other party, which sounded as if it was going to be awful.'

'It was.'

'Let me introduce you; Peter, this is the famous Jazz who I talk about a hundred times a day. Jazz this is Peter, my fiancé.'

There is a record player at the bar and soon the room is filled with a jazzy vibe. After a few glasses of glass of arrack, she is floating and almost happy.

She sees Sonny approaching and her heart lifts. He sees her at the same time and for a moment everyone else fades; it's just the two of them in the room facing each other, eyes locked, the heat rising between them.

'Here he is, at last!'

'Only Sonny would arrange a party but come so late!'

'The bugger will be late to his own funeral!'

'Okay, okay, now that Sonny is here, we can get down to the speech.' Everyone groans as Walter moves to the centre of the room.

'Go on Jazz,' says Sonny, 'you too.'

'But I don't want any fuss.'

'Not like the dress you were wearing earlier,' calls Suresh, eliciting howls and catcalls.

'Well, Jacintha – or may I, now you have officially left the *Courier*, finally call you Jazz?' She nods her assent over the laughter.

'Three words to describe our first female reporter: 'Tenacious. Talented. Tigress.' The room has grown quiet. She feels her eyes welling up. 'When your uncle informed me at the end of last year, that I had to take his niece on as a junior reporter, I had no idea what to expect from this unknown girl. My wife suggested that she might want to contribute a piece on new modern household cleaning implements and whatnot, and I thought vaguely that she might do a couple of pieces on jewellery or cosmetics.

'Boy, was I wrong!' He shakes his head in mock disapproval. 'When I first met her in the office I thought for a moment, yes I would get her to do those things and then I suddenly saw her eyes flash and I thought...no. Let's see what she's made of. And so, for an easy life I paired her with Sonny.'

The room erupts with laughter.

'You should have seen her push her way into the room when Sonny had the tip off about the body in the Lanka Samudraya. There was no stopping her. Sonny tells me she has always been meticulous in her note taking.' Jazz looks at Sonny who winks at her. 'He also tells me she has a natural curiosity, charm, and imagination. And she's a good listener. But of course, all these things are very evident as soon as you meet her.'

Sonny raises his glass to her.

'We all know that it was Jazz who got the story of the Veddas. And of course, that is why I know she is going to be a big hit in England. So, everybody, raise your glasses. Jazz, here's to you.'

There is a roar of good humour. The arrack is flowing freely and her colleagues swarm around her, wanting to know her plans; where would she be living, exactly how cold would she expect it to be in the winter? And would there be snow?

Walter comes to her for a few private words. 'You are sure you are doing the right thing? It's not a definite job offer, is it? I suppose it is not easy for you here with your uncle constantly clipping your wings. I wanted you to work alongside Suresh, I think that would really have made you a name in the business. I did my best to persuade Mr Crozier. I just wanted you to know that.'

She pats his arm. 'Thank you Walter. It's for the best'.

'But it won't be easy in England, you know'.

'Easy life is a boring life, no?'

Almost all in the room are drunk. Sonny comes to stand beside her, and they share a secret, hopeless smile. From the corner of her eye, she sees Pearl advancing, her hips still hopefully swaying, one eye on Sonny, carrying a parcel tied with string.

'A little something for you.' She smiles at Jazz stiffly. Sonny nudges her to open it. She rips open the paper and brings out a knitted jumper in a terrible shade of mustard.

She gives Pearl a genuine smile. 'I will definitely be needing this. It's very thoughtful of you.'

Pearl says, 'my sister lives in Birmingham. I've slipped her address inside in case you get a little homesick for some good food. She's a very good cook.'

'Well,' says Jazz politely, 'thank you, that is very kind of you.'

Pearl pulls her away from Sonny to one side. 'I am sorry if I have been rude to you.'

'It's okay, Pearl. No hard feelings.'

Pearl's eyes bore into her. 'I saw him first, you know. But it's okay, you are going away now.' She stalks off.

'So, this is it? The big goodbye.' Suresh wanders over holding a roughly wrapped package. 'Go on, open it,' he urges.

She tears away the wrapping and looking down at the gift laughs out loud.

'*Fifty Rice Recipes*' she reads aloud with a groan. 'Good one, Suresh. I can confidently say that I don't expect to ever have to write about rice again.'

'I thought I'd get you something that would make you smile, and also think of me. And if you are doing your own cooking it will be useful.'

'Suresh, I don't need a book to be reminded of you.' She smiles at him.

'You're doing the smart thing, you know. I'm sure of it. And who knows, I may spread my wings too, one of these days. Come and join you in England. Maybe get to Fleet Street.'

'I got you this.' Douglas has ambled up in his usual unassuming way and shoves a package wrapped in newspaper, into her hands. When she opens it, she finds a set of mechanical pencils. 'They last longer, you don't have to keep sharpening them,' mutters Douglas.

Jazz's eyes meet those of Sonny's. The pencils must have cost Douglas a week's pay.

'I...thank you so much, Douglas. I will treasure them'.

'What a marvellous present. You know something, Douglas.' Sonny takes him to one side, 'now that Jazz has gone, her position will be up for grabs.'

'I couldn't,' muttered Douglas, 'I mean, me?'

'Yes, you,' Sonny says, 'your spelling and handwriting are immaculate. You just need to be a bit more forceful. Write a few articles and show them to Walter before he starts to look around for somebody.'

'You really think so? I say! Thank you.' He toddles off to linger over the remains of the food.

'That was nice of you,' says Jazz.

'I can be nice sometimes.'

'Sometimes,' she says and then says softly, 'thank you for my jolly party.'

'Anytime, Jazz,' he says. They smoke companionably for a while. 'Are you free one day before you leave? We should have a talk.'

'Yes,' she says after a long time, hoping she will not regret it, 'we should definitely talk.'

39

He is waiting for her on the same bench they had sat on back in January, before the dead man had floated into the Lanka Samudraya, before she had really known Sonny and the chaos he would cause in her heart.

'Good to see you, Jazz.' He kisses her on the cheek.

'Sonny, what is this news about the silver bowl? Must be significant, no?'

At breakfast she had read Sonny's latest report about the murder in which a woman in Kalmunai, the wife of a wealthy Tamil businessman, had come forward and identified the bowl as being her sugar bowl, part of a silver tea set. The bowl had gone missing from the household a couple of years ago. There had been no break in and nothing else had gone missing from the house.

'Yes. It's all very strange. But you don't want to keep thinking about the case now. You are free of it.'

'I will always be interested in the case, Sonny.'

She sits down beside him and slides a package across.

'For me? It's not my birthday.'

'Open it.'

He undoes the string and pulls out a small box. Cufflinks. Each one an intricately wrought gecko holding a golden heart. He makes an inarticulate noise and takes her hand.

'Do you like them?'

'I'm not sure I deserve them, but I love them.' He pauses and fumbles for his cigarettes. 'Damn, I must have finished the packet.'

'Here, have one of mine.'

'You never fail to surprise me, Jazz.'

For a while they stay silent, close together, stranded among Colombo residents, families promenading and picnicking at the tail end of the weekend. Then he draws away from her, a serious look on his face. She wonders if he is going to talk about their future. Whether he has changed his mind.

'I'm going to tell you Gail's story.'

'Oh, but Sonny there's no need.' She is suddenly tired of Sonny's insistence on always bringing his family to the table. She doesn't want to think about Gail, silent and sedated. Dread, like the rising of a flock of startled wood pigeons, comes upon her.

'I need to.' His eyes glitter.

'Okay.'

'I told you of the visit to the Hindu temple and the swami?'

She nods. Difficult to forget the grim tale locked in the pages of her journal.

'Daddy and I of course didn't believe what the swami was telling us about a curse. We thought it was some kind of magic trick. We didn't understand it, but we made a pact to never speak of it again.'

'You did the right thing,' says Jazz. 'I've been thinking that the whole scene was some kind of staged trickery. The swami fellow saw a way to feed on your grief, perhaps providing some twisted source of fun for himself.'

Sonny shakes his head. 'No, Jazz. That's not it at all.'

She looks at him anxiously.

'A while after the visit to the temple in the forest, my parents went over to Gail to lend a hand. Bernard was away, the twins were about a year old, and it was hard for Gail to keep an eye on them and also give Joe all the help he needed.

'When they entered the house they were confronted with something alien in the middle of the room: a metal cage which a well-meaning neighbour had built, the intention being to put Joe in it during the day so that he would not fall and hurt himself while she was caring for the twins. Joe was at the stage when he was playing up, shouting, and screeching, frustrated, becoming aware of his own differences.' Sonny pauses gazing at her with troubled eyes.

'Daddy says to this day, he doesn't know what came over him, sadness perhaps that Joe was forever locked in his silent world, how awful it must be for Gail to bear. While my mother was playing a game with the children he found himself telling Gail about the swami in the forest temple, and his claim that Joe had been cursed.

'Like you, he thought it had been some kind of cruel joke. He assumed that Gail would laugh and exclaim over the ridiculous tale. What actually happened was that Gail stood up, dropped the jug of lemonade that she'd been about to pour and started to scream.

'He tried to pacify her, but she screamed some more. Then my mother came in horrified because Gail was scaring the children.

'Eventually Mummy took all three children out for ice cream, hoping that my father would be able to calm Gail down while she was gone. After a long time, Gail finally stopped crying and began to pace up and down, staring up at the ceiling or maybe the heavens, as if there might be something there that would help her.

'In a quiet voice she said finally, "It's my fault".

'What? Why would she think that?'

'She confirmed the story,' says Sonny.

'She what?...What do you mean?'

Sonny looks so pale, Jazz fears he might faint. 'We don't have to continue the story if you don't want to,' she says, saying this as much for herself as for him, so that she doesn't have to hear it.

After a while, Sonny says, 'It was true. Just the way the swami told us. Gail admitted that she had been a little thoughtless towards a sannyasi who had come to the house begging for food when she was pregnant with Joe. She had forgotten all about the incident until Daddy told her what the swami had said about the curse. Since then,...' he shakes his head, 'she has never been the same. The moods, the hysteria, the insomnia. Well, you know.'

'My God. How awful.'

Sonny looks so dejected she just wants to hold him. 'When we left the temple, Daddy and I shrugged the whole incident off. It was never our intention to tell Gail, we said to each other that there was no point telling her something so cruel and obviously untrue. Of course, we had no idea that the swami's vision was real.'

Understanding dawns. She puts her arm around Sonny. 'That is why things are not always well between you and Artie.'

'Yes.'

'And what about Bernard? How did he react?'

'Gail made us promise not to tell him. She was so ashamed of her unkindness towards the sannyasi, she thought he would blame her.'

'She did nothing wrong! It's the sannyasi who should be blamed. And punished,'

says Jazz fiercely. 'How can somebody like that, ever be classed a holy man?'

'Indeed.' Sonny says after a long silence.

After a while she says, 'Sonny, you are not responsible for your family, you know. You have your life to live.'

'Ah Jazz. We are a family ruined by devils. What else can I say?'

'It's not your fault. Come to England. Please. A new life, a new start. For both of us.'

His face twists. 'I should come before it's too late, shouldn't I? Before everything closes in on me. But I just can't. Not even for you, Jazz.'

'Don't do it for me. Do it for yourself. Look at the state of you.'

'I want to be with you. I want to be happy. But it's not possible. It's just the cards we are dealt, right, Jazz?'

She tries one last time. 'It's the hand that you play, that's important.'

'Exactly. My point, exactly.' They both draw on their cigarettes a final time.

Galle Face Green is quieter now; the sun has dropped into the ocean and the families have dispersed. Under cover of darkness, they kiss for a long time.

40

For once, on the day she is to leave she is greeted by leaden grey skies across the city. 'The skies are always blue above the clouds though, isn't it?' her father says.

When she had gone to book her passage to England, she had been surprised when Ajit had instead driven her to the offices of Air Ceylon.

'Uncle's orders,' he had said in a voice that could not be disobeyed, 'come, come.'

She has always wanted to fly. It is very generous of her uncle.

From Bimali she has heard that her aunt Ada had tried to dissuade Angelo from this bountiful act, no doubt still miffed that she had been unable to secure a marriage for her niece with an eligible Burgher bachelor. Jazz is glad that her uncle has stood up for himself in this instance, wondering what her life might have been like if he had done it more often.

On the morning of departure, Ajit places her two suitcases almost reverently in the car. The rest of her belongings, packed into trunks will be sent by ship once she has settled. The house has been in turmoil all morning, Jazz alternatively weeping and elated, her sensible head in a spin.

When it is time for her to leave, the household gathers outside the car. Bimali is crying, ugly rivers of snot running down her face, and is sent inside by Aunt Ada. Jazz runs to her and gives her a wrapped package, a new dress purchased from Millers that she knows Bimali will never be able to afford to buy for herself.

'Open it later,' she says, 'thank you for always looking after me.'

'Send postcard,' says Bimali, over and over like an echo.

'Time to go,' calls Ada tapping her watch, exasperated to the last minute by her niece. 'I wish you a safe journey. Be sure to write and let us know how you are getting on. Make sure you get in with the right crowd in England.' A peck on the cheek and then a quick, regretful hug.

Jazz peers over at her uncle who is striding towards her with what looks suspiciously like tears gathering in the corners of his eyes. He gives her a tight embrace.

'Thank you for everything, Uncle,' she murmurs.

'I wish,' he says softly, and then stops. He clears his throat. 'Be sure you write often, keep warm and send me all your cuttings. I will be looking forward to hearing how you progress.'

'Thank you, Uncle, I will.'

'Come, Jacintha.' Her father is waiting patiently. She takes his arm and settles in the car and before long they are on the road towards Mount Lavinia and Ratmalana Airport.

'Will you miss it?' Her father gestures out of the open window to the crowded streets. They have slowed down as traffic is heavy going past the bazaar. The riotous colours of the silk stall assault her eyes, her ears ring with the bartering cries of the customers and the pleas of roaming hawkers, the scents of sizzling garlic and chillies, herbs, and spices pervading her senses. She tries to take it all in. Panicked she realises she has never written such scenes, always taking them for granted. She starts rummaging in her handbag for her notebook.

Her father stills her arm. 'Relax. It will stay with you.' He gestures to his heart, then brushes her forehead with a kiss. 'And if you are unhappy, you can come home, and it will all still be here.'

When they arrive at the airport they discover the flight has been delayed for several hours. Jazz looks across bravely at her father.

'Daddy,' she says.

'I know, child. No point waiting. And I can't keep Ajit here for hours.'

'I have my book. Better go.'

'Very well.' They hug for a long time, and both sets of cheeks are wet when they disengage.

'Daddy, you will visit? When I am settled?'

'Try and stop me. God bless, Jacintha.' He goes to the exit, turns, and waves his handkerchief, victoriously from afar.

She has been sitting on an uncomfortable seat staring into space for the past hour. Somebody brushes a hand in front of her face. 'Go away,' she says irritably, thinking it to be one of the fruit sellers.

'That's not very polite,' says Sonny sitting down beside her, lighting cigarettes for them.

'My gosh. I didn't realise it was you.'

'Have you seen the *Courier* today?'

'It's been such a chaotic day; I haven't had time. I'll try and buy a copy before I board.'

He is staring at her. She feels disquieted, wanting to break the mood.

'Well, not long to wait now. Luggage all checked in, the aeroplane is there on the tarmac, waiting for me to climb the steps and board.' She falters. 'You...you haven't changed your mind?'

He looks at her. 'Maybe one day, Jazz.'

She gives a deep sigh.

'I want to ask you for a favour.'

'Of course. Anything.'

'It's about Joe.' He shuffles in his seat. 'Joe should be at school by now, but it turns out there are not many options. Gail and Bernard can send him away to Colombo, but he would be alone and far away from home. He is on a waiting list for a Blind and Deaf School nearby, where he will receive some kind of education, but it will be basic at best.'

'I see. That is awful, but what can I do to help?'

'I was wondering...could you...would you be able to send some books for him in braille?'

'Of course, I will. Anything I can do. You just have to ask. I hope things improve for him. If I send you my address, you will write and let me know how everything is?'

'Yes.' They give each other a long look as they try not to think of the dark origins of Joe's affliction. Sonny blinks, breaks the mood, handing her a package tied with a gold ribbon. 'For you,' he says softly, 'something for you to remember me by.'

'I will wait for you, you know. In case you have a change of heart.'

'Best not.'

'I hope you can banish your demons, Sonny.'

'If they don't get me first. Goodbye Jazz. Take care.'

An air stewardess is approaching, checking people's tickets. She nods when Jazz produces hers. 'It's time to go through to Departures.'

'Well, this is it, then.' She senses Sonny's eyes lingering on her as she passes through the barrier. It feels like a promise.

~

She slides into her window seat, shunning the attempts of the neighbouring passenger to chat about the cricket, the rice subsidies, the inconvenience of the flight having been delayed.

'Damned nuisance, I will have missed my connections now. I don't know why these buggers are so disorganised. I know it's a new service but always they blame air traffic control. Where exactly is the evidence of any control I ask myself?'

The passenger is riled up with indignation. Having not garnered a response from her, he turns his attention to his newspaper.

Jazz turns her attention to the package from Sonny. It feels reassuringly solid. She slits open the wrapper. A notebook with thick, creamy pages. On the front is embedded a gemstone, a tiger's eye in the shape of a heart.

The plane is taxiing, commencing the long journey to London. First stop Bombay, then Karachi, Tel Aviv, and Rome. They rise above the teardrop island, the silks, scents, and spices of a thousand markets, tea pickers strung like pearls across the hilly plantations, waves crashing on the palm-fringed beaches of the Eastern Province, the sprawling mass of Colombo with its colonial past and its sky-scraping future, all disappearing from view.

Tears are streaming down her face.

'Tea or coffee for you madam?

She wipes her eyes and asks for a cup of plain tea, wishing she had a hip flask of arrack as Sonny would have done.

Her neighbour has discarded his copy of the *Colombo Courier* in the pocket of the seat in front of her. 'May I?'

He waggles his head. She opens it at the page her neighbour had been looking at and reads with a catch in her throat, Shyam's excellent piece about a famous foreign cricketer who has been persuaded to come and coach the Ceylon team. An article by Suresh hints at trouble from the massed workforce who it is rumoured, are banding together to protest at government policies. And then she turns to the front cover.

MURDER VICTIM IDENTIFIED?

Mrs Anjelica Dias, living on the outskirts of Kalmunai, has come forward to say that a few years back she remembers giving some scraps of food to an old sannyasi who had arrived in her village, offering prayers for people in exchange for food and water. She had been surprised that instead of the wooden bowl such holy men carry, his had been made of metal with an unusual pattern. She was unable to give the police a name or supply further details.

Her neighbour sees her reading and gestures at the article.

'Who on this earth would think about killing a sannyasi? An innocent holy man! Are these the sort of tactics now that are being used against the Tamils - some kind of warning from the Sinhalese? This country is imploding and for that you have to blame the government...'

Her blood runs ice cold. She doesn't want to think about why somebody would have murdered a sannyasi. Her thoughts spiral towards their inevitable conclusion. She seeks a distraction from the devastation, opening her new notebook, pen in hand almost giving in to the lure of its blank pages. She sees that Sonny has written something at the front, an inscription:

Jazz – I know you are going to write a great novel...make sure you choose the right story to tell.

She turns to look out at the skies. A single bead of condensation trickles down the window, where it lies, resting in the middle of her vision, like a teardrop.

PART IV

HOLY MAN

41

It is the wandering monk's sole purpose in life to meditate on his identity, forever seeking his inner core. Sometimes, when the astrological signs are favourable, he assembles with other monks to fast and pray, but mostly he will travel, eat and sleep alone in caves and forests, traversing the roadways and the hills, friendless and unloved, his only possessions the robe on his back and his own pure thoughts.

As he wanders the country begging for alms, he is willing to teach those who wish to learn how to meditate and sometimes performs spells, always keeping his mantras secret, never losing sight of his eternal spiritual quest.

At his death, the sannyasi should neither be cremated nor buried but instead become immersed in the river where he will hope to eventually become absorbed into the Universal Soul.

From the notebook of Jazz Barthelot

42

OCTOBER 1953

'No, I'm getting these, it's my turn.'

'But—'

'No arguments. Okay?'

'Thank you.' She looks down with greedy pleasure at the glass cup Vera places in front of her, anticipating the sweetness of brown sugar against frothing warm milk. She thinks she's becoming a coffee addict. She lights up a cigarette.

'Not been in here before, I've never had coffee like this,' Vera says cautiously lifting her cup to taste. 'It's rather nice.'

'It's Italian. New place opened last week. At night it's full of young men with quiffs and drainpipe trousers but the daytime is respectable enough.'

Vera takes a satisfying gulp. 'Now, I want to hear everything. How are you getting on?'

'You don't need to worry about me' Jazz assures her, 'I'm enjoying it. Everything is going well.'

'I can't help but feel guilty, though. I lured you over here on what turned out to be biggest wild goose chase.'

'Don't be so ridiculous', Jazz assures her, 'I chose to come, even though it wasn't a firm job offer.'

'Somebody less brave would have come over for a holiday rather than leaving everything behind.'

'I was ready to make a change. It was very nice of the editor to think so highly of me that she wanted me to come and interview. Honestly, everything has worked out for the best. Besides,' she waves expansively outside to the Soho streets, 'I am in love with London.'

'I must say, I envy you. I miss London with a passion. Manchester is grim, really.'

Jazz looks out at her adopted city with a proprietorial air. She's been in the city for five months now and her heart is gladdened every day by the twist of fate that has kept her in the capital.

When she had touched down at London airport, clutching her purse filled with unfamiliar currency, and a train timetable, she was tired but ready for the next part of her adventure. She was not expecting to be met by Vera, almost in tears at the arrivals gate.

When Vera had told her that the newspaper had decided they were not after all, ready for a women's page, her knees almost buckled. Vera took one of her suitcases from her, hailed a taxi and took her to her parent's rambling four-storey house in a road off Camden High Street.

In shock, she had wanted nothing more than food, bath, and a bed, all of which were offered with immense tact and kindness by Vera's parents, Alan, and Maud. The next day, she and Vera had sat down to discuss her options. 'Firstly, Mum and Dad want you to stay as long as you like.'

'I don't want to be a burden.' Jazz had tried to steady her voice.

'You wouldn't be a burden. They have three bedrooms standing empty!'

'Why don't I come with you to Manchester and see if I can find another job?'

'The problem is, Jazz, I don't know how easy it will be to find another job up there. I think you would be better off staying here, at least London is starting to climb out of the depression now. Mum will like having you around, she misses female company now that I'm in Manchester most of the time. My brother Bill, you probably remember him, he got married last year and lives the other side of London, so you really wouldn't be in the way.'

'Okay.' Jazz really had very few options. She fought back the sinking feeling that threatened to engulf her.

'I have to go back to Manchester this afternoon. Settle in here and I'll come next weekend and take you out. Relax and make yourself at home.'

For a week she had roamed the streets of London, anxious to be out of the house and not make a nuisance of herself. Having only visited London a few times in her university days, it was mostly uncharted territory, and she knew nothing of Camden and its environs. During the day she spent hours in the market, wandering among the fruit and veg stalls, noting the latest fashions, learning how the English loved browsing for bargains at a stall selling what Maud referred to as 'crockery'. She bought herself some cardigans and even managed to find a ladies' overcoat that didn't swamp her slender frame. Slowly she reacquainted herself with the vastly differing dialects; Irish, Cockney, Scottish (which defeated her) remembered from her university days and others that were new to her: Yiddish which she was told was the language of the Jewish people, and Italian.

Every day she found herself growing more charmed by the energy and optimism of the city, although occasionally she was brought up short when she saw an ominous sign posted on a window or a shop door where a vacancy was being advertised: 'No Coloureds.' She had been sheltered from this on her previous visit, now faced with having to find somewhere to live and work, she grew worried. She assumed she would be classed as Coloured, although she wasn't entirely sure. Now and again her optimism faltered, before being bolstered once again by a friendly word or smile from those who weren't affronted by her brown face.

She worked for a few days on a stall selling knitwear, she had made friends with the girl who ran it who was about her own age and didn't seem worried by the fact that Jazz was so glaringly different. The girl, Elsie, was going up North to see her mum and needed someone to keep the stall running for her, otherwise she'd lose her pitch.

'You can stay in my flat too, if you like,' said Elsie, 'I'll give you the address, duck. Keys are under the mat, just let yourself in.'

She had proceeded cautiously after work, catching a bus which she loved to do, riding upstairs where she could see every-thing, to Kings Cross which she imagined Vera describing as 'a bit of a dive.' Dismounting and following her nose, she found the street after a few wrong turns, littered with dog mess and rubble and junk. A small dog barked ferociously at her when she arrived at the subdivided house where Elsie lived in a single room, sharing a leaking bathroom and a kitchenette on the landing, with seven other people.

Jazz had bent down to retrieve the key from the mat as instructed only to be met by movement at the front door, a couple of rough looking young men, in laced up boots and donkey jackets. One of them had nudged his friend, 'Look, Malc, the entertainment has arrived. Exotic looking, ain't it?'

She had pretended she had the wrong house and had fled.

'Do you want another coffee?' Jazz asks Vera, 'what time is your train?'

'Not until three. So, tell me, are you really enjoying the new job?'

Jazz grins at her. 'The job is great. I love it. I'm learning so much. Stop worrying.'

Vera looks at her thoughtfully. In a big collared coat over a pale pink twin set and dark slacks, her hair much shorter and worn in a loose pony tail, Jazz does possess the air of somebody thriving.

A couple of weeks after Jazz's arrival, a friend of Alan's who lived outside London, heard of a temporary vacancy on a newspaper in his local village. The *Mallingford Times*, was a provincial newspaper in South Buckinghamshire, covering the small town of Mallingford and the surrounding hamlets and villages. She had to take the tube out as far as Amersham and then catch a bus. It was a different world.

Sitting in the waiting room for her interview, she had been unnerved at first by the interested stares that came from the reporters' room as she perched on the corner of a chair waiting for the editor to call her in. A secretary came over and gave her a broad smile. 'Good luck.' Jazz looked around. 'Where are the other candidates?' The woman did a wide, exaggerated sweep with her eyes around the room. 'Just you.' She winked.

'Miss ...er...Bath-a-lot?' A broad man in tweed trousers had come into the room, looking around.

The woman burst into laughter. 'Is that really your name?'

'The 't' is silent.'

'Go on,' her new friend urged in a low tone 'don't keep Mr Satchell waiting. Oh, and Miss Barthelot?'

'Yes?'

'If he asks, and take it from me, if he does ask, it's a good sign; make sure you say you own a pair of wellies and you know all about libel laws. Alright?'

She knew next to nothing about British libel laws and had no idea what wellies might be, but by the end of the day she had been taken on as the newest reporter in the pack. While the country's national crime reporters were being kept busy in the Old Bailey with the harrowing case of John Christie, on her first day, she found herself reporting from the Mallingford County Show, delivering five stories: 'The Winning Cake', 'Summer Knits', 'Oxford Down Sheep', 'The Largest Marrow' and 'Tractor Maintenance'.

At the end of the day, she had collapsed in a heap in her rented room above a village pub, kicked off her wellington boots, a present from Maud which left her practically lame by the time she sat down, devoured a home cooked shepherd's pie (entirely fitting) from the landlady and laughed for a long time.

When the job had come to an end after four months with the return of the regular reporter, she had the confidence and the credentials to apply for local newspapers in the London suburbs and was taken on as a court reporter for a large North London local weekly.

Now she spends most of her time in the North London Magistrates Court or sometimes in one of the Crown courts if the senior court reporter is otherwise engaged.

Sometimes she sits there, shivering even though it is the English summertime and thinks of Sonny and the heat and dust and feels a pang. But then the feeling disappears, and she goes home to Alan and Maud's place where she is now at her insistence, a paying lodger, and looks forward to weekends roaming the National Gallery and the Royal Parks, Saturday nights with work friends at The Tottenham Royal, or the pictures with a tub of Lyons Maid.

She is learning not to mind if people are unkind, or rude or unfriendly when she encounters them on the streets, on the bus or the tube, in the park, in shops and cafes and pubs. She once asked one of her colleagues why some were so enraged by brown and black faces and was told it was mainly fear of the unknown. Another said that the increasing number of immigrants was perceived as an employment threat. She tries not to take it personally. Sometimes she wonders if a place exists where she can truly belong. Before, she was in the East with her Burgher heart and mind oriented to the West, and now she is in the West, she is perceived as being from the East.

She has always had a tendency to overthink things.

'Not lonely?' asks Vera.

'Not especially.'

'Nothing you're missing about home?'

'My father. Sometimes the weather and the food. But I love the energy, and the history of the place, and the people. It's energising.'

'Give it some time, and we'll get you to Fleet Street, yet.'

'Actually, I may have other plans,' says Jazz casually, but refuses to say more.

43

FEBRUARY 1954

She sits in her bedroom at the back of the house, swathed in a chunky gold and black knit, a Christmas gift from Vera. It's February, a bitingly cold day but the sky is blue with a pale wintry sun over the back garden. What she now knows are snowdrops have sprung up gleaming white amidst the small patch of lawn.

A fire burns generously in the grate. She has a week off work, her first since she started at the newspaper back in October. She has made so many plans; long lie-ins, walking in Clissold Park, shopping for a new dress in D. H. Evans in the final days of the winter sales, taking Maud for tea and cake in the local ABC.

She does none of these things.

Alan has brought her a desk and chair which fit nicely under the window. In the desk drawers are her notebooks which have been shipped over with the rest of her belongings. She has been sorting through them, picking up each one randomly, reading, remembering. This time last year, she had been with Sonny in the Eastern Province, chasing the story of the dead man in the lake. It seems long ago and far away. All except Sonny. She carries the secret knowledge of him around like a stone in her heart that will not be dislodged.

She has heard from him once when he wrote a short note to say thank you for the books she had sent for Joe. She had written back a chatty letter, asking him if he was still in Kumburapola, staying out of trouble and whether there have been further developments in the case. She has yet to receive a reply.

Vera thinks she should be dating and has arranged a couple of evenings out on double dates whenever she has been home, which have been a lot of fun, but she can hardly imagine herself with a chartered surveyor called Wilf, or Terence, an insurance broker. She doesn't know why.

There are a lot of people now in London from back home, the majority of them living around the Earls Court area. She has been put in touch with a few and has spent some happy evenings with them, reminiscing, complaining about the British weather, laughing about the cuisine. They have cooked for her; rice and curry, difficult as it is to achieve in a cramped room, with a single cooking ring, battered saucepans and precious spices from home used very sparingly. One of them, overseas to study but with culinary dreams, and rich parents, has a plan to open a Ceylonese restaurant in London. Jazz thinks the idea is, to use one of Maud's favourite phrases, 'pie in the sky.' The English have had a long while to accept Indian curry houses, she thinks it will confuse them if the Ceylonese contingent introduce another foreign variant into the mix. But she hopes she is wrong.

Although it is fun socialising with people from home and there is no doubt that her palate is in agreement, when a room becomes vacant in the block where most of them reside she resists all invitations to move in. 'Why ever not?' says a pretty, married Sinhalese girl, Anuradha, now going by the name of Annie.

She makes an excuse, letting them believe the family she

lodges with is reliant on her in some way. She doesn't want the friends from home to think she is being judgemental, but she believes assimilation is the best way to win over the aggressors, rather than being part of a large impenetrable tribe. She is glad she has made English friends who she can celebrate her differences with and learn from theirs.

Just the other day one of her colleagues, Dot, had asked her why she doesn't wear a sari. The question has prompted Jazz to think that perhaps she needs to write a Ceylonese novel, bring the whole glorious, trembling, confusion of her teardrop island to the place she now calls home.

Standing up, stretching, sipping a cup of coffee, her eye falls on a folded newspaper on her bookshelf. She goes over and picks it up. One of her Ceylonese friends had given it to her, thinking she might be interested. They had all been so impressed to learn she had worked on the *Colombo Courier*.

She looks at it now closely, an edition a couple of weeks old, sent to Britain by a relative wanting to share the cricket news. A jolt of electricity goes through her as she turns to the front and is confronted with Sonny's headline:

BODY IN THE LAKE LAID TO REST

Police Superintendent Ludowyk has gone on record to say he does not believe they will ever formally identify the man found dead in the Lanka Samudraya in January 1953. Speaking to journalists at a recent press conference in Colombo, he explained the body had only recently been given a burial in an unmarked grave in the city. Last year, hopes for identification of the mystery man had been raised when a woman in the Eastern Province had come forward to identify him as a sannyasi. Unfortunately, police have been unable to confirm this and the witness, a ninety-year-old woman, has since died. 'It is good to be able to put the fellow at rest, even if the same cannot be said for the case,' said the genial superintendent with just a hint of disappointment on his ageing brow. Superintendent Ludowyk will be retiring at the end of the month, after a long and distinguished career. The case remains open.

She waits for her heart to stop hammering, lighting a cigarette with shaking fingers. She wonders if she will ever be rid of the presence of the shadowy sannyasi. Sonny's gift to her, the tiger's eye notebook with his written message, lies unopened, like a challenge. She opens it to the first page, uncaps her fountain pen and begins to write.

44

JULY 1955

'Canapes?' says Jazz. She is seated in a café on a street in Bloomsbury, the summer day outside a wet splash of gloom. The waitress delivers a plate of ham sandwiches with a few strands of limp lettuce and a dash of salad cream, and a pot of tea. She has been in the country for two years and still cannot reconcile herself to the limited choice of ingredients, in the face of continuing rationing. 'Yes,' says her companion, 'you know, finger food. Tinned sausages, cheese, crackers, that sort of thing. Potato crisps. My wife's got everything arranged.'

'Tinned sausages...I say...' says Jazz faintly.

'The bookshop will stay open an extra hour so that guests can buy a copy of your book before the party. The party will start at seven with champagne and as discussed the er...canapes. Once the guests have circulated and settled, you will be introduced and then we'll have your reading. Have you chosen a section you feel comfortable reading aloud? I think we agreed that the part where they discover the body would be the most intense, and most likely to grab the audience.'

'I'm still considering it,' says Jazz with a lying smile at her literary agent.

Monty Baxter is a fairly new, relatively inexperienced agent. As Jazz is an entirely new and inexperienced novelist, it is almost inconceivable that her first novel is actually being published. It has happened in no small part due to the fact that Jazz had drunkenly confided to a journalist at a party that she had written something and he, in his capacity as Arts Editor, had been intrigued enough to track her down the next day, and ask her for a date.

When she immediately said no, he had grinned and asked if he could see her novel instead. After reading it, he had firstly told her how good it was and secondly put her in touch with an acquaintance of his who had recently started a literary agency with two friends. The firm had had a small taste of success, managing to sell a rather unusual detective novel set in Egypt. There was some logic therefore, that they might be able to sell Jazz's book, also set in exotic climes, and they agreed to take her on as a client.

When the small independent publishing company who had published *The Egyptian Detective* were sent Jazz's novel, they initially turned it down. They were anticipating more to come in the Egyptian series and didn't want to take on a more literary kind of novel. One lone voice on the Board had a change of heart and had championed her novel as being extremely modern in its diversity and had turned the tide in her favour.

'Well,' says Monty, 'don't forget to practise beforehand. We've got a decent number coming, around thirty so I'm told. It should be quite an event.'

'It sounds marvellous,' says Jazz, giving him a genuine smile. She is fond of Monty, but she has her own ideas.

'I'm simply green with envy,' says Vera, 'but at the same time, I'm so proud of you. It's a marvellous book, Jazz.'

'You're possibly a little bit biased,' grins Jazz, but she is pleased with the compliment, she knows Vera is not one to throw praise around. 'You know, I'll be glad when this party is over and done with.'

'This is just the beginning,' says Vera, 'you might have to get used to this kind of thing.' She pauses. 'Now, there are about sixty people coming according to my tally. Have you managed to bypass the dreadful sausages?'

'Yes indeed. My friend's husband in Earls Court will be bringing what we call short eats. It's been a little tricky for him, but he's been very creative with vegetables, eggs, and pigeon, would you believe. All lightly curried'.

'And much more in keeping for a novel about Ceylon, than cheese and bloody crackers.'

'Exactly.'

'I'm so sorry your father is unable to come. You must be so disappointed.'

'Yes. The main thing is he is healthy now and as long as he takes it easy, he will be fine.'

Guy Barthelot had suffered a heart attack the previous month, a mild one which was the only reason Jazz had not immediately flown back to be with him. On the telephone he had sternly made her promise not to worry about him and she had promised to come back in the autumn for a visit.

'What about your aunty and uncle?'

'They know I have a book coming out, and I'm sure my aunty is telling the entire Burgher community on the island about it, but as it will not be available to buy in Ceylon, it's a bit muted for them.'

'I'm sure your uncle will buy copies and have them shipped

across. Who knows, maybe he will set up his own publishing company for your future books.'

'Perhaps,' says Jazz shortly, remembering how it had not wholly worked in her favour, the last time he had played a guiding part in her career, 'we'll see.'

'I take it George will be coming?'

The previous month, Vera had come down to London for a party and had taken Jazz along. Not knowing anybody, and with the front room a bit of a squeeze, Jazz had taken refuge in the tiny kitchen amid myriad bottles of pale ale and stout, and a couple who were getting friendly with each other in a corner. A good-looking fair man with soft eyes had come to find himself a drink and seeing Jazz had insisted on scrabbling around looking for a bottle of sherry for her.

'Please don't worry, I've had a glass of shandy.'

'I insist. You look far too stylish to be drinking shandy. Aha, what have we here?' A seasoned partygoer, he had rooted around in the pantry and discovered a bottle of Babycham hidden at the back, and the remainder of the evening spent with him, had taken on its sparkle.

Intrigued by her career, George had taken her through a number of his favourite crime novel plots and had mock-plunged a kitchen knife through his heart when she confessed she had never read Margery Allingham. The next afternoon, he had turned up on the doorstep with his copy of *The Tiger in the Smoke* and had been invited to stay for tea.

Jazz has seen George a number of times; for a drink at the pub at the top of her road, to a party given by one of his work colleagues, to the pictures to see *East of Eden*, and they have spent a few evenings staying in to listen to *Hancock's Half Hour*, sharing a bar of Fry's Chocolate Cream, and crying with laughter.

'Yes,' she says, 'George is coming.'

'That will be nice,' says Vera pointedly.

'Stop fishing,' says Jazz, laughing but she will be drawn no further on the subject.

'Alright, I'll mind my own business. Now, which part of the novel are you reading tonight? The teardrop?'

'Of course.'

'Well, then I think you're ready. An exciting evening ahead, Jazz.'

She goes upstairs to her room where she had first had the idea to write *Teardrop* eighteen months ago, coming home and writing each night after work and at weekends for month after month, until she had amassed what turned out to be a two-hundred-and-twenty-page novel. After she had finished it, drained, and hating it, she had put it away in her drawer with her old notebooks and danced, drank, and partied in order to forget it, until the fateful meeting with the Arts Editor.

When her agent had announced the publishing deal, she had immediately written to Sonny and explained the nature of her book. She wasn't seeking permission, after all, it's a work of fiction but still...what had started out merely as a story of a Burgher family spun across three generations, also ventured into some darker corners. There is an awful lot of heavily-disguised-Sonny in the book.

She sighs. Of course, he has not written back. She knows from occasional sightings of the *Colombo Courier* that he does not appear to be working on the newspaper. She has been too proud to ask her father or her uncle if they know of his whereabouts.

She washes her hair and dries it in front of the fire, the nerves slowly building as she tries not to think of having to read aloud in front of so many guests. A new dress, a spit of Maybelline against her lashes, lipstick, heels, a dab of perfume behind each ear, and she's ready.

Downstairs, the family are waiting, puffed up with pride: Vera, Alan and Maud, and the next-door neighbours, Jean and

Jim. An enormous bouquet of yellow and white roses, carnations and daisies has been delivered for her. 'Look,' says Vera, 'from your father, and your aunt and uncle. They asked me to arrange it on their behalf.'

'It's really very thoughtful of them,' says Alan. Maud twists one of the roses away from its setting and arranges it in Jazz's hair. 'There, you look lovely.'

A figure steps in from the hallway with a bottle of champagne tied with a red bow.

'I've got a couple of cabs waiting outside. I thought I would accompany you in one of them. I hope that's alright,' says George, offering her his hand.

Surprisingly she thinks it is.

45

Mr Peterson, one of the directors at the publishing house claps his hands to hush the chattering crowd. Clearing his throat, he steps forward. 'Well, good evening ladies and gentlemen. Welcome to this little gathering that we at Cobblestones Publishing are proud to be holding here, in the wonderful Bookish bookshop.'

There is an enthusiastic round of applause. Jazz looks around the room at the familiar faces of Vera and her family and George, friends and neighbours in Camden, newspaper colleagues, the Earls Court crowd, her agent, Monty and his wife, publishing house representatives, and the charming staff of the bookshop.

'When I first read the manuscript of *Teardrop* the thing that struck me most, was the fresh and authentic voice of the narrator, safely guiding us through the landscape, customs, and culture of the teardrop island of Ceylon. With vivid descriptions that jump off the page and a cracking family mystery to boot, I'm sure you will all agree that the book is a highly enjoyable read.

'Anyway, that is quite enough from me, I'm now going to hand you over to the author of *Teardrop*, Jazz Barthelot.'

More applause as she takes centre stage. For a moment her voice fails her. She takes a sip from the glass of lemonade beside her, fixes her eyes on the page and begins.

My niece, Maria was not always blind. For the first ten years of her life she was just another ordinary girl, going to school, playing with her friends, running in the garden with the dogs. And then one weekend, my sister Frederica the girl's mother, went on a trip to the East Coast to visit family. She had been gone for two nights when in the morning, Maria woke the house with her screams. Her father, Willy came rushing to her side to discover she couldn't see.

For months, an army of doctors in Colombo carried out tests. Nobody could say why Maria was suddenly blind. And nobody could make her see again. Naturally the family were devastated by this occurrence but as time went on they learnt to adjust, if not wholly accept the situation. Of them all, Maria coped with it the best, with the resilience of the young, but her parents, Willy and Frederica remained utterly distraught.

One day cousin Cyril came for a visit, the same cousin my sister had been visiting when Maria had so tragically become blind. Cyril worked as a guard on the railways, travelling from Batticaloa to Colombo overnight and he usually had a humorous or interesting tale about the people he had met on his journeys.

Willy and Cyril were chatting while Frederica was supervising in the kitchen, and the conversation turned to Maria. Willy was despairing about what the future would hold for his blind daughter.

Cyril wondered if there was a cure and Willy explained that all the tests had been done and nothing had worked. And that was when Cyril suddenly said he knew somebody who might be able to help.

The conversation stopped at that point. Willy didn't press him but about a month later, he received a rather mysterious letter from Cyril, alluding again to somebody who could help Maria, and inviting Willy to Batticaloa that weekend.

Jazz pauses, lets her eyes play across the audience. They seem wholly engrossed in the story. George, who has been attentive but not intrusive throughout the evening, gives her a discreet thumbs up from his seat in the front, next to Vera. Jazz swallows and takes another sip for her dry throat. She is not at all sure how the next section of the novel will be received. At one point the publishers had wanted her to erase it and she has had to fight hard to keep it in.

Cyril met Willy at the train station in a borrowed car. He seemed a little tense. At first, they travelled along the coast, just an ordinary day, the ocean smooth and calm, fishermen mending their nets spread wide across the sands, school children in their white uniforms walking to their lessons.

But inside, the car was filled with tension, although Willy was not sure why. After a while Cyril changed course, heading inland into the forest. He seemed to know exactly where to go, even though to Willy one clump of trees seemed much like the next.

Finally, Cyril stopped the car at the edge of a plantation, where a small Hindu temple was almost hidden beneath tree branches. 'Make your way inside,' said Cyril.

'Inside the temple?'

Cyril gave a small nod and reaching across, opened the door handle. Willy stepped outside and waited.

'Just you,' said Cyril.

'I'm confused,' said Willy, 'Why would I go into a Hindu temple?'

Cyril shifted in his seat. 'I've heard things about this place. They might be able to help Maria. You have nothing to lose, no?'

Reluctantly Willy moved towards the entrance, past some small deities and an arched recess. His heart jumped violently when a monkey launched itself from an overhanging branch with a wild shriek, vaulting down to the path where it stopped to pick up grains of rice from the ground, recently used in rites of prayer.

He stopped at the entrance of the temple; a Christian man reluctant to enter an unknown realm. He uttered The Lord's Prayer under his breath which gave him courage. Thinking only of Maria he entered.

There were oil lamps blazing upon a stone altar. His eye was drawn to the panels dedicated to the god Shiva, the god he had always perceived to be of darkness, anger, and destruction.

At the side of the altar a swami stepped forward, about forty years old, kind eyes and thinning hair. He turned to Willy and bowed his head, who did the same out of respect. The swami indicated a bench. They sat.

'You come with a troubled heart.' The swami spoke in a gentle tone.

'Yes. That is true.'

'A young girl is blind.'

Willy gave a start. 'My daughter.'

'Daughter's name?'

'Her name is Maria.'

'What happened to Maria?'

Willy looked at the swami and gave a sad shrug.

'Nothing happened.'

'No illness or accident?'

Willy shook his head. 'One morning she awoke and was blind. That is all.'

The swami gave a deep sigh. 'I understand.' He rose and scattered flowers around the bench on which they were sitting. The cloying scent filled Willy's lungs. He coughed. More lanterns had been lit and placed on the floor, offering an ethereal glow. When Willy finally stopped coughing he looked around, but the swami had disappeared. Sweat broke out on his face and he wanted to leave but felt unable to rise.

Jazz pauses. The room is silent. She suddenly thinks of Sonny, his face when he had told her this story that she has borrowed and embellished about his beloved nephew, Joe. She sees George in front of her reassuringly solid. She takes another long sip.

All of a sudden the swami reappeared holding two objects. The first was a betel leaf which he placed in his palm, perfectly flat. He showed it to Willy and smiled.

'Let us see what we will see.'

He took up the second object, a little brass bottle and from it, poured forth a single drop of liquid which eventually settled in the centre of the betel leaf like a large teardrop. Willy's immediate thought was that he should look away. He wondered if the swami could sense his fear. Gathering his courage, he kept his eyes on the teardrop, determined to witness whatever was about to take place.

The swami closed his eyes, gently moving the teardrop from side to side, chanting, by now in some form of trance. Willy blinked and held his breath, unable to take his eyes away from that teardrop of liquid. Shapes were beginning to form into moving images, a grainy scene, like an old film. In the middle of the teardrop, he could see the figure of a young woman seated in a garden. With a start, he realised it was Frederica. He blinked, not understanding how this could be happening.

He could hear her softly sighing to herself, sipping a cool drink in great contentment. Suddenly there was another figure in the garden, an old man, a sannyasi with scrawny hands, standing over her. He started gabbling at her asking for food and water but Frederica, comfortable in her chair waved him away and closed her eyes. The sannyasi's face filled with rage as he stood over Frederica who remained impassive until he finally left, walking slowly away, chanting, and muttering under his breath.

The images faded and the teardrop disappeared. In the palm of the swami's hand, the green gloss of the leaf was fading, its edges crumpling like used paper. He opened his eyes and flicked the leaf onto the ground.

'You saw?'

Willy felt sadness, shock, and rage darting through his veins. He had seen enough to know the truth.

'I can lift the curse, but the woman must come and ask for this to happen.'

'I see.'

'It's a very strong curse, you see.'

'I will do what I can, but my wife is a devout Roman Catholic and also a stubborn woman. I don't know if she will be persuaded.'

As he was leaving, he said to the swami, 'I suppose you are expecting payment?' but the holy man shook his head in great sadness. 'Get your wife to make prayers to the gods,' indicating the statues in the temple, 'the charm is very strong, but I can try and help and maybe the girl will see again. Bring your wife here to make her prayers.'

Jazz stops reading to briefly assess the audience. She thinks it has gone well, no signs of restlessness from the seated guests. She's glad it's almost over.

A month of rains passed before Willy could bring himself to talk to his wife about the temple in the forest. Hopeful that Maria could have her sight restored, he finally plucked up the courage and told her what he had seen in the teardrop.

Her face turned chalk white.

They say she screamed for a day before the doctors came to take her away to the asylum.'

She closes the book. The pages meet with a soft slap, the audience stirs, and the applause begins, led by Mr Peterson. 'I'm sure everybody agrees that was wonderful, Jazz. Now, ladies and gentlemen, there is still a tiny portion left of that rather splendid rice and curry, there are also plenty of sausages and cheese and a bottle or two left of champagne, I dare say. Jazz will be available for questions shortly.'

She moves swiftly across to Monty. 'I need a drink,' she mutters. He fetches her a glass of champagne. 'Make it two,' she finds herself saying while she lights a cigarette.

He pushes her gently back to her place in the centre of the floor, where her editor is inviting the audience to ask any questions they may have. They come quick and fast and after an hour she is still in the midst of a crowd.

Every now and again she glances up at either Vera, or her

Earls Court friends and once or twice at George who is a calming presence in the loud chatter.

There had been a point while she had been reading, when she had felt the atmosphere in the room was suddenly different, the feeling of the surrounding space inhabited by something, or someone almost forgotten. She had shaken it off, but now she sits alert, waiting. She feels a hand on her shoulder, and she turns, and there he is, standing looking at her with an inscrutable stare.

'Hello, Jazz,' he says quietly.

'Hello, Sonny.'

'You certainly told a story, there, Jazz.'

'Yes I did.' She is not going to feel any guilt. She has tried for so long to reach him. Perhaps she has been trying ever since they met.

'Would you sign my copy for me, please?' She signs with shaking fingers. From the back of the room, she sees Vera and George coming towards her, feels the coming collision of her two worlds.

'I have to go,' she murmurs, and she feels rather than sees the surprise in his eyes.

'Can we meet tomorrow?'

'Yes.'

She tells him of a place that she knows before moving away briskly to join her friends.

46

She will not hurry; she tells herself sternly. Sonny is always late. She spends hours planning what to wear, disregarding everything in her wardrobe except a black chiffon cocktail dress which she puts on and pulls off a dozen times before realising she is now in danger of being late herself, and puts it back on. Coming downstairs carefully in her high heels, she hears a man's voice in the parlour. Vera has gone back to Manchester so it can't be one of her friends. Perhaps Jim from next door has stepped in to talk about the previous night with Alan and Maud. She puts her head around the door to shout goodbye and stops.

Seated in an armchair, glass of whisky in hand, is George. He breaks into a wide, open smile at her arrival.

'Hel-lo' she stutters, overdressed and embarrassed, 'I didn't realise you were coming over, I'm afraid I have plans this evening.'

'That's quite alright. It's my fault. I should have asked you last night if you were free, but we didn't get much of a chance to chat and in the taxi you were exhausted, and I didn't like to disturb.'

Disturb is such a good word, she thinks, a word that immediately brings Sonny to mind. George has by now drained the contents of his glass and got to his feet, holding out a hand to say goodbye to Alan.

'Come again, old chap,' Alan says with a wink at Jazz.

'I'll walk you out, shall I?' says George, 'don't forget your brolly, it's due to rain this evening.'

'I lent mine to Vera. I think she took it back with her. Never mind I can make a dash if I need to.'

They step out into the summer evening, and he takes her arm, navigating her safely around the worst parts of litter and dog mess on the pavement. Sounds of revelry fly from various pubs and gardens as they walk along.

'Did you enjoy your night? I thought you coped with it all very well.'

'Thank you. Surprisingly I did enjoy it, especially once the reading was over.'

'I started to read my copy last night. You paint such an enticing picture of your homeland. I could almost taste the spice and feel the heat on my cold, London face.'

It begins to drizzle. Dismayed, Jazz puts a hand protectively over her hair. George steps off the kerb and whistles to attract a black cab. It comes gliding across. He opens the door for her.

'Oh, I was going to take the Underground.'

'Where are you headed?'

'The Strand.'

'In you get. Driver, please take this lady to The Strand. I'll pay the fare upfront if that's alright.'

'Suits me, guv.'

'Oh, but really, there's no need.'

'You are looking so nice and smart it would be a shame for you to arrive looking like a drowned rat.'

'Well, thank you very much, it's very kind of you.' She stops. 'I'm so sorry I can't see you tonight.'

'That's alright, Jazz. There will be plenty of other evenings for us. Have a lovely night.'

He remains waving on the pavement until they have driven away out of sight.

'That your fella, love? Seems like a nice chap. Cares a lot about you. Paying your fare and all that. I always say to my daughters, if you've got yourself a good'un, hold on to him, they're as rare as hen's teeth.' The cabbie gives a wheezy burst of laughter. Sensing she is not in the mood for chat he obligingly falls silent.

The journey should only take twenty minutes but then they find themselves in heavy traffic on the Euston Road and eventually she gets out of the cab opposite Aldwych, twenty-five minutes late. She is mortified but thinks it will be fine, he is probably still on his way.

The summer rain is coming down heavily. She dashes inside into the dry. She has not been to this Indian restaurant before but so many people have told her how good the food is. To reach the entrance, she has to make her way through the hotel. She peers through the foyer as she passes but there is no sign of Sonny. She climbs the stairs and comes face to face with a waiter who asks if he can help. Flustered she says she is waiting for somebody and then she hears a chair being pushed back sharply and her name being called.

'I'm sorry I'm so late, the weather is terrible, and we got into a traffic jam.'

'It's okay Jazz. You are here now, finally.'

She feels she could say the exact words to him.

'This place is very plain, no? Not much decoration. I expected more in London.'

'It's all about the food, Sonny, not the interiors. Good hot curries don't necessarily need to be enjoyed amongst silk and marble.'

He looks thoughtful. After they have ordered, Sonny drinks a couple of bottles of beer and Jazz has a large glass of white wine, so acidic it makes her gasp. Relaxed by the alcohol, they feel their way back to their natural rhythm.

'You are not married yet, Jazz?'

'No, I've been too busy. What about you?'

'I'm too lazy.' He skips a beat. 'I'm only kidding. Of course I'm not married.' He stares at her.

'So, what have you been up to? Not working at the *Courier* anymore?'

'I lost my appetite for it, after the hartal in '53. You must have read about it?'

'My gosh, yes. The Ceylonese over here talked of nothing else. I remember thinking of Suresh and his obsession with rice subsidies. He was right all along; he always thought the workers would rise up against the government. Even the university students protested, didn't they? We heard about the violence of course, people dying during the demonstrations.'

'Yes, there were casualties. But Jazz, it wasn't just about rice sanctions. It wasn't as widely reported but the Tamils also used the demonstrations to highlight the government favouring the Sinhalese.'

'You can't blame them.'

'I understand how they feel but I do worry sometimes how it can ever be resolved. When I left I got the impression that things were still simmering.'

'I like to think that some kind of agreement will be reached in time. Our island is such a peaceful place.'

'It used to be. But since the hartal, I'm not so sure. The spirit of the people has been stirred, whatever grudge they may be holding.'

'Well,' she says, greatly saddened, 'let's hope you are wrong.' She wants to change the subject. 'So, what have you been doing with yourself since you left?'

'After Serena's wedding, I went on tour with Mateo's band, you remember my upstairs neighbour?'

'I remember.'

'The band had a series of concert bookings across Canada. I helped them out on the road, moving their instruments, booking the accommodation, that type of thing. From there I went to stay in Toronto with Victor for eight months and picked up odd jobs, here and there.'

'How is Victor?'

'He's doing well, managing a small hotel now which will probably get bought up by one of the big chains before too long. Then with luck, he will really hit the big time. He's married to a Canadian girl, and they have a daughter.'

'Burgher girl?'

'Of course.'

They give each other a sly grin.

'Sonny, tell me, how is Joe?'

'Gail and Bernard have moved the family to Colombo so he can attend a suitable school.'

'That's good news.'

'If I get myself settled somewhere, who knows, maybe he could even come over here.'

She nods, naming a school she thinks might be suitable. 'So, Sonny, how long have you been in London?'

'Only a few weeks.'

'I see.' She is dying to ask if he has come because of her, but she stays silent. Unexpectedly the image of George's face as he had put her into the taxicab, flits across her mind.

'I'm sleeping on somebody's sofa in Earls Court, one of my old journalist friends. I didn't know where you were but once I had my bearings and got used to the coldness of what I'm reliably informed is the British summer, I began to hear of your name before I even needed to ask around. You are becoming famous, Jazz.'

'Don't be silly. Every Ceylonese bugger in Earls Court knows every other Ceylonese bugger.' Finally, she asks the question. 'You didn't want to come and see me sooner?'

'I was going to. And then I thought I would come to your book party and surprise you.'

'Well, you succeeded.' She pauses. 'Or maybe you were the one who was surprised.'

He nods slowly.

'Look, if I had known you were coming, I would have chosen a different part of the story to read, last night.' She looks him in the eyes. 'I did write to you about the novel, but I guess you were away and never got the letter.'

'My fault. I should have stayed in touch.'

She doesn't disagree. He finishes his beer and promptly orders more. The food arrives and they fill their plates with bhuna chicken, rice and chapatis.

'Are you still working on the newspaper now your book is out?'

'I've been given leave to promote the novel, but I don't think I will go back. Monty would like me to write another book, I'm sure. I was given a small advance so I can live on that for a while.' She takes another eye-watering mouthful of wine. 'So...have you read any of it?'

'I stayed up all night to read half of it and finished it before I came out this evening. It's a great book, Jazz. I have to pay tribute to the fruits of your assiduous note taking.'

'Now you are making fun of me.'

He sighs heavily. 'I'm sorry. Honestly it's a wonderful book. It just makes me aware that I'm nothing, I'm a nobody.'

'Not to me.'

'You've always believed in me. That's what I loved best about you.'

She notes the past tense with a pang.

He picks himself up instantly. 'What I still love best about you. There is a lot to love about you in general, now I come to think of it.'

'I wonder...is it too late for us?'

'I really don't know. But I'm here now and I'm not planning to go anywhere. I want to win your hand, Jazz.'

She can't help laughing. He fixes her with a stare. 'I noticed last night, my rival sitting in the front, his eyes fixated on you.'

'Oh.' She blushes.

'What would Aunty and Uncle say? He's not a Burgher boy.'

'No. I've wondered since I arrived in England, whether or not that is important. And I remain unsure.'

'So, come on then, tell me all about the non-Burgher boy.'

He sounds nonchalant but she notices he chain-smokes as she tells him about George. 'He works as an assistant architect for a firm based in a large practice in Holborn. I think eventually, from what he's said, he would like to work in commercial architecture. He lives in a bedsit in Kentish Town, about fifteen minutes from where I stay. He's funny, kind, and considerate,' Jazz concludes, 'comfortable I think is the word I would use'.

Sonny grunts. They finish the meal off with coffee and brandy and conversation of a less contentious nature.

'What now?' says Sonny as they walk out into the night. The clouds part to reveal a lustrous pearl moon.

'Shall we walk?' They stroll arm in arm among the Saturday night revellers, teddy boys with hard faces, girlfriends in pleated skirts and bobby socks, singing and screeching at the tops of their voices, owning the night.

'Let's go and sit by Tower Bridge,' suggests Jazz.

They sit for a while in companiable silence, looking across the water at the bridge in the moonlight.

'Have you seen it open? It's quite a sight. I once saw a beautiful sailing ship pass underneath. It reminded me of the yacht the superintendent told me he once gave you for your birthday.'

'He told you that?'

'Yes. He took me to Makara Kata on the drive back to Colombo.'

There is a long silence.

'Did he talk about the body in the lake?' asks Sonny eventually.

She looks away. 'Not really. He was talking more about you.'

She lights two cigarettes and passes one to him.

'But one could say, the two are inextricably connected.'

She gives a deep sigh. 'Yes.'

He takes a long draw on his cigarette. 'Do you remember what I wrote in the notebook I gave you?'

'You told me to make sure I told the right story.'

'What made you write about the teardrop? I'm not angry, just curious.'

'I don't know. Maybe I needed to be rid of it.'

'Remember when I took you to meet Gail that weekend? She's quite hard to like, in some ways, but I know you did your best to get along with her.'

She gives a start. 'I didn't dislike her. I thought she was very intense.'

'Gail was the first daughter in the house. My mother gave her the stars and the moon and a piece of sunrise on the side. Then of course when she met Bernard, he also worshipped her and so the baton of goddess-keeper was passed from mother to husband. I try not to make judgements but…she can be selfish. Thoughtless. Sometimes a little unkind.

'But as you know, life changed for all of us, one hot afternoon when a sannyasi came calling, begging for a little food and water, and my sister, lying out in the garden, closed her eyes and her heart and denied him.'

She sits silently. It seems as if all their conversations have been leading to this one.

'Your hands are shaking, Sonny. Are you cold?' She takes them gently in hers.

'I think I will forever be cold.'

She looks at him with sadness.

'We both know that back home there are events that transcend explanation. A man can go a whole lifetime without encountering such things, but then, if you are unlucky, if the gecko falls on the right side...who is to say what may happen? You once called the East Coast a place of devils. How right you were.'

'I'm sorry for writing about things that maybe should not be out in the open,' she says softly, 'can you forgive me?'

He gives a snort. 'You want me to forgive you? We are part of each other's story, now. There's really nothing to forgive.' He pauses to stub out his cigarette and light up another. 'Did you know my godfather retired? Without solving his last big case?'

'Yes, I knew.'

He stares at her. 'Remember that day in Kumburapola when you followed me into the church? Ah, I bet you thought I hadn't seen you. I smelt your perfume on the way out and realised you were there.'

'Oh, my gosh. You knew I was there all along.'

'I imagine you thought I was following up a lead and were annoyed that I hadn't shared it with you.'

'Yes, that is what I thought. Well, you can tell me now.'

'I was talking to the highest authority of all, Jazz. Asking for forgiveness. Praying.'

She steadies her voice. 'I think you've had far too much beer this evening, Sonny de Roye. You're not making a lot of sense.'

'Jazz, you could have written an entirely different story about the body in the lake and the teardrop.'

'I wrote the story I wanted to write,' she says quietly.

A stain of deep crimson spreads slowly across the sky like a wound. 'It's dawn,' Jazz says after a while, 'we've been up all night.'

They watch the sun rise, warm and golden as it washes away the blood, the blue sky revealing itself slowly, like a blessing.

ACKNOWLEDGMENTS

I would like to thank all those who have patiently read earlier drafts, given advice, and continuous encouragement, especially Lucy Amos-John, Tricia French, Maurice Landsberger, Daniel Lansbury, Jenny O' Neill, Jo Sinclair. Special thanks also to Maurice Landsberger and Daniel Lansbury for Burgher history and family tales.

Thanks to the fam in the UK, Sri Lanka, and Australia for feeding me so well on my visits...my curries will never be as good as yours. Massive thanks to Damien Mosley and everyone at Indie Novella for all their support.

And finally, to Mike and Luke for technical troubleshooting, patching up plot holes, keeping my glass topped up... and for always being there.

ABOUT THE AUTHOR

After a freelance television career, **Sue Amos** took a career break and began to write in her spare time. Inspired by forgotten, misremembered scraps of history, she wrote two novels under the pen name Sarah Roux. Her first, *A Painted Samovar* is a homage to her maternal Jewish grandfather while *The Chronicles of Harriet Shelley* gives voice to the first wife of the poet, Percy Shelley.

Submitting her 3rd novel to the **Watson Little x Indie Novella Prize,** Sue decided she needed to come out from the shadows to write under her real name, having an inkling this would prove to be auspicious! Born and bred in North London, and now resides in the Chilterns with her husband, son, and dog, *Teardrop* also represents a tribute to Sue's Sri Lankan heritage and her work shedding light on the post-colonial culture of her ancestors.

Teardrop won the 2023 Watson Little x Indie Novella Prize.

THE ROCK 'N' ROLL OF INDIE PUBLISHING

We're Indie Novella and we were founded by a group of friends with one mission, to make publishing more accessible to everyone.

We love literary fiction, but we don't love the snobbery that gets associated with it. Great literary fiction comprises of stories that capture our imagination and resonate with us. Stories that shed light on modern issues, which use relatable and understandable language, which are about characters who speak for the communities we live in.

That's why we're publishing novels which make literary fiction less elitist and get readers as passionate about books as we are. We're also revolutionising publishing by doing something so few others are. Levelling the playing field. Our writing course is funded by the Arts Council and has been designed in collaboration with leading literary agencies such as Watson Little, David Godwin Associates and Georgina Capel and is completely free.

When it comes to writing and storytelling we believe there are so many voices that go unheard. Therefore we made a vow: We won't sit down. We won't shut up. We will commit to being our authentic selves. Just like our authors.

Stories of identity, community, belonging, and being proud of who we are. Our authors write the stories that represent what they stand for, in a truly authentic voice.

If that's not Rock 'n' Roll, I don't know what is.